Sujata Krishnan hails from India and was raised in Kuwait. After working for about 12 years and then becoming a full-time mother, she has decided to concentrate her skills on writing. Now settled in Dubai, Sujata has written her first book, *The Dynamic Doorway*, which started as a night-time story for her son.

For my son, Ranbir, who lit the fire of imagination in me.

Sujata Krishnan

THE DYNAMIC DOORWAY

AUSTIN MACAULEY PUBLISHERS™
LONDON * CAMBRIDGE * NEW YORK * SHARJAH

Copyright © Sujata Krishnan 2023

The right of Sujata Krishnan to be identified as author of this work has been asserted by the author in accordance with Federal Law No. (7) of UAE, Year 2002, Concerning Copyrights and Neighboring Rights.

All rights reserved. No part of this publication may be reproduced, stored in a retrieval system, or transmitted in any form or by any means, electronic, mechanical, photocopying, recording, or otherwise, without the prior permission of the publishers.

Any person who commits any unauthorized act in relation to this publication may be liable to legal prosecution and civil claims for damages.

This is a work of fiction. Names, characters, businesses, places, events, locales, and incidents are either the products of the author's imagination or used in a fictitious manner. Any resemblance to actual persons, living or dead, or actual events is purely coincidental.

The age group that matches the content of the books has been classified according to the age classification system issued by the Ministry of Culture and Youth.

ISBN – 9789948797791 – (Paperback)
ISBN – 9789948797807 – (E-Book)

Application Number: MC-10-01-1737816
Age Classification: E

Printer Name: iPrint Global Ltd
Printer Address: Witchford, England

First Published 2023
AUSTIN MACAULEY PUBLISHERS FZE
Sharjah Publishing City
P.O Box [519201]
Sharjah, UAE
www.austinmacauley.ae
+971 655 95 202

I thank my family and friends for their faith in me and for supporting me.

Chapter 1
The Storm

About a fortnight before Christmas, it was very stormy. Everything had shut down, even the shops. All were advised to stay at home. I wasn't feeling too festive and welcomed the chance to rest.

The storm, with its dark and dreary ambience, was making my mood just as dreary. I was watching some cartoons, imagining myself in that animated world. Would be a lot of fun if it was real; cartoons can genuinely lift-up my spirits!

I often had the propensity to imagine myself in the animated world. It's a childhood passion that refused to go away. I may be 24 years old, but whoever put an age to finding happiness!

Alright, so I did get ridiculed by peers through my teens for my strong interest in cartoons. But when I decided to take it up professionally, I was suddenly the voice of wisdom for those very same friends, who were struggling to zero in on what course they should consider.

I was born in Brooklyn, New York, to migrant Indian parents, Arvind and Radha Rajan. My parents had moved there as a newly married couple to chart out a new life for themselves. It took them a few years to find a footing and set up a nice decent life for themselves, with a row house for a home in Bay Ridge and comfortable amenities.

So about seven years later, I was conceived, as a symbol of a settled life. It was time to start a family and I marked that beginning. Welcome Siddharth, aka Sid! A fulfilment of all their wishes.

Life was good, normal, and wholesome. My parents were very hard-working, and that value was taught to me from the very beginning. A lot of importance was placed on prioritizing my schoolwork. Yeah, I was a NERD! But nerds need fun too, and cartoons gave me that escape.

"How come you're still watching cartoons when your friends have moved on to other interests?" They frowned.

But that penchant for single-minded focus stood me in good stead when I opted for the animation industry as a profession.

Although they were skeptical of my choice (Indian parents in those days only considered engineering, medicine, medicine, and computer programming as viable professions), they understood my passion and gave me their blessings. Later, of course, the trend was catching on and they were happy.

I now live in a snazzy, urban neighborhood lined with skyscrapers on every street. These tall towers look so intimidating and powerful against the skyline. The modern steel cladding on the concrete structure makes it gleam in the sun at daytime and reflects the shimmery bright lights of the night.

My home is in one such imposing building – an apartment at the top, the 45th floor! Looking down from the window makes the world seem small and gives me an overpowering high. I know it does not seem logical, but I feel like being up so high gives wings to my imagination. And I need loads of it in my profession.

As for that furious, festive (or not!) night, the storm seemed to be increasing in intensity. The sky blinked frequently like a flashlight, thunder roared and echoed through the neighborhood, rain pattered against the windows at a fast pace and loud rhythm, and the wind howled. It made the atmosphere seem so eerie.

I lived alone and the lack of interesting, spirited company and conversation didn't help. Suddenly, the rumbling and crackling thunder went BOOM! The lightning seemed too bright and close. I felt, as though for a split second, the building shook.

The lights just went out. As I looked out the huge French windows for signs of light, I saw the neighborhood enveloped in darkness save for the flashing lightening. There was a power outage in the entire street. My anxiety was rising by the minute.

Random questions popped in my mind: *What just happened? Did lightning strike the building? How is it possible? Is my imagination getting out of control?*

Then I heard another sound. This was much closer, in fact, from my apartment. It sounded like a grating, static noise which kept on playing without any change in frequency.

Again, I was hit with confusion and myriad thoughts ran through my mind: *How can I hear sounds? Isn't the electricity out? It can't be my television. Nah! Televisions don't make that sound anymore.*

I tried to follow the noise and was shocked to see where it was originating. Glowing in the dark with that annoying sound frequency was my vintage, old 29-inch CRT television sitting on a wooden stand, all lit up with white noise.

How is this possible? This television has not worked in years, not to mention that there is no power.

The television belonged to my late grandfather, and I have preserved it as a memory of him. CRT televisions are those old TVs that had a big box-like compartment behind the display screen and weighed a ton.

I loved my grandpa, my father's dad. My strongest memories of him include watching movies and comedy shows on this TV with him. He was a man who laughed easily, and that happiness resonated around him.

I loved doing things with him, and since he enjoyed his evening time in front of the idiot box, I enjoyed sitting with him and dissecting the content on screen. These were my vacation times in India, full of joy and stories. Maybe that's what helped fire up my imagination.

When he left for his heavenly abode peacefully in his sleep, we were devastated, and the family rushed to complete his last rites. After completing the rituals, we sat together in the living room, and I gazed at the TV.

"I want to take his television back home," I insisted.

It took a lot of cajoling with my dad, as technology was already rendering these picture boxes obsolete with the advent of flat screens. My grandpa had stoically refused to get a new updated version. Anyway, I managed to convince my father and we shipped it to our home in the United States.

Coming back to the white noise, as I went closer to the television to investigate, I realized that it was not even plugged in. I looked around – quizzical and apprehensive, searching for the reason that sparked off the TV.

I came around to the screen, to see if I could try turning the knobs around for answers. The light seemed to grow stronger and stronger, until it became a blinding blaze.

I started to feel lighter, as though I was losing consciousness. I desperately tried to fight that feeling but was unable to hold on to my senses. My head was spinning, and I felt like I was being sucked into a bright hole.

Chapter 2
A New Dimension

I had blanked out. As I came around, I woke up feeling dizzy and a little tired. It felt like I was awakening from a dream after a deep drug induced sleep, and everything was still hazy. I tried my best to get on my feet but found that I couldn't feel the ground; I was floating! I was beginning to freak out!

What's going on? What's happening to me? Where am I?

I began to recall the bright light and being dragged into it. But now I was engulfed in darkness, like an intense black hole. I could see nothing and only sensed that I was moving forward through the air, and the only way I can describe it would be to say that it was an endless passageway full of nothingness.

I felt trapped, mortified, scared, terrified! My hyperactive imagination envisioned some dark supernatural being trying to steal my soul. Or maybe I'm headed towards the smoldering cauldron of a satanic witch!

Am I going to become human stew on some ogre's plate? Oh my God! Help!!!

Before I could visualize any more horrors, out of nowhere, I felt a slight push from behind and I was hurtled towards some brilliant light! At first, I thought it was a way out and felt some sense of relief. As I approached the light, my feet touched the ground and I quickly collected myself and walked towards that glare.

I looked around and behind me, trying to make sense of what was going on. It looked like a cave and the opening of the cave was almost invisible with the blinding light. I staggered toward the entrance in a daze, and just as I reached the edge of the cave, I lost my balance again.

Again, I found myself falling headlong down a swirling candy cane-like slide. It was a splash of colors, almost hypnotizing me. By now I was incapable of any thoughtful analysis and just waited to see where I would land.

I plonked bouncing onto a soft bubble.

Really, a bubble? Is that even possible?

Yet it was true! A bubble that obviously should burst, but it was bouncy like a ball. I tried to get a hold of my senses, looked around and saw in front of me this wondrous fantasy world. It was like the cartoons I was so hooked on to since childhood and what I created at work. Colorful and vivid – the two-dimensional animations that I grew up watching with so much glee.

I couldn't believe my eyes or my sanity. Maybe I was losing my mind. I pinched myself to know I wasn't dreaming. I could sense excitement building up inside me. Slowly but surely, the exhilaration was mounting, and my energy was escalating. My fatigue had almost disappeared with the sights I beheld. I was raring to get up and about.

In recent times, my life had become sad, mundane, mundane, and drab. I had been through a personal rollercoaster and that drained me of all my joy. I was living but not feeling alive with passion, emotion, emotion, and fun. I was left alone to deal with my life. And the only saving grace was my profession, my escape route. Why?

After losing my grandfather, we had returned home to Brooklyn and life went on. I did always miss my partner-in-joy, my grandpa. My father too was deeply affected as he felt responsible for leaving his father alone in India after my grandma passed away.

But really there was nothing he could do, because Grandpa refused to move out of his home. Grandpa held on to the memories and the life he shared with Grandma. They were so endearing together, with the silly bickering and loads of concern, and the amazing, fun aura that Grandpa always created around him.

And Grandma was the perfect foil, enjoying the fun but keeping the reins in her hands! I can't stop smiling when I think about them.

Back home, Dad had become more serious in his demeanor, and that affected my mom too. He would return late from work every day and be too tired to do anything else.

One day, Mom waited as usual at the dinner table for Dad to return home. He'd normally come home just in time for dinner and then shuffle up to his room to sleep. After he freshened up and sat down to eat, Mom tried to strike up a conversation.

"Arvind, Diwali is around the corner, and I want to do something special at home this time. Would you take me shopping for some decorations and groceries? I'm thinking of inviting our friends over for a party."

"No, I'm too busy at work, you'll have to manage it on your own. And by the way, why do you want to host a party? I don't have any holidays around that time."

"But you always take a week off for Diwali!" My mom sounded concerned.

"Yes, but this time there's some project deadline to meet. I can't take any time off. I suggest you just think about the preparations involving decorating the home. I doubt if I can be present for any festivities other than the pooja time."

Mom was disturbed, I could tell. Diwali is a major five-day festival, and before now, we made it a point to be together as a family and plan happy celebrations. It was a tradition in our home. But circumstances were changing for the worse after Grandpa. I don't know why Dad was drowning himself in guilt.

Mom tried again. "Arvind, please…understand…it's not your fault that Papa went. He lived his life with happiness and went in peace. It was his time to reunite with Mama. You've not neglected him, nor could you have done anything more. We used to visit him every year!"

Dad replied in a sullen, low voice, "You don't understand, he was lonely. And I couldn't be there for him. Whereas he did everything possible to be able to send us here to start a new life. I couldn't live up to my duties as a son, and I'll never be able to forgive myself."

"What about your duties towards us, Arvind? You still have to be with us too," Mom countered softly.

Dad silently finished his dinner and went up to sleep. The next morning, he was having trouble waking up. He opened his eyes, but his body was heavy and refused to cooperate. He made unintelligible sounds till Mom heard him. And by the time I was awake, I saw him being carried into an ambulance.

He had had a stroke that left him paralyzed on the left side. And this stroke paralyzed our 'family life' too. Mom's routine now ran like clockwork. Wake up at 5.00 am, …prepare my lunch for school, …go to work, …visit the hospital, …return home to prepare dinner for me, …and sleep by 10.00 pm.

I didn't ever see her smile after that. I was mostly left to my devices in figuring out what to do with my time and life. And I was all of 12 years old.

But I didn't blame her, she was doing her best. It's not like she didn't care, but she just couldn't spare the time. Once a week, I too would go and visit my father.

I think that's what helped me to continue with a positive mindset. The good memories, and the unflinching love and care that I could sense. But it was also the reason, I chose to move into this tall tower once I started earning enough to pay for my own accommodation.

Mom had decided to take a small room on rent closer to the hospital, so that she could spend more time taking care of Dad. And I couldn't bear the deafening memories in the house, that just amplified my sad life now.

When I found this urban high-rise apartment, I was filled with an old exhilaration that I was almost forgetting. That sealed the deal for me. Our suburban home, after that, remained locked.

And now…as I stood in this great big fantasy, this world of my dreams…my childhood joy rushed back. I felt like I had gone back in time, when I daydreamed about cartoons and the funny, quirky characters.

The buildings, the people – in fact, everything had black outlines filled with color. I was reminded of my drawing classes in school; I was pretty good at it. This was so unreal! It was like a 3-D version of comic books.

I had to explore and find out more, so I decided to talk to some people and try to understand this world. I walked around aimlessly taking it all in, until I saw a group of kids nearby. One of them spotted me and headed towards me; I was apprehensive but stood my ground.

As he approached me, I could see him smiling, talking, and trying to communicate, but I couldn't understand a word he was saying. It seemed to be a different language. Gibberish actually.

And his voice (I chuckled in my mind), sounded like a fast-forwarded version of a conversation, ha-ha! So, does this world speak a different lingo? I tried using sign language to get through to him.

One thing was clear…that they were friendly. So, I went closer. All of a sudden, he touched my face. It caught me off guard.

Hey, what the…what is he trying to do? Maybe he's surprised to see my form just like I'm surprised to see them and wants to touch and feel the human skin. Or maybe he's sending some invisible vibes…hmmm!!!

Chapter 3
The Enchanted Forest

Strangely, whatever he said after that I could hear in English, and I could understand them. I think his touch was to help me comprehend their language. This was a strange technique. But I guess logic does not form a part of the cartoon world.

"Hi there! You're a human right? How did you get here? What's your name?" he asked.

"I'm Sid, and what about you? Yes, I'm human. How I got here, even I'm not sure. I'm confused and trying to understand the situation and your world. Would you help me?"

"Sure thing! Come along and meet my friends." We walked over to the others. "I'm Jim and this is Steve and Roy," he introduced.

Jim was a lanky teen with blonde hair, blue eyes and round face marked with freckles. He had a friendly demeanor and easy gait. Steve was handsome, tall tall, and muscular with brown hair and eyes, like a rugby player and possibly a little older. Roy had olive complexion, dark hair and eyes and smiled with a goofy grin.

And me…I'm Sid…curly black hair, black eyes, good looking (so my mom says) and light brown skin. I'm about 5ft.'10in." in height.

After our round of introductions, I got to know that Roy was 18, Steve 20 and Jim 17. I may be a little older, but these guys looked like they'd be a fun bunch to have around. Besides, I'm here now and this adventure calls for good company. They can help me understand what's going on.

"Guys," I spoke up, "I have had the strangest experience in my world, and honestly, I don't know how I came to be in this realm. But I'm really glad to have met you, and want to experience your life with you, if you don't mind."

Roy grinned. "Hey! We're surprised to see you too, it isn't every day that we see a human but that's okay, life is strange and funny. Let's just enjoy it while we can." He looked at Jim. "Jim, when are we going to the carnival?"

They don't seem as shocked to see me as I am to be here. Are they used to this?

"You don't seem that surprised. Have you met other humans before? And there's a carnival on?" I asked with excitement. "I'd love to see that!"

"Sid, life in the Toon World is full of surprises. We're used to it. So, let's go to that carnival then." Jim waved his arm to all.

Steve, who'd been silent until now, piped in, "Let me draw up a car."

Just as I waited for him to go towards a parked car or call for one, he pulled out a sketch pen from his pocket and started to literally 'draw' a car on the street. My eyes widened as he artfully drew a swanky sedan in fast motion. It was done within about ten minutes flat.

He zapped it with his pen, and we had a vehicle in front of us. We drove off quickly to the street in the adjoining district and joined the cheering crowds that had gathered there.

"What is this carnival about?" I asked. Jim told me it was a ritual held once a month. "Won't I stand out among the crowd? I don't want to be stared at."

Steve reassured me, "Don't worry. It's a carnival, they'll just think you're in a human costume. Lots of people come in costumes."

Life in the animation world was apparently very vibrant. My own life had been very sedate till now, and in fact lonely and sad the past few years; so here was my chance to find my mojo with some exhilarating experiences.

Let the adventures begin!

We walked into that sea of laughter and cheer, street raining with confetti and streamers, and found a good spot to view the parade. Elaborate floats rolled down the street, people in amazing costumes, band, characters – everything like the carnivals in our world. I was having a great time!

Roy caught my hand, along with the others and, in an instant, we were on one of the floats. It was created like an enchanted forest and helmed by a witch. Other characters waving out were an ogre, a fairy, a dwarf, and a gnome.

And then there was us…waving out to the swirling currents of heads smiling, shouting, and singing in incomprehensible sounds. The euphoria I felt was unimaginable. I had never felt anything like it in my life. My heart soared and I felt a happy light in my soul.

I haven't been this happy since Grandpa died. And these experiences are unreal, like my childhood fantasies come to life.

I smiled to myself, and totally submitted to the events unfolding.

The float continued down the street. About half hour later, it was to turn right towards a demarcated ground where all of them were to be parked. I was told they'd be dismantled the next day at this ground.

However, after turning right, instead of heading towards the ground, following other floats, ours turned left into yet another street. All four of us looked at each other confused.

I tapped the 'witch' on the shoulder to ask. She turned around giving an evil smirk…and POOF! We were no more on the street in a float.

We were in an enchanted forest, with the witch before us, and the other beastly characters surrounding us. Looking perplexed, Jim caught a hold of my arm and signaled me to do the same with the others.

As soon as we clasped our hands, I realized that I could hear their thoughts and they could read my mind too. It was the same Jim earlier, who touched my face, after which I was able to understand what he was saying.

Is this some kind of power he has?

The moment the thought crossed my mind, Jim confirmed it. That's when they made me realize another feature of this strange universe.

That most of them have some unique power. So much like the toons where nothing is logical, and anything can happen. Altered Physics. …Yes, that's what they call this unique characteristic of the toon domain.

Jim's power was telepathy I guess, and Steve could draw like a dream. Oh yes, and Roy can appear and disappear, sort of like moving by teleporting. That's how we ended up on the float.

Not just that, being physically linked meant that the others were included in on the effects of those powers. That's how we were communicating by telepathy so that the witch wouldn't know what's on our minds. Not much to hide at this point though.

Jim: "Stay together guys. It looks like we're in for some trouble. This witch has tricked us here."

Roy: "Plus she's got these goons to help her too. Aren't fairies supposed to be the good guys, or gals?"

Me: "Why don't we just ask her what she wants from us?"

Steve: "Yeah, that's a start. If you hadn't mentioned, we never would've thought of it." I could see him smirk slyly.

Wise guy!

"Who are you and why have you brought us here?" I asked the witch.

She laughed a loud raucous cackle and announced in a commanding tone, "I am Selene Kouris, the ordained priestess of the Enchanted Magus Forest." Her voice grated like sandpaper scraping wood. "My word is law! These are my trusted subjects, and YOU are here to help me become high priestess of the Toon World!"

Her evil laugh reverberated through the woods, and her loyal creatures joined her in the cacophony.

The witch had a very angular wrinkled face, a sharp long nose and bony body. She looked every inch the typical witch with her dry red hair, and beady green eyes. In fact, her creatures had a clichéd look too. The forest, on the other hand, was truly enchanting. Mystical and mesmerizing. I wish we could explore under better circumstances.

But this situation was getting creepier by the minute. And before we could say anything more, she ordered that we be chained and locked in the secret room of the Black Temple.

I looked at my three friends with a 'what do we do' look; surely there was something they could do to get us out of this. Why weren't they using their powers? Roy…he's the one who can teleport right? But he did nothing.

We were led by the gnome and ogre to an ancient dilapidated, yet grand, temple, and then blindfolded. After that, we were walked into what felt like a long corridor, turned left, again walked for a bit, turned right and pushed into a room.

Our blindfolds were taken off and we found ourselves in a dungeon like space. They locked us up and left, their surly, monstrous voices trailing off slowly.

Chapter 4
The Evil Scheme

We started talking all at once, trying to make sense of what was going on, and couldn't understand a damn thing. I asked Roy why he didn't do something to get us out of that place.

"I did try, but I was unable to. It wasn't working. I don't know why," he said. "Do you suppose she has put a spell on the forest, so no one else's but her powers work here?"

"That's very likely. She said herself she controls the forest, and all the beings here won't be able to go against her," I opined. "What shall we do then? How do we get out of here?"

Jim sounded somber. "She intends to take over the Toon World too. We have to work this out."

Steve fished out his pen and tried drawing a key to open the door to the dungeon. He was able to draw but couldn't zap it for use. The power wouldn't work. Come to think of it, it was so dark, we weren't even sure what Steve drew. We sat there in darkness for what seemed like a very long time. I was beginning to feel hungry.

Do the people in the cartoon world feel hungry?

I spoke my thoughts out loud, and Jim said that they did eat food and he was starved. Steve was unable to materialize his drawings, or he could've drawn up a feast. We walked around the room looking for cracks, secret openings or anything that might give us a clue of the possibilities; but to no success.

Just then, we heard someone approaching. It was the fairy. She had brought us some food. She didn't look harsh, so I was surprised that she was with the witch on her despicable plans. I thought of striking up a conversation with her, but she gave a stern look of unapproachability, kept the food and walked away quietly.

We ate quickly and again started discussing our plan of action. I asked Jim if he could mind-read the fairy to know what she was thinking. I recall that we were able to have a telepathic conversation when we held hands. So that still worked; maybe because the thoughts transmitted upon physical contact. We certainly can't try it out with the other unpleasant looking beasts. I don't fancy becoming an ogre's lunch.

He said he'd surely try the next time she came around. We chatted and whiled away our time and eventually fell asleep. There was no way of telling what time it was, or even if it was day or night. When we awoke, we were still enveloped in darkness. It was getting scary now. The toon boys were worried as well. But we were stuck in limbo. The time just stood still.

After what seemed like forever, we heard some footsteps and hoped it was the fairy with some food. At this point, it was the only hope we had of getting any answers, and something to eat as well. Our hopes were dashed when the door opened, and we saw the gnome enter with a flaming torch in his hands. But at least it was better than seeing that huge hideous-looking monster, the ogre. He scared me to death.

The gnome looked kind of gentle in comparison, a tiny version of Santa Claus, but without the cheerful, cherubic face. His eyes held fear…I wondered why. Lit up by the torch, we could see that the corridor outside was very similar to the room we were in – old red-brick walls, musty and dingy. The door was made with ornately carved heavy wood, held together with iron hinges, and the large latch held a thick chain with an iron padlock.

He kept some food and informed us that the witch will be coming soon. We had to do something fast, and now. It struck me that we could try to read the gnome's thoughts too. I caught Jim's arm and communicated my idea.

Jim quickly got up and held his hand. "Please, why are you holding us? We can't help you in any way. Let us go."

The gnome shrugged him off with a disgruntled growl and left. As soon as he was gone, Jim told us that the gnome was just following orders out of fear. His family was being held captive by the witch, and he was being blackmailed into working for her.

I'm sure there's more to his story, but we would need more time with him.

We ate and waited with some trepidation till the witch showed up. We could hear her gravelly voice echoing as she headed towards us. All four of us were feeling collectively curious, cautious, and craven, all at the same time.

We heard the padlocks being unlocked once again, and the heavy door opened with a groan. Selene Kouris stood before us in all her evil glory, baring her yellowing sharp teeth. She was flanked by the gnome and the fairy. For some reason, that felt hopeful.

"Now, it's time for me to tell you how you will be of service to me," she started. "You, toon people, you will come with me. I have arranged a ceremony to invoke the Henosis of myself with the One, the Monad of your world."

"What mumbo-jumbo is that?" asked Roy, totally confused. None of us understood her but didn't have the courage to voice it quite in that manner.

She sounded annoyed. "I intend to be one with your universe, and so I shall be THE ONE for your people! I will rule, I will be YOUR universe! Do you understand now?"

She gave me a look and sniggered. "I'll come back to you later. Human world is my ultimate aim."

She left with instructions for the gnome and fairy. "Jinzic, Flora…prepare them for the theurgy."

The pair brought special robes to be worn for the ritual and gave them to Jim, Steve, and Roy. And as they reluctantly wore the garments, I took a chance and spoke to Jinzic, the gnome, "I know why you are doing this for her. If you help us, I promise you we'll help you get your family back, safe and sound."

Jinzic froze, and Flora's reaction told us, she had a similar tale. She looked incredulous and sneered. "What can you do? She's very powerful. At least we're alive, you'll just get all of us killed. But how do you know anything about us?"

"That's not important, what's important is that we do something about it. Don't you want a life of freedom and happiness? Helping her takeover is just going to make things worse…for EVERYONE! What I mean is, not only should we try to stop her from taking over the other realms, but we have to make sure she loses power over this one. That's the only way you will get your family back."

By now, everyone was paying attention to me. "If we don't take these boys with us now, she's going to kill us and our families," Jinzic spoke up softly.

I reassured him, "I'll make sure it looks like we escaped despite your best efforts. But first you have to tell us, she must be having a book of magic that she follows to cast her spells and follow other rituals; where is it?"

I had heard legends and stories about witches, wizards and the like using a book of spells while researching for one of my projects. Apparently, they are incomplete without it.

"Oh, that's the Grand Grimoire. It is at the Altar in the inner sanctum of the temple. Be warned, no one can use the grimoire other than Selene. It is ineffective in the hands of any other. However, without it, she is also ineffective. Any power she may have yielded using the book is rendered useless if someone else touches it."

He looked around cautiously. "And that is why she has summoned demonic guards by using necromantic spells, to protect the Book. Come on…The ritual she intends to hold with these boys is in the courtyard of the temple. If we don't get there soon, she will see something amiss and come here to find out," he informed.

"Perfect! So now let's go out together. We don't know the way out since we were blindfolded when brought in. And as you near the entrance with the boys, they will push both of you and sprint. Just pretend to chase them, and then say they got away."

Next, I turned towards the toon boys and said, "The three of you run and hide, and meanwhile, I'll stay back in the temple to get the book from the inner sanctum. When they are all out searching for you, I'll escape the temple grounds."

Flora was more forthcoming now. "There's a cave in the hills behind the temple. You can hide out there till all of you get together again. I'll come there later to help you out."

Now that sounds like a plan!

Chapter 5
The Grand Grimoire

We walked out together, and I was glad that we didn't have to find our way out by ourselves. The dungeon area was well hidden by a secret door disguised as a wall.

One of the iron sconces for the torch had to be turned around to slide the door open. We would never have figured it out on our own. Once opened, we walked through a narrow corridor till we reached an open area lit by sunlight through stained glass windows.

"This is the priests' court," said Jinzic, referring to the large hall. Pointing to another small room in the center of this hall, "That is the inner sanctum that holds the grimoire. On the other side…you see a doorway? That leads to the plebeian court, which opens out to the entrance of the temple."

He explained the layout so I could escape and then reminded me, "Do not forget that the book is guarded by evil spirits."

I thanked him and told them to move on to the plebeian court. I headed towards the inner sanctum, keeping an eye towards the rest of the gang headed outside. I also noted a well-hidden niche behind a wall, towards a corner.

I could hide there in case of a problem.

Then I walked into the sanctum sanctorum. The moment I stepped into the room, the air felt cold, dark, and heavy. I wanted to get out of there immediately, but I had to get that book. I continued with a sense of foreboding, not sure what I should be doing.

"Never be afraid of the dark, there's nothing there that you don't already know. Remember you just cannot see it," Grandpa told me once, after I expressed fear on walking into a dark room at night.

I thought of his ever-smiling face and encouragement, and also the love between my parents, and my heart was filled with positivity. The sense of commitment that they showed towards each other, had taught me the value of looking out for each other. It did not matter what we had to face, to do so. I had to help my friends; besides, it would affect my world too eventually.

I remembered I wore a bracelet with a religious insignia and felt a little relief, or should I say, protected. God was with me.

I walked past the dilapidated walls, towards the darkly decorated altar. Black sheets, lit candles that cast ominous shadows, some skulls and an inverted cross were set up. Everything about the ambience in the chamber screamed evil.

In the center, was placed a large book with the cover in red leather and an imprint of a black serpent with blazing red eyes. It was bound by a brass clasp with a keyhole. I couldn't see keys around; I suppose the witch must not be entrusting anyone with it.

I closed my eyes and said a quick prayer. I proceeded toward the book, continually chanting the Gayatri Mantra. It is supposed to be the most powerful mantra in Hinduism dedicated to a sun deity. It bestows enlightenment and empowers the sunshine within us. In simple terms, it helps drive away darkness.

I slowly inched forward my hand to take the book. The moment my fingers touched it, I heard deep growls. I retreated, and saw dark shadows begin to loom large around me. Eerie howling began to ring in my ears.

I had never encountered anything like this ever and was quaking in my shoes. But I continued my chants and slowly but surely, the light in my heart grew stronger.

I picked up the book, and the shadows became belligerent. They started to flow around me in a circle of impending doom. They moved faster and faster, and the sounds became more and more ungodly. The screeching and hissing sounded violent.

I'm not going to survive this, I thought.

I was expecting, any minute, to be overpowered and killed. Then I realized that they were frightening me enough to have a cardiac arrest but weren't physically touching me. A few things in the room came hurtling toward me, but I managed to dodge them. I was perplexed. The howling was deafening now. But there was nothing more.

Amid my chants, I hugged the book close to me and walked towards the exit. I still wondered why they didn't harm me. I think it was my chants and my bracelet that protected me from the evil spirits, so I had no intention of stopping – my mantras or my mission.

As soon as I crossed the threshold of the inner sanctum, I felt like I could breathe. The air was lighter. The howling was behind me now, though it didn't stop. Maybe, the spirits were bound to that chamber.

In fact, I heard an extremely loud screeching cry. Only this time, the sound came from outside the temple. I realized the witch may have, somehow, got wind of what had transpired. She must have been informed by the dark depraved souls. Like a telepathic connection.

I quickly rushed and hid in the niche I had spotted earlier. I saw the old hag rush in, flailing her arms in angry despair. She ran into the chamber, and I could hear her wailing loudly and angrily.

Without wasting another moment, I ran out as fast as I could through the plebeian court and out to the temple courtyard. I quickly noted a gazebo area with a burning pyre, possibly the arrangements for the intended ritual that was to be performed. Running out of the grounds, I saw Flora pointing towards the hills. I took the cue and ran for my life.

Chapter 6
In the Hideout

I couldn't afford to stop even for a minute. Not even to think.

What if the witch saw me running just in time as she came out of the temple and is following me with her entourage? What if she had found out we were helped, and forced information out of Flora or Jinzic? What if she got a monstrous army to track us down?

Lots of troubling thoughts and questions, but not a moment to spare and slow down. I summoned all my energy to keep running, till I reached the hills, and tried to find the cave that Flora mentioned.

It took several minutes, before I saw a soft light emanating from a large crevice. I had to crouch in and was relieved to see my friends waiting with a torch in hand.

"Did you get the book, Sid?" Steve asked.

I valiantly brandished the book in front of them. They let out a little victorious whoop and hugged me happily. I told them to extinguish the torch, so no one would be able to spot us. Once more in the dark, there was just a subdued evening light from outside to help us see.

I asked them to relate the details of their escape. Jim said it went as per plan. When they pushed the Jinzic and ran, Selene instructed the gnome to follow us.

"As expected, Selene told him to run after us and get us back. But we also heard her shout out 'Vozig!' Once we were out of her sight, Jinzic showed us which direction to take, and informed us that Vozig was the ogre. He told us to hurry because Vozig would soon be on our tail with his ogre community. They are Selene's soldiers."

Just as I thought.

"We had almost reached the hills, when we heard the combined roars of a torment of ogres in the distance. We became wary of making noise that would give us away if we were too fast. We had to slow down our run and make sure we remained hidden as we headed toward the hills. Believe me, it was a double-edged sword as we made our way here. Didn't want to be seen, didn't want to be slow either."

Steve continued, "Luckily, we managed to stay together and reached this cave without been spotted. We did have a close shave once though. One of those ghastly creatures walked past us in search, as we remained hidden behind a huge oak tree. We were afraid to breathe, for fear of being found out!"

I quickly told them about my encounters with the dark spirits, and they congratulated me and backslapped me. They were amazed how I dealt with them. …Hell! I was amazed at how I dealt with them!

"Now we just sit quiet and wait for Flora to come," I said.

As the sun went down and the cave was enveloped in absolute darkness, we started wondering if the fairy would make it to us. But she didn't disappoint us, when we heard her voice outside informing us of her arrival.

She had brought us something to eat and drink – God bless her! She also told us something that felt like manna for the soul. She had spoken to the Fairy Queen in Fairyland, about the situation, and assured us the complete support of her clan.

"But," she forewarned, "no one must know, until it is time that we can do something. Or Selene will harm our families."

"We promise our discretion. Unless we have a definite plan in place, we shall not discuss the involvement of the fairies," I gave her my word. "We need to unite all the forest communities. Only then can we overthrow the reign of Selene."

I paused in thought and spoke, "Can the gnomes join your herd? And what about the other creatures? There was a dwarf as well when you brought us into the forest. Tell us about him."

"That is Gibel," informed Flora. "He provides the weapons for the soldiers. The ogres, the trolls and the gremlins form the army. The dwarf and his ilk are not bad, but they are cousins of the gremlins who fight for Selene. The gremlins are very nasty, while the dwarves are a community that prefer to live their lives in peace. They are more interested in the fruits of their labor."

She continued, "Gibel has joined hands with Selene on the promise of being offered the complete management of the armory. His gain would be gems, and honor and importance among his people." We nodded in understanding.

"As for the gnomes, I haven't had the chance to meet Jinzic after you fled. Tomorrow, I'll talk to him about joining forces with us against Selene. But he's a friend, and it looks hopeful."

She left us to rest and said we'd meet before sunrise the next day to chart what should be our next plan of action.

We were extremely tired and slept well despite the rocky floor, but not before doing a little brain storming. Roy came up with the first idea. "Hey, doesn't the witch lose her power if someone else has the book? That's what the gnome told us. Does that mean we have our powers back?"

"Oh my God, yes! Good thinking Roy. Actually, she will not lose her own powers, but the spells she cast will be cancelled. The shield of overriding power that she had put over the forest must have dissipated. Try to see if it works," I implored.

He looked down in concentration and, poof, he was outside the cave. He crouched back in looking smug with excitement. We almost did a happy dance. Steve was glad that he would be able to use his sketch pen again to advantage. With that satisfaction, we dropped off to sleep.

Flora woke us up again the next morning, while it was still dark. She was a woman of her word! She came into the cave with her gnome buddy.

We were happy to see Jinzic, because that spelt hope. We discussed the gnomes' support, and he was in favor. But he would need time to work it out with his people. Fair enough.

Score! So, what do we do until then?

Chapter 7
Enter...the Dragon

Jinzic mentioned that we must hide the book in a safe place.

Oh yes, hadn't thought of that.

"Should we dig up a hole some place and bury it?" I asked. Everyone nodded their approval. "Also, please tell us what happened after we left."

He quickly related the events. "I allowed the Toon boys to escape as we had decided. Fortunately, Selene did not suspect anything. She asked me to chase them and bring them to her, and then called out to Vozig.

"Flora mentioned to me later that while I pretended to chase the boys, there was a moment of turbulent wind where they stood, and Selene suddenly screamed."

That must be the moment I managed to get the book out of the inner chamber and heard her scream.

"She rushed into the temple in a fit of rage," he went on. "When I returned to inform her that they had escaped, she was walking out looking totally devastated. I understood that you had succeeded. She got angrier when I told her the boys had fled and instructed Vozig to seek you all at any cost."

"Yeah, it wasn't easy for us to reach the cave when we saw them combing the area," said Jim; he continued after a pause, "I think you should leave before the sun comes up, or you may be seen."

I agreed. "Yes, you know what you have to do. Whenever you have some news for us, you know where to find us. Start talking to your people and other friendly fraternities of the forest as well. We need to garner as much support as possible now."

They quickly left, and I noticed a twinkle of hope in their eyes. I felt happy, and more determined to make this work.

We too got out to scan the area and decide where we should keep the book. Steve quickly drew and materialized a strongbox with a key. Close to the hills, was that huge oak the boys talked about. I thought it was the perfect landmark. We locked up the book of magic in the strongbox and took it to the oak.

It was a magnificent, enormous, possibly centuries-old tree. We were about to dig up, when I noticed a hole in the trunk about an arm's length above the ground.

Perfect! Oaks are supposed to be sacred too. It will be safe here.

I told the boys we'll hide it in the hole and cover it with leaves. Once done, we were on our way back towards the hills, when Gibel saw us and raised an alarm.

"Hey you! Stop right there. I know you've escaped Selene. I'm going to let her know right now that I've found you. Gibel sets things right!"

We were taken by surprise and, instinctively, wanted to make a run for it.

Instead, I walked towards the dwarf and said, "Calm down, and listen to us, please! You know that we were tricked into being brought here and were held by her to fulfil her wicked ambitions. Is that fair? What do you have to gain from all this? She wants to take over the entire universe, and by harming the inhabitants. Why are you with her on her devilish game?"

He adjusted his collar with an air of importance. "I will be the prime supplier of all the weapons and tools she needs. There is a lot of profit and prestige in it for me. I can become the leader of my colony. The hills will be my kingdom."

"Gibel, you're blinded by your personal ambition. She has been holding families to ransom to get her way. Do you honestly believe that she will reward you for your loyalty? Once you have served your purpose, she will not only abandon you, but she will also usurp any power you hope to hold, perhaps even endanger your life." I tried my best to caution him.

"Remember, her primary aim is to be the sole sovereign over the entire universe! Are you happy to be the cause of ruin of your people and other dwellers of this land?"

"That will not happen to my people. As a leader, I will ensure that they are taken care of," he insisted, stubbornly confounded by his aspirations. "And I shall soon inform her that I've seen you here." Saying so, he rushed towards the other side of the hills.

"Guys, we have to leave this place immediately! Once he lets them know we're around here, they will scan every inch of space and find us," I warned.

"But where shall we go now?" asked Steve. "And how?"

"I think Fairyland would be a safe bet for now. That way, we can keep Flora informed of our whereabouts too. And Roy can do that without us getting noticed," I said.

Roy argued that we don't know where it is located, but there was no time to lose. We had to disappear before anyone came there. We held hands, Roy concentrated, and in a flash, we were in…the cave of a dragon! Yikes!

We saw a dragon snorting fire ahead of us. Gosh, he looked angry! Luckily, he had his back to us, or we'd be barbeque. We were still in danger of his tail hitting us like whiplash. He was moving it around wildly and roaring loudly.

It seemed like he was in pain. I scanned him and saw that a thin, possibly prickly, tree branch had jabbed into his ankle area.

The dragon was a huge bat-winged, scaly serpentine creature with four stumpy legs, red in color and every bit as scary as they're made out to be. Especially the fire-breathing kind. We were not looking forward to being found out, so I told Roy to get us out of there.

And I learnt something new. Roy said if he has used his power, he has to wait for half an hour before he can use it again.

OH NO! How do we get out of the cave now without becoming toast? If not that, we're sure to get swatted like flies with his tail.

Just then, the dragon turned around and his piercing green eyes spoke, "Get out of my way." I most definitely want to do that, but without getting singed or scorched. Jim, without warning, ran towards the dragon and touched his legs.

Is he brave or what?

It worked and the dragon's roar simmered to a deep purr. I guess he understood that we meant no harm. Jim signaled to help him pull out the tree branch. So, he noticed it too; good thinking on his part.

We struggled for a bit and finally managed to pull out the dragon's thorn; but not before feeling the heat from his nostrils. Luckily not directed at us. He calmed down immediately and asked us what we were doing there. I told him we reached there by mistake and were headed towards Fairyland.

"Could you tell us where it is?" I asked for his help.

"I will take you there myself," he offered. "But you must tell me why you want to go there. You may find this hard to believe, but I am their protector, and I must ensure their safety."

Shocking revelation, but a relief, and I was ready to seek his support.

"Oh wow! Then you're the right person— err…dragon to talk to. We're hiding from Selene and her army. She had kidnapped us and wanted to use us to get control of our worlds, just like how she rules yours."

I saw him wince at the mention of Selene. "We managed to getaway and neutralize her shield of power here. But we need the unity of the inhabitants to end her reign. Fairy Queen is on our side. We're looking for a place to hide, now that her army has been alerted near our hideout. We also need to get in touch with Flora and let her know."

"You can hide in my cave. No one will ever know. I will take you to the Fairy Queen myself. You see, in spite of my strengths, I am unable to quash the witch because of her spells. I feel defeated. It's a pledge I made to my father, that I shall protect the fairies come what may. I will help you."

Chapter 8
The Savior

I couldn't believe it! We had a dragon on our side. This was definitely going to be a big advantage.

He told us to hop on to his body and brace ourselves as he took us to Fairyland. Frankly, I think I was looking forward to the aerial view of the forest and the ride. I felt like I was about to enjoy a ride in an amusement park.

We walked out of his cave and stood on the precipice of the cliff and the sight just took my breath away. We scanned the lush green landscape that was spotted with other brilliant shades of red, blue, and yellow. The Enchanted Magus Forest was truly magnificent. Somewhere to the left side, was a village. "Is that the homeland of the fairies, to the left?" I asked.

He confirmed it and pointed out to other villages at various distances as well – the villages of the elves, the gnomes, the ogres…and there was a glass-like blue lake as well that glistened in the sunlight.

He took off, gliding smoothly into the air, and started to relate his tale. "My name is Archon. When my father was young, he was greatly revered as a promising prince, who eventually succeeded my grandfather as the beloved King of the Skies. We lived in harmony with the land dwellers. Until…Selene started to slowly gain power."

As his story went, he was a fledgling, when she started to create trouble between the dragons and the other creatures of the land – the giants, the ogres, the dwarves, and others. I think she feared the strength and power of the dragons. She maligned them as evil and malevolent.

There was a greatly feared giant called Balor. She manipulated and hypnotized the one-eyed Balor into believing that the dragons are going to kill him. Balor was known to wreak mass destruction with a just look of his eye. When angered, the pupil of his eye would enlarge to the size of his iris and emit a poisonous, incendiary beam, reducing everyone and everything in its path to ashes.

"One day," Archon continued, "when my father was called upon to appease the rain gods for the ogres, Balor saw opportunity and attacked my clan. He felt that offense was the best form of defense. He unleashed his terror on the dragons and killed and wounded many."

Archon became a little emotional. "In the mayhem, my mother was also killed. I was playing near the path of his roving, killer gaze. She rushed to get me out of danger and got caught in his deathly stare."

Now he was nostalgic. "Suddenly, Titania, the Fairy Queen came and picked me up just in time, as Balor turned towards the spot where I stood. She ran with me and hid inside the nearest cave, waiting till the bedlam was over."

"What happened when your father returned?" asked Roy.

"When my father returned, he was aghast upon seeing the dying embers of death and destruction. He went after Balor, and after a horrible and bloody battle, he managed to kill the giant with some intelligent strategy.

"Once it was all over, the survivors slowly walked out of hiding and Titania handed me over to my father. Both of us felt deeply anguished when we saw my mother's lifeless body. He shed silent tears as he held me close."

We were shaken to hear about his heartbreaking story, as he ended his tale. "My father was profoundly grateful to Titania for saving my life and pledged to protect them for life. When he was breathing his last, he made me promise to honor that pledge."

We reached Fairyland and Archon touched down, so we could get off. We were greeted very cheerfully by an ethereal, silver-white unicorn, with a mane of pastel pink, blue and purple, and a long spiraling golden horn on its forehead. It was the most beautiful creature anyone could ever see!

"Hello strangers! What brings you here?" She glanced at Archon. "Okay, I know that thing brought you here," she said grimacing and half-hiding behind Roy, "he scares me to death."

Archon snorted a laugh and almost missed searing Roy. Roy and the unicorn let out a unified 'ouch!' and everyone burst out laughing.

"Come, let's go and meet Queen Titania," Archon said. "I don't need to seek her audience, she's like a mother figure to me, and I'm always welcome."

We could see the care in his eyes, and his pride at being special to her. We walked into the Fairy Castle, so dreamy looking, the kind that little girls love. A portly soft-faced Queen Titania lit up as she saw Archon and seemed to recognize us instantly.

She welcomed us, with a little surprise glistening in her eyes, "Hello boys! How is it I see you here with my dear Archie?"

As we introduced ourselves and told her we had to leave our hideout, she asked her staff to summon Flora. "It's good that you're in the cave with Archie now. There can be no safer place for you. Meanwhile, I have to tell you that the gnomes are joining us in our crusade against Selene Kouris."

We were overjoyed that things were working out in our favor.

"Oh wonderful!" piped in the unicorn, and then with some comedic concern, she quietly whispered to us, "Are you sure, he won't burn you when he snores?"

Queen Titania continued, "Dulcea can take you anywhere you need to go, in case Archie is too big to go, right Dulcea?"

The unicorn acceded, "Yes of course, my queen, I would be delighted."

Just then Flora walked in, and she looked relieved upon seeing us. She respectfully curtseyed in front of the queen and turned back to us. "Boys, do you know that Gibel had seen you and alerted Selene? And she has her army scouring the entire area with a fine toothcomb."

"Yes, we accidently met him. I tried to convince him to help us, but we couldn't persuade him. So, we immediately fled," I informed her. "Flora, I'm curious, where has she kept your family?"

Flora's expression quickly saddened as she thought of her kin. "She has all the people she's holding in the basement of her mansion. They're locked up together with food that she replenishes every two days. The entrance is chained and padlocked and, as usual, she has put a spell on it."

I winced at the information, as she spoke, "Anyone who tries to tamper with the lock dies. We have, unfortunately, lost a few people who tried to save the captives."

"In that case, our first course of action should be to get everyone out of that basement." I was determined to get the hostages freed.

Having their families with them, would definitely give the forest dwellers confidence to oppose the witch. Also, she will not be able to harm them if she feels defeated and without leverage.

"Operation Freedom. Tomorrow!" I boomed in announcement.

Chapter 9
The Dark Woods

We sat together to understand how best we may be able to enter Selene's mansion and get to the basement without being detected. I asked Flora to describe the location and security.

"Selene's mansion is in the Dark Woods, which is a small area in the deeper recesses of the forest, where the darker spirits prevail. A singular trail leads up to the mansion atop a small hill. But the trail is full of peril. A dense fog envelops the entire area, and you can easily stray into the woods because of zero visibility. If that happens, you cannot escape the demonic spirits that roam the woods."

We were taken aback with her cautioning narration. She went on to recount the lore behind it.

"In ancient times, those who were found indulging in evil practices were ostracized and sent into exile in those woods by the Emperor of the Enchanted Magus Forest.

"The Emperor, Leonardo Maximus, was a beast with a human body and the head of a lion. He was a brave-heart and a good leader. On one of his rounds around the kingdom, he ventured towards the Dark Woods and met a mysterious and beautiful nymph, Aegeiros.

"It was strange that within a few days of meeting her, he decided to get married to her. Even though his trusted courtiers advised him against it. He silenced them from discussing her in a negative light.

"He was in raptures over his new bride; but the enamor didn't last long. He accidentally walked into her private room, one day, and witnessed her witchery. As he soon came to know that she was practicing black magic, he banished her to that mansion, where Selene now lives.

"Since then, all those found indulging in the dark occult practices were excommunicated and sent to that region. It is believed that their malefic spirits continue to haunt those woods.

"The emperor was heartbroken and became growingly despondent with time. He did his best in his capacity as the sovereign ruler, but his spirit was broken. He didn't live very long after that.

"After his death, the Magus Forest no longer saw a strong unified leader. Every region and community had their own leaders. That didn't create major problems for several years, until the rise of Selene.

"In fact, it is popularly assumed that Selene is a descendant of the nymph. The Black Temple was initially a Temple of Faith, which Selene took over. In the absence of an absolute monarch, she converted it into the Black Temple."

She concluded the folklore with an account of the present situation of those woods.

"Anyway, those are the dangers of the region. Since it is almost impenetrable, she does not have security at the mansion. She personally takes the prisoners in, including any necessities of life. The trail leading to the mansion, however, is free from the menacing specters that haunt the woods.

"Apparently, the nymph left the road untouched by black magic, in the hope that the King would forgive her and come to take her back. But the fog makes it unsafe and, therefore, untrodden."

I told Flora that we would need her and Jinzic to help us with the route and other information as we go the mansion. With much trepidation, she agreed. Her family meant more to her than this life of subjugation to a sorceress, out of fear.

I listed down the supplies that we would need to carry and asked her when Selene leaves the mansion. Apparently, Selene went to the temple every morning around 10.00 am to perform a ritual that sustains her powers. She continued to stay there or visit other regions of the forest till sunset.

So, we had enough time to work to our advantage. I told everyone we'll gather at the Fairy Castle again by 8.00 am. Then we returned with Archon for the night.

Once we were back in the cave, I discussed the nitty gritty with Jim, Roy, and Steve and what we would need to be prepared for. The air was rife with apprehension, and yet, a certain must-do attitude. The boys were totally supportive and gung-ho.

Archon watched us indulgently and offered to help. But that wasn't really possible with his size. We needed to do it undetected, and he was like a gigantic banner of an announcement.

We were all so anxious, it was hard to sleep. I think I finally fell asleep because I was tired of thinking and got up early too. I told Steve to draw us some flashlights. We definitely needed those to get through the fog.

Archon took us to the Fairy Castle in good time. The others were there, waiting for us, and preparing the bags we needed for each person. Ropes, flashlights, religious insignias for everyone and a truckload of faith.

Roy couldn't get us into the mansion using his powers, since he had no idea where it was exactly. Though he would be able to get us out of there unseen. So, we needed to brave the perilous walk.

Everyone exchanged hugs and good wishes, and we started out. Archon flew us and stopped to drop us a little distance away from the woods. From there we walked silently and as inconspicuously as possible towards the trail of the woods.

When we were almost there, we hid behind a huge rock nearby that gave us a clear view of the trail. And we waited to see Selene leave. Every minute seemed slow and stretched, but finally we saw a carriage pass by.

A look at Flora and Jinzic confirmed that it was Selene. In fact, it was being driven by Selene herself. Once the carriage was completely out of sight, we waited a little longer to be sure. When there didn't seem to be any probability of her return, we rushed towards the same road.

I instructed everyone, "We need to walk in single file, tied to each other with the rope around our waist. The purpose is to keep all of us from straying away from the safe trail. That way we can keep a check on each other's safety."

We tied the ropes and checked the knots and the allowance it gave us to move. "Everyone, please carry your flashlights to light the way ahead of you, or to the left and right side. It will help us keep an eye on all sides. WE CANNOT LOSE SIGHT OF THE PERSON AHEAD OF US. All of you wear your religious amulets."

The trail and woods were clearly demarcated with the fog, almost as though a line was drawn around it to create the borders. It did not permeate outside the region.

We checked everything once again and entered the thick haze ahead of us. I told everyone to continually say prayers under their breath. Good faith would keep us safe.

We were to be no more than 3–4 steps behind the person ahead. I was leading, with Flora behind me, followed by Roy, Steve, Jim and Jinzic. We walked slowly and carefully, ensuring that we stayed on the right track.

The trudge stayed uneventful for about fifteen minutes. We kept calling out to each other every couple of minutes to check if all was okay.

Then, all of a sudden, I heard Flora talk, "I'm coming my dear, I'm coming to get you."

"Flora, who are you talking to?" I asked.

"My daughter called out to me; she's in Selene's mansion. But I'm surprised I can hear her," she said.

"Please don't pay any attention to any voices. The spirits are playing tricks to get us off track," I reminded her.

"You're right!" she agreed. And we continued.

A few minutes later, I heard my name being whispered. It sounded like my dad's voice. I felt a lump in my throat. I was yearning to hear my dad speak to me again. But I knew this wasn't true.

Every few minutes, one of us was being lured with a call that made us emotional. Steve almost started to follow the voice. But the rope helped to keep him away from veering off the trail. The walk was emotionally draining us and felt tiring.

We had been plodding along for almost forty-five minutes now. The fog was so thick that if we hadn't decided to be just a couple of steps away from each other, we surely would not have been able to keep them in sight.

After another five minutes had passed, we heard a loud, deep, yet shrill roar. It continued for a while and then stopped. We stopped moving, and I turned around to check with the others. Jinzic immediately said, "That sounds like Archon!"

Chapter 10
The Homecoming

"Yes, he's right. It sounds like a warning roar. Did you ask him to keep a watch over the area?" Flora questioned.

"No, we told him to return because he's too large and that could alert Selene or her henchmen," Jim spoke.

Roy opined, "I think he decided to help anyway on his own. But the point is what is he warning us about, if that is indeed what he is doing?"

"I think he may have seen Selene come back this way," I sounded out my worry. "How much longer do we have to reach?"

"It's hard to say," said Flora, "with this thick fog. Let's just continue and get there."

We started again, but luckily, shortly after that we saw a step. I guessed that we had reached the mansion. We climbed up the low stairs and the air was miraculously clearer now. In fact, the mansion was in clear view. A very large, ominous looking home. It reeked of gloom and had a sinister aura. It looked straight out of a Halloween poster.

We untied the ropes, and quickly went around the back, to avoid being seen by Selene, just in case, the warning was in fact to alert us of her return. There was a door at the back, which was locked. Steve materialized a crowbar and opened it.

It led into a very spacious kitchen. But it looked more like the witch's lab. Large cauldrons, jars containing vile looking things. I think they may have been parts of living creatures. Creepy does not even begin to describe it. We walked in silently, not knowing if there was anyone else in that house that we needed to be wary of.

Cautiously, we walked from room to room, until we saw a staircase going down. Surely that led to the underground chambers. Every room spoke of a lost grandeur that succumbed to centuries of evil shadows that pervaded the spaces. It was filled with an unholy stench.

We continued down the stairs undisturbed, gratefully, and walked past a pantry and a lumber room, until we reached a large door that was chained and padlocked. This is what Flora had described to us. Definitely, it is the room with all the hostages.

Just then we heard some shuffling sounds of approaching feet. The lumber room being closest, we darted into it. As it turned out, that was a smart move. We could easily hide behind the various pieces of old furniture stored in there. We could also clearly hear the sounds as they amplified and echoed in the empty passageway.

As we held our breaths to avoid any sound, the chains clanked when keys clicked lightly into the iron padlock, and then the large door creaked open. As soon as the door opened, we could hear a wave of pleas and soft cries.

Sadness grabbed my heart, and I could feel the immense grief that Flora, Jinzic and all the others must be feeling. I could feel the pain of living every day with the despair of separation with loved ones, who are captivated and in danger.

Just then, Selene heckled in her grating voice, "Quiet, you…bumbling buggers! Here's your food." And we could hear the shuffling and shifting of, possibly, gunny sacks. The door creaked shut again, and the clanking and clanging of the lock and chains reverberated.

Footsteps echoed for a bit and slowly faded away. We were afraid to move, in case she returned. After, what seemed like a long enough time, we finally spoke to each other to come out of hiding.

"I forgot that she was to restock on food today," said Flora. "God bless Archon for signaling to us."

I urged everyone, "Come on, let's do this quickly now. Steve, can you please draw up a door on the wall? We can't open this one as it's been hexed."

"Yes of course!" Steve quickly got to work and as he brandished his pen like a magic wand, the door became a reality. Flora and Jinzic gasped with joy.

They opened the door, and the sudden surge of wails, to surprise, to happy tears was heavy with emotion. I requested everyone to stay quiet and come out quickly. What if she returned? We couldn't take that risk.

There must have been roughly forty to fifty people there of various forest communities and of various ages. Jim told everyone to hold hands and they all quietened down and looked ready to follow our instructions.

As quietly as possible, we made our way back the same way we came in, shepherding the captives towards the back door. Roy went out front to check if Selene had left. He returned almost immediately to tell us all was clear. We took everyone towards the steps and told them to wait a moment.

An elderly dwarf, who was already at the last step, didn't quite hear me, and continued to walk into the fog. No one realized until it was too late. A few moments into the fog and we heard him let out a horrifying scream.

Everyone was aghast; I ran upfront to stop anyone else from following to check on him. The shock of the sudden loss brought tears to their eyes. I'm sure they had all formed strong bonds in confinement.

I told everyone to stay rooted and hold each other's hands to form a chain. "Roy, work your magic."

Roy took a few seconds to concentrate, and we were not only out of the woods, we were teleported directly to Fairyland. There were cheers of jubilation as everyone celebrated their freedom. Everyone was hugging everyone, and it was a happy sight.

Dulcea glowed with joy when she saw all of us and traipsed off to inform Queen Titania. The queen came immediately to congratulate us and led everyone to the castle courtyard. She wanted to formally address everyone.

News spread like wildfire in Fairyland and all the fairies joined the congregation to welcome any members of their family or friends, who had returned from their ordeal, and hear the queen's address.

The courtyard wore a festive atmosphere. Tears of joy, and squeals of glee filled the air. I saw Archon and ran to him to thank him for his help, despite my instructions to not stay around the Dark Woods. After all, it was his timely warning, that helped us avoid any complications in the already difficult mission.

Refreshments and blankets were passed around for the returnees. The happy families thronged around us to express their gratitude. The Toon boys and I were being treated like heroes!

The queen stepped out onto her balcony, and her attendant shouted, "Hear ye, hear ye all!"

Chapter 11
The Queen's Address

The excited crowd silenced quickly, and Queen Titania cheerily waved to the people. She started her speech by addressing the freed hostages, "It is with immense joy that I welcome home all those who have been suffering since long."

There was a wave of deafening applause.

"The brave silence, with which our families have been enduring pain, has finally been rewarded. For this, I thank these four boys, who I would like to call our guests from heaven. These God-sent angels have confronted extreme danger to bring us happiness and reunite our families. I extend my heartfelt gratitude on behalf of the entire Enchanted Magus Forest.

"For years, we have silently watched the unbridled and steady rise of Selene Kouris and her negative forces. We have been living in the shadows of darkness and gloom for a very long time. But no more!

"These heroes have shown us the path to a happier future, freed us from our constraints, and now…we must not lose this opportunity to take back our lives, that was curbed under her oppression.

"We have to take that step forward to negate her forces and bring an end to her tyranny. We must amalgamate our strengths and fight together. We must unite to return the Enchanted Forest to its former glory.

"To all of you, who have returned, I implore you to convince your communities to join hands with us in this war against evil. But first, I will make sure you return home in safety to your families. And there's not a moment to lose, to reunite you with your loved ones.

"Then, you must convene immediately with your leaders and persuade them. It is imperative that all the communities act together, to be able to stand up to the despicable powers of Selene.

"On behalf of the fairies, and as their queen, I hereby pledge allegiance to this mission to exterminate the hold of Selene Kouris on our lands and lives. From this day on, I announce that we shall once again celebrate Christmas, and start all preparations towards a happy celebration of our faith in the Supreme! God bless you all!"

The crowd was overjoyed and shouted out loud enthusiastic approvals. The queen acknowledged the ovation, and then went in to start making arrangements. She had undertaken the responsibility for the safe return of the escapees from the other communities to their villages.

The gnomes, the dwarfs, the elves, the imps, even the ogres…they had all been affected with a similar grief. Their weak faces streaked with distress, now showed a glimmer of joy. Flora's daughter was over the moon that she would enjoy her family's pampering.

Jinzic looked gratified after reuniting with his parents and nephew. It was the first time I saw him smile. He took on the responsibility of taking all the other gnomes back with him as well.

Dulcea was appointed take the elves; their village was very close to Fairyland. Archon would return the imps to their home.

We were wondering how the ogres would go back to their village. Flora said she would go to Vozig and bring him with her, to pick them up. That seemed to be the only way to ensure their safety, since they were so huge.

Besides, that had an added advantage. We could try to make Vozig see the importance of veering away from Selene.

"What about the dwarfs?" I asked the queen.

She contemplated for a bit and said, "Why don't you boys take them?"

I was surprised with her suggestion because she knew that Gibel was not in our favor, and he was the one to snitch on us.

I looked at her, quizzical, and she explained, "These dwarfs have been saved by you. You have their trust. And they will be able to prove to Gibel that you are genuine and mean well. I will handle Vozig here when he arrives."

"But Gibel is also driven with his ambitions of gain from Selene," I reminded. "Would he be willing to lose that?"

The queen was reassuring, "You can remind him how undependable she is. Also, with everyone ready to go against her, he might end up losing out on his ambition anyway. Tell him he has more to gain by applying his skills for the progress of the forest dwellers."

That sounded like a risk worth taking, and I agreed. "What about Selene? Do you think she has found out by now, or what if she sees some of the people going back home? Maybe someone else would inform her. Won't she attack them with her army?"

"Sid, even if she knows, by the time she reaches them with her army, their village will be up in arms to tackle her and we'll be there with them. Also, she cannot overpower now with her spells and magic, since the Grimoire is in your custody. She can only use her powers for minor things. I'm sure we can deal with that."

I looked at the boys. "Let's go!" We formed a chain with the dwarfs, holding hands, and Roy took us back to the hills where we first hid. The dwarfs informed us that the village was in those same hills, just behind the particular hill where we hid in the low cave.

No wonder we were spotted by Gibel, I thought.

As we entered their domain, the other dwarfs emerged from their homes and looked at us incredulously. The families, who were missing their loved ones, broke the silence with their cries and rushed to hug them. In a matter of moments, their leader along with Gibel also joined the crowd.

Explanations done, I turned to Gibel. "We are here to ask you to reconsider what we discussed earlier. As you can see, your own people have been tormented by her."

Gibel cut me short. "You don't have to explain further. I'm with you."

Introducing the leader, he said, "we were just talking about it now, when you arrived with our people. After I informed Selene about seeing you in the forest near the hills, she sent out a search party, but could not find you. And she blamed me for it."

He hung his head and gulped his emotion as he went on, "I was humiliated in front of my clan. At that moment, I realized you were right! She is not trustworthy. My ambitions were misplaced. And I cannot tell you how happy I am to see our people back home."

We were ecstatic. "That's wonderful to hear from you! We are garnering the support of all the communities."

In a more somber tone, I informed him, "There is bad news though, about an elderly dwarf, whom we lost in the Dark Forest. It was very unfortunate. Please convey our condolences to his family."

One of the dwarfs who came with us, related the incident. They shook their heads with a twinge of sadness.

And I continued, "The fairies and gnomes are already with us. Very soon, we shall convince the imps, elves, and ogres too. United, we can destroy Selene. But…She would still have the gremlins on her side."

The leader spoke, "Don't worry about them. They are our cousins. Hard to convince, but I can handle them and make sure they do not support her."

"We'll take your leave now, and get back to you soon," I said as we shook hands to their agreement.

Chapter 12
Christmas Prevails

We returned to the Fairy Castle, just in time to see Vozig leaving with the ogres. He didn't see us, which was just as well because he frightened me.

I looked at Queen Titania and she was smiling. I heaved a sigh of relief. This meant that Selene now had no army. The ogres and the gremlins were both going to be walking away from her. This was working out very positively. I asked if the fairies were planning a celebration that night.

"Not tonight. I'd like them to spend some family time together, which will help in their healing. From tomorrow, the fairies will get busy with Christmas preparations. It has been years since our faith was usurped, and there have been no festivities. It's time we reinstated our faith. Christmas this year will mark the return of our beatitude."

I remembered again the Christmassy stormy night that took me to the Toon World, when she spoke of Christmas celebrations.

"We have just a couple of days left. It would be a pleasure if you join us. I shall be extending this invitation tomorrow to all the other communities as well. In fact, I think we should stake claim on our Temple of Faith too."

It did cross my mind earlier that there was no sign of the festive season in the forest. Now I understood why. The queen was right. We must reconvert the temple back from black magic to the magic of God as it was originally intended to be. And my thoughts were running amok.

How were we going to do that? How do we cleanse the sanctum sanctorum from the evil spirits? And is Selene going to give up without a fight? I don't think so. Seems too good to be true.

For now, I didn't want to take away from the joyful feelings that the day had brought. So, I didn't bring up my doubts. And it had been a long day, we needed the rest too.

We returned to Archon's lair. He was already there after leaving the imps at their abode. He greeted us with gratitude and said he felt indebted with our sacrifices. He could now fulfil his duties as protector of the fairies in earnest.

The next morning suddenly felt brighter than usual. A heaviness seemed to have lifted from the air.

We were all set for a day of fun at Fairyland. We reached there with Archon, and Dulcea met us with an extra spring in her step. It seemed now that she was warming up to Archon as well.

The villagers were active with work, centered around a huge Christmas tree placed in the village square. The fairies were decorating the tree and the square and, in fact, the entire village was in the process of being festooned with flowers and ribbons.

The aroma of delectable bakes wafted through the air. The fairies involved us in their decorating errands, and we were enjoying ourselves. I, myself, had been missing the festive cheer too for several years. I got nostalgic reminiscing Christmas time in my neighborhood as a kid; it was a beautiful feeling.

Flora came to meet us with her daughter, who thanked us for getting her back to her family. All of us got involved in the activities around us, and we saw the leaders of the other communities come in with some of their people, from time to time.

It was nice to see all of them join in, and it struck me that the forest ought to have an absolute sovereign once again, one who could keep them together in harmony. It would also dissuade the uprising of any other destructive force in the future. But first we needed to get rid of the current disruptive force.

Just then the queen came to the square to inspect the goings on and invited all the guests to a royal feast. I was excited and really looking forward to the royal banquet. It was something I had never even dreamt of experiencing.

The arrangements were amazing; an elegantly set up dinner table, a delicious meal followed by those fabulously aromatic fresh cakes and pastries we could smell earlier. I had never had such a grand meal ever. The Toon boys were also enjoying themselves.

We were all engaged in cheerful banter and laughter. The other guests spoke of their Christmas preparations as well. After getting news of Fairyland's special announcement, they decided to re-establish the old traditions too.

After a fabulous time at the castle, we once again joined the fairies in the square, and their fun. I saw some of them rehearsing for a dance and noticed that Steve had joined them.

Now that was a surprise! I had never thought that a serious and strong looking Steve would be interested in dancing. What astonished me even more, was his partner…he was dancing with Flora's pretty daughter!

In the hullabaloo, I hadn't noticed how pretty she was…oh, she was a cute looker, and those gossamer wings just added to her pixie-like appeal. And he was looking absolutely smitten!

I was amused and couldn't wait to rib him about it. All said and done, I was also happy to see them enjoying each other's company. It was an affirmation to me how positive emotions can transcend the worse of situations.

The day had been exciting and enjoyable and was ending on a beautiful note. It was getting late, and all the boys caught up with me. We found Archon relaxing near the castle and all of us returned to the cave.

We were in a good mood and continued our conversation about the activities in Fairyland. Sitting around a cozy bonfire, we exchanged notes about what each of us did; Archon included.

He was looking so compassionate and caring, a far cry from the angry fire-breathing dragon that we first encountered. The ambience was easy and homey. I took the chance and brought up Steve's budding romance.

He looked sheepish. "I liked her from the moment we rescued them from the dark mansion. She was shaken up when that elderly dwarf walked into the fog and met his end. Instinctively, she clung to me for reassurance. And I felt very protective towards her."

Jim and Roy teased him incessantly. Archon was listening to our conversation, and then took out a book from a little hidden corner of the cave.

Handing it over to me, he said, "Sid, this is the bible my mother used for praying. We should use this and other cleansing items to rid the Black Temple of its demonic souls. We need a place of worship and faith. And it's the same faith that will return the temple to us."

"You're right, Archon. It is always faith that keeps us protected. You've just reconfirmed to us how we can get this done."

Chapter 13
Exorcising Demons

We returned to Fairyland the next morning to strategize the takeover of the temple. And we needed all the leaders to be a part of this mission. Everyone was summoned, once again, and we did some brain storming, and worked out all the requirements and how to go about it.

It was a terrifying thought, that we'd have to deal with those satanic souls. There was no telling what would happen. Everyone had more than their share of apprehensions. Much as we all believed it needed to be done, we also feared the backlash.

No doubt I had stepped into that room once before, but it was one thing to avoid those spirits and get the grimoire, and quite another to get rid of them altogether. That would be like a head on collision. I just remember that wearing the symbols of God on my person, kept me safe from them.

However, if they are being forcefully expelled, it is a direct offense. And I wasn't quite sure how effective we would be in evading their attacks under such circumstances.

I was just praying that everyone's joint effort would be powerful enough to remove them from the temple and cleanse the place of worship. We would also need to set up a watch outside the temple, so that Selene would not be able to foil the procedures.

That also brought to our attention that there had been no sign of her, post the rescue of her hostages. No counterattack, no confrontation, no communication at all. That was worrisome. Surely, the silence was the one before a storm. It was open war now.

The only blessing being that she was not in possession of her book of spells and could not exercise powers that restricted anyone. But I'm sure she did have some powers of her own, and we did not know the extent of her abilities.

In my opinion, Archon was the best bet to keep her at bay from the temple. She would not be able to go past his aggression. Therefore, he was entrusted with the responsibility of keeping her away, while we completed what we set out to do inside.

So theoretically, we were all set to start. We now needed to figure out when was the best time. As we were contemplating, Vozig and his leader suggested we do it right away.

"There is no time to waste, or we may end up having to deal with other obstacles that Selene will create," they said.

And they were right, so we decided to head towards the temple as soon as possible. Queen Titania sent out some of her fairies to the forest, to collect large quantities of herbs and woods considered helpful in repelling negative energies; like white sage, cedar and palo santo. We also needed some coconuts to make the natural bowls to burn these materials in.

Next, we wrote down the prayers and incantations that we would recite during the ritual. All the religious symbols and amulets were gathered for everyone to wear.

A large cross that would replace the inverted one placed in the inner chamber was arranged. We asked for a big bowl of sea salt and, together, blessed it to empower it's cleansing properties.

"Almighty God, we ask you to bless this salt, as once you blessed the salt scattered over the water by the prophet Elisha. Wherever this salt (and water) is sprinkled, drive away the power of evil, and protect us always by the presence of your Holy Spirit. Grant this through Christ our Lord. Amen."

In the same way, we blessed a container of spring water. Next, we added some of the salt to the water. Making the sign of a cross as we sprinkled it in, we recited a protective chant.

"May this salt and water be mixed together; in the name of the Father and of the Son, and of the Holy Spirit. Amen." Our holy water was ready to be used.

Our groundwork done, we proceeded to the temple. All the leaders of the dwarfs, ogres, gnomes, elves, fairies, and imps along with us boys and Archon. We also took along two of his dragon friends. I think we formed a formidable group.

We reached there to see the remnants of a ritual that was likely performed by Selene that morning. Luckily, she wasn't around at the time. And again, I wondered what underhanded plot she was working on now.

Archon and his friends took on their position in vigilance. We entered the vestibule, went through the plebeian court and into the priests' court.

We prepared the coconut bowls with the burning herbs and woods and double-checked if were wearing our protective symbols and amulets. I passed on the wafting smoke to everyone to smudge themselves with the purifying fumes.

I cautioned them, "Under no circumstances are we to stop our prayers before completing it. Every prayer, every incantation must be recited in full. The situation may look bleak and dangerous, but we must continue, no matter what is happening around us. Please fortify yourselves mentally and 'Do Not Stop'!"

The ogre, dwarf and gnome chiefs carried the cross, while the others held the coconut bowls with the cleansing smoke. The Toon boys and I carried the blessed salt and holy water. Together all of us said the prayers addressing the Heavenly Father to protect us from evil and keep us safe.

Continuing our prayers, we entered the inner sanctum. I had seen it before, but it was a first for the rest of the group, and they gasped in shock as they took in the dark vibes. We placed the cleansing bowls in all corners of the room and on the altar, as we chanted.

Within a few minutes, the air started to feel heavier and gloomier. We could hear soft groaning. We took our positions near the altar and started our prayers invoking God and the Holy Spirits. Holy water was sprinkled all around.

"Being of earth, in the name of the ineffable God and Goddess consecrated in the service of the Highest, guard and protect this temple and everything and everyone in it from all evil."

The groans soon turned into a howl and the atmosphere became more vicious. Objects randomly flew about the room.

The Ogre Chief got hit and bruised when he got in the way of a chair that seemed to have been flung towards him and Queen Titania. He was trying to save her from the impact. But he was strong, and slowly stood up to continue what we had started.

We made an adjuration addressed to the spirits to force them to abandon the chambers and the temple. The tumult in the room became more intense and violent.

We held hands in united power and started chanting prayers of expulsion continuously, amidst the roars and growls and deafening howls. The noise was reaching a crescendo, as was our chanting. Even during the chanting, various objects hit several of us, but we refused to let it stop us.

We would also get thrown off with the force of the spirits. We decided to sit down in a circle holding hands, to avoid a forceful push. Everyone was determined and fully committed to seeing this through.

Chapter 14
Emergence of a New Era

After some time had elapsed, the spirits suddenly quietened down. But the aura I felt was still bleak and thick, after a moment of assessing the surroundings. I urged everyone to continue, because I suspected that they were trying to deceive us into believing we were successful.

Once again, we repeated the invocation persistently, and the screeching and howling resumed to extremely loud proportions. Just as I expected.

It took a few hours of praying tirelessly, when all of a sudden, the stained-glass windows shattered, and we felt an enormous gust of dark wind exit from the door and the windows. Everything became very still.

The ambience turned light and bright and there was a fleeting scent of roses. We could tell with conviction now that we had managed to successfully complete our mission.

We pulled down the inverted cross and set up the cross that we had brought with us. I suppose we could just turn the other cross around, but I didn't think it was worth taking a chance of leaving any remnants of darkness. What if the wood had absorbed the negative energies?

So, I suggested we submit it to flames while praying. We could do that in the verandah outside.

We sprinkled the salt and holy water, and smudged with holy smoke, every conceivable corner of the chamber. We came out exhausted and bruised; but continued cleansing the other areas of the temple.

Alighting from the temple, we burnt the cross that we had pulled down inside. All the leaders rejoiced that they had finally reclaimed their Temple of Faith.

Archon and his friends looked very pleased to see us; they could tell that everything went well. Taking bold steps to preserve their faith, and doing it together, had given all the foresters a very strong sense of unity.

And the Toon boys and I held a very special place for them.

This was the resurgence of a good period. New relationships had formed. An integrated society, such as this, needs to be preserved for posterity!

As we started to go back to Fairyland, Archon mentioned that Selene did, in fact, show up during the exorcism. But it wasn't difficult to get rid of her. Breathing fire was enough to make her beat a hasty retreat.

She did, however, threaten consequences. By now, everyone was sure she's going to create some trouble soon.

Nevertheless, this was a time to commemorate this special victory. Christmas was the following day, and that made this achievement a lot more special.

Once back in Fairy Castle, Queen Titania called upon all the fairies to gather at her courtyard for her address once again. In fact, all the leaders quickly returned to their villages to do the same.

"To all my beloved subjects, I have the most astounding news to share with you. This day marks a new beginning for all of us."

With a suspenseful pause, she continued, "We have reclaimed our Temple of Faith! This is a confirmation of the wondrous time ahead of us. And though, we do not have ordained preachers at this time, as a community we should jointly pray for continued blessings.

"It is Christmas Eve and I implore you all to please go the temple tonight, to pray together and bring in Christmas Day. All other communities, all the dwellers of the Magus Forest are expected to do the same.

"Thank you and God bless us all."

The crowd displayed their euphoria with unabated applause and screams of triumph. Soon after, they rushed to their homes to make suitable preparations.

The village was now looking beautiful with all the decorations and lights put up. The tree looked amazing with the baubles and ribbons, and the star on top shone in all its glory.

I saw Steve talking to Flora's daughter, Aurora. Jim and Roy were goofing around with Dulcea and checking out the shops selling Christmas goodies.

I wanted to have a word with the queen. After I was done, I joined Jim and Roy. Dulcea, I had noticed, had taken a liking to Roy, and was always ambling around him.

"Dulcea," I asked mischievously, "what do you think of our Roy?"

"Oh, he's so cute," she replied.

"Really? You think I'm cute? So, what you're saying is…Jim is 'not' cute?" Roy grinned looking at Jim.

Dulcea looked sheepish. "No, no, no…that's not what I meant. But you're cuter!" We laughed heartily.

Meanwhile, Steve and Aurora walked arm in arm, and went and sat on a bench near the Christmas tree. I could see them from afar. They were quite engrossed in each other.

They talked for a while, and then walked towards the archway that led to the tree. It was decorated with a mistletoe. Yes, I saw them steal a kiss. Romance was in the air!

Why am I being so creepy and eyeing them? They need some privacy.

I focused once more on our banter, and we decided to share some desserts. I couldn't help but think of my grandparents and their funny mock fights.

"Come and have your dinner. You sit there all day and grow only one leaf in two weeks," Grandma would sound annoyed, calling him for the fifth time.

"Can't you think of anything other than food?" he'd reply, half laughing, while he was busy dirtying his hands in the garden. "And don't exaggerate. You're just jealous that I'm the one with the green thumb in the house."

After a while, Steve and Aurora joined us and we talked for a bit. He informed us that he would be going to the temple with Aurora and her family.

Dulcea wanted to join us. I wanted to get some rest before we left, and sweet Dulcea offered to take us to her home for some much-needed rest.

When it was time to leave, we were feeling nice and refreshed. We walked out of Dulcea's home, and it was quite a sight, as we saw everyone walking out in their best finery.

Large groups headed out of the village together. We went out and we saw hundreds of dwellers from the other villages also joining in. Multitudes, moving in the same direction.

All roads lead to the temple, I thought to myself and smiled.

When we reached the temple, it was like a sea of heads. The courts of the priests and the plebeians, and in fact the entire temple grounds, were crowded with happy faces. The leaders who had gathered earlier in the priests' court lit candles at the altar in the inner sanctum.

They came out and started to sing hymns, and the population took a cue and joined in. The entire shrine and its grounds echoed with pious, soothing melody. They sang soul-stirring carols and said prayers.

The lack of so many years of festivity was erased with the vigor they displayed that night. The celebration of worship continued till midnight, after which they were all wishing each other 'MERRY CHRISTMAS!'

Everyone's faces were lit up with radiance when they returned home.

Chapter 15
Christmas Day

"Mom, I want more laddoos."

"No. Finish your breakfast first. Who eats laddoos first thing in the morning?"

"C'mon, Radha, it's Diwali and he's a kid. That's what festivals are for. That's what celebrations are all about." My dad took up for me and started feeding me my favorite sweet.

****

I woke up almost feeling the taste of the laddoo. I realized I'd been dreaming. Dad and I loved most Indian sweets, but this was a favorite. The memory of that rich spherical dessert made of flour, had me drooling.

How I miss those festive celebrations with Mom and Dad! It has been so long since we did anything together.

It was Christmas Day; the sun was up and so was everyone else. I squinted my eyes open and saw the boys wishing each other with bear hugs.

"Come on, sleepy head, wake up!" Jim shook me hard.

"I'm up, I'm up, don't get violent." I laughed sleepily.

And they swooped down on me, like they were tackling me in a game of rugby. Any remnant of sleep was all gone now. But I wasn't annoyed at all. I quite enjoyed their madness. I felt like our friendship had steadily strengthened with time.

"Merry Christmasssss!!!" I shouted out.

"Merry Christmas!" they shouted back and there was a big round of hugs.

Just then Archon came into the cave and there was another round of hugs and greetings. He was carrying four boxes. He handed one to each of us, saying, "This is my Christmas gift for you. I hope you like it."

"Wow! Christmas gifts! Thank you so much Archon. We love you too, but we don't have any gifts to give you," said Roy.

"Oh, you boys have given me the best gift you can. And not just me, all of us in the forest. Our families, our faith, the festivals, friendship, and most importantly FREEDOM! Thank you, my dear friends," he sounded emotional.

We opened our boxes. Four identical hampers. Each one had a mini-Christmas cake, a freshly baked loaf of bread, a turkey pot pie and a snow globe with a forest and a Christmas tree in it. I thought it was an extremely thoughtful gift. The food was a considerate and apt Christmas meal, and the snow globe was a befitting souvenir to preserve the memories.

"I love it! Where did you get this stuff? Okay, don't answer that, must be from Fairyland, right?" I guessed.

"Right!" He smiled. "And please get ready soon. Today is a going to be a big day for you all. I'll be taking you to visit all the villages to see their merrymaking. It will be a Christmas to remember. We will end the tour with Fairyland being our last stop. Queen Titania has planned a special dinner for you."

"Wow! Sounds like a fabulous day," Jim spoke for all of us.

After enjoying our wonderful Christmas breakfast, we hopped onto Archon and flew off to the first stop – the dwarf village.

The skies were looking so blue and clear. It looked like a fabulous day to get our tour on Archon Airlines!

Below, we could see the most lusciously colorful landscape. Trees of various colors covered the land – green, red, orange, purple and yellow. We flew above the thick canopy of the forest and passed a huge glistening lake. It was the same lake I'd seen earlier from outside Archon's lair.

"What lake is that?" I asked Archon.

"Oh, that's Lake Arcane, the only lake in the enchanted forest. Its water has healing properties," he informed. "If anyone is ill, they are asked to drink water taken from Lake Arcane, to help them heal faster. The healing properties have been bestowed by the mermaid Narissa, who is a protector of the lake."

I have to go to this lake one day. It looks so tranquil and beautiful.

Soon we saw the hills loom ahead, which housed the village. As we got closer, we saw the stony hills were completely transformed with streamers, adornments, and a decorated tree. There was a cheerfulness in the air, which was missing the first time we went there. The harsh landscape was lent some softness. And so was the village.

The dwarfs were smiling and mingling with each other. The atmosphere was very much like a community fete. A line dancing performance was on near the Christmas tree with a cheering crowd. Womenfolk wore jewels and kids ran around happily. It was an endearing sight to behold.

We walked around like happy tourists, until we saw Gibel and rushed to greet him. He was far cry from the individual we first met. He was warm and welcoming, and together we went to greet the leader.

We also saw the gremlins having a joint celebration with the dwarfs. They were small and creepy looking creatures. Large blood shot eyes, sharp teeth and claws, scaly skin and lacking the elegance of the dwarfs.

It was hard to see how they could be cousins. They, apparently, lived like nomads, and didn't have a fixed place to call home. For this reason, their leader chose to celebrate along with the dwarfs.

After spending some time with the leader, it was time for us to move. Before going, I asked Gibel if he still aspired to become the leader of his people. What he said to me told me that, indeed, he was now capable of handling the duties of a ruler.

"Earlier, I was driven by personal ambition and was blinded to the requirements of my people. I have realized that I would gain their respect, only if, I could give them stability and prosperity as well." We agreed.

"I'm happy to be second-in-command, as I trust the ability of our leader. And in this position too, the people look up to me. So, I did get what I want – their respect. And any further progress will only make things better."

The village was in good hands.

With that, we moved onto our next destination – the ogre village. The houses were larger here; not so surprising seeing their stature. As expected, the festivities were on, the decorations were up.

To be honest, we didn't feel very comfortable in their village. They were all so huge and scary looking. If we hadn't been instrumental in their freedom, I'm sure our equation with the ogres wouldn't have been very pleasant.

But it was Christmas Day, and they were all attired in extravagant robes and ornaments. That definitely softened their personalities. We met the leader and exchanged greetings.

Surprisingly, Vozig came up to us and thanked us for our contributions to their wellbeing. That helped to still our fluttering hearts. We shook hands, wished them well, and took their leave.

"Phew! That's a relief," said Roy, "I was afraid one of them would come and crush us."

"They know who you are, and that will never happen, especially with me around." Archon smiled.

Chapter 16
Party Hopping

Subsequently, we flew out to Gnomesville. It was located in a heavily wooded area and hidden from open view.

Jinzic noticed Archon, as we were nearing, and ran over to greet us as soon as we got off. We exchanged friendly hugs, and he insisted on showing us around. Their homes were small, simple stone structures, quite unlike the somewhat elaborate woody homes of the ogres.

I enquired after his parents', and he happily said they were doing well and resting at home. "Their age does not allow them to actively celebrate, and they need the rest after years of captivity. My nephew is enjoying himself with his friends. Would you like to meet my parents?"

"Yes, definitely!" I said cheerily.

All of us walked together towards an alley behind the village square and stopped outside a home with a beautiful wreath on the door. Archon, meanwhile, went to greet the leader. We had to bend low to enter; the doorway was small.

The home was simple, but warm, and there was table laden with Christmas goodies to welcome anyone to came to meet his parents. We were led inside to his parents' room. His mother sat on a rocking chair knitting, while his father sat on a chair next to the window to get a view of the revelry outside.

They broke into warm smiles as they saw us and invited us to make ourselves comfortable. We enquired after their wellbeing and made some pleasant conversation. We didn't stay too long and excused ourselves, to allow them to continue unwinding.

Jinzic took us on a house tour, and we were pleasantly surprised. The simple exterior belied the functionality within. The home was spacious with a staircase leading under the ground to another level with a few rooms. Like a basement level. Apparently, this was the norm for gnome homes.

Quite an architectural feat for a simple race, I thought to myself.

He brought us back upstairs to the food table and insisted we try his mother's cooking. We enjoyed a few snacks, while chatting, and complimented his mother's cooking skills.

It was time to meet and greet the leader now. Jinzic led us to the town hall, where Archon was in conversation with their chief. Our wishes exchanged, we headed back outside and saw a magic show in progress.

The audience was laughing and applauding, as the illusionist showed tricks and laced his dialogue with humor. We watched the show, and Roy was even called out to volunteer for a trick.

"Sir, can you pick out a card?" Roy randomly picked one from the deck stretched out in front of him. "Now please look at your card, show it to the audience and tear it up. You can pretend it's a note from your teacher."

The audience laughed heartily. Roy did as he was told.

The magician waved his hands about and said some magic words, "Alakazim…Alakazam…andddd…here's your card…Shazam!!!"

He pulled out the exact same card from Roy's pocket. He was rewarded with wild applause and whistles. It was an amusing show, after which we said our byes and headed to see the imps.

The imps did not have a proper village with houses. They actually lived on trees in a secluded area of the forest. So, we did not have the same festival experience with them.

We reached there to see a whole lot of tiny, thin, bony, unattractive creatures moving up and down on trees. Their structure could easily camouflage in the trees, except their red body color gave them away. Some of them were gliding around spreading their leathery, bat-like wings.

There was one imp perched on a high branch, singing a melodious tune. Some of them watched him and swayed with the rhythm, while many of the others looked like they were busy in a game of 'how to annoy one another.'.

A few of them saw us and rushed to get our attention. Each one was insisting, only he had the authority to take us to the leader. While they tried to convince us, the leader swooped down and shooed all of them away. They sniggered and ran away.

"Merry Christmas, boys!" their leader greeted with a flourish.

"Merry Christmas to you and all the imps too!" we said in unison, and I continued. "We have the pleasure of visiting you today and be a part of your merriment."

He waved his hands around to show us and informed, "Well, as you can see, we don't celebrate in the usual manner. But do you see that imp singing there? To us, that is celebration. Music is a big part of our lives."

We continued chatting for a few more minutes and then left. We only had the elves left to visit before heading out for our dinner date at the Fairy Castle.

The Elfin Village was very close to the fairy domain. It was not surprising that their homes were just as pretty. Their houses twinkled with colorful lights and streamers, as did their lanes.

They too had a lovely tree placed in the square. There was another centerpiece of attraction placed alongside the tree. A wooden sleigh with wooden reindeers was specially constructed by them, for the occasion.

They had done this at lightning speed considering, until two days ago, they had no clue that Christmas was going to be celebrated. In spite of having just a couple of days at their disposal, it was fabulously done, and totally brought the spirit of Christmas alive.

The elves with their diminutive size and pointed ears looked like Christmas toys themselves – an endearing but mischievous bunch. They also seemed to be very hard working.

They had set up various little stalls with games and activities to entertain their people. One pretty elf-maiden came up to Steve and urged him to get his fortune told.

"I will as soon as we are done meeting your leader, Lord Avery," Steve promised her.

"Don't forget to come. Surely, you want to know your future with Aurora," she said naughtily and skipped away grinning.

"How did she know?" He looked astonished.

"C'mon, did you think no one noticed the sparks? Your vibes can be spotted a mile away!" Jim teased. "Okay, let's go and wish Lord Avery."

Lord Avery was seated on a throne, placed on a podium. The podium was set up in a corner that could oversee all the village activities. A few guards stood on either side, to ensure that nothing went amiss.

He welcomed us as soon as he saw us, and we greeted him. After exchanging pleasantries, he thanked us for all our help and encouraged us to enjoy the activities.

Chapter 17
Reviving Life

We decided to try out some games and pushed Steve to go to the fortune teller. He said he'd do so if all of us went, and we agreed.

One game was like a competition. We had to paint little sleighs, and the first one to complete it would win a small jar of gum drops.

We needed twelve people to start. So, we waited for a bit until other elves joined in. I felt like I was reliving my childhood. It was fun.

Some of them tried to get their way by hiding our paints – mischievous little critters! However, the winner was an elf who did his bit fair and square.

After a few more games, we went to see the clairvoyant elf-maiden. She was happy to see all of us there, waiting to tell us what was in store for us.

"I will start with you." She looked at Steve.

"Yeah, he's always a hit with the ladies." Roy laughed.

She gazed into her crystal ball for a few moments. "You will not be together for a very long time, and yet, you will always love each other," she told Steve. "But do not be disheartened, you will find your happiness."

That was a cryptic revelation. Who was she referring to, was she talking about Aurora? We asked her, but she said nothing. I suppose it would be clearer with time.

She looked at me and said, "You will find your future in the Enchanted Forest. I cannot elaborate further at this point."

Why did she make such obscure readings?

It was a bit annoying, but we left it at that. She told Jim that he'd become an ambassador of sorts, and Roy's future was in entertainment according to her.

With those sketchy disclosures of our fortunes, we got ready to leave. It was time to freshen up before attending our royal dinner with Queen Titania. We quickly returned to the lair to freshen up. We were lucky there was a waterfall nearby that helped us.

The day had been so enriching for us. It felt like all the hardships we had been facing since our entry into this realm, had been washed away by this one soulful day.

Our spirits had also been refreshed, and we were ready for new challenges. We just couldn't stop recounting our experiences of the day's whirlwind tour.

Our impending dinner was the icing on the cake. Besides, Fairyland had started to feel almost like home now. We had become so familiar with the space, their faces, camaraderie, and hospitality.

'Archie boy,' as the queen called Archon, had been such an entertaining and compassionate host to us. Even though we were staying with him in a hard and bare cave, we were not left wanting for anything.

This unplanned adventure has actually been very healing.

I reflected on all that I had gained and felt during this time.

We went to the castle and were welcomed like celebrities. We had noted that the castle was beautiful before, but today it exuded such joyful vibes. The walls and railings twinkled with lights interspersed with red, green, and gold decorations. Grandeur permeated every corner.

The queen descended from the staircase to greet us, looking elegant in her elaborate gown and crown. She held a black and gold staff adorned by a gleaming crystal at one end. We had never seen her like that – looking so very majestic.

"My dear Archie" – she first headed to Archon and lovingly stroked his face – "wish you a very merry Christmas."

She turned towards us. "And thanks to you boys, we have the pleasure to wish each other this Christmas. I wish you all every happiness."

She touched our heads with her staff, bestowing her blessings.

We were led to the dining hall and shown our seats. An array of delectable food was laid out in fine tableware. Queen Titania was being more loquacious and jovial at dinner. She was an extremely gracious host.

We had our fill of food, wine, and dessert; and continued to chat. She had so many stories to relate about happier days. These included funny anecdotes of Archon as a gawky, fledgling dragon. He was almost embarrassed.

"Once on his birthday, I arranged a cake for him. As is customary, I put some candles on it and lit them. Even though he puffed air to blow them out, he could not do so. He was too soft, I thought."

She paused for effect as we chuckled, and continued, "Then he tried hard, and he turned the cake to cinder." We laughed out loud.

"It didn't strike earlier, that it was his hot breath that refused to let the candles extinguish." By now, everyone was laughing uproariously.

Finally, it was time to bring the mirthful evening to a close. We bid goodbye and joined the fairies outside. We wanted to take part in the festive activities arranged for the day.

Flora was waiting nearby to wish us, as she knew of our dinner invitation. We were touched with her friendship. She too had a gift for us – a little fairy charm, that she advised we should wear at all times, for good luck and healing. Gratefully, the charm was a man fairy.

I would've found it hard to explain to people back home why I'm wearing a female fairy.

I tittered at the thought and wore the charm, that was strung on a chain to wear around the neck. The Toon boys did the same.

"You are brave and it's a pleasure to see your family celebrate together," I said.

As expected, Steve excused himself in search of Aurora, and found her a little distance away. They headed to the dance floor that was set up near the tree. Music filled the air, and the arena was filled with couples and children dancing the evening away.

Jim, Roy, and I headed towards the bake stall. No, we weren't hungry after that scrumptious dinner we had. It was a stall to bake cookies together and decorate them. And it seemed like a very Christmassy thing to do, so we wanted to try it out.

Besides, this was our chance to do something for Archon; we intended to make the cookies for him. He was busy meeting and greeting the other fairies he knew well.

A half hour later, I had renewed respect for all those who baked. I certainly wasn't cut out for it. It tasted fine, but that's because we were guided on the amount of ingredients to be used.

The presentation, however, was another story. Jim and Roy were just a tad better than me. Between the four of us, Steve was the one with an artistic bent of mind. I'm sure he would've done great in this workshop.

We packed our labor of love in a gift box and took it to our benevolent host and guardian. "You have been very protective towards us, like a big brother. And this is a token of our love and appreciation. From the four of us."

He was surprised to receive something. He gave a wide smile and sniffled quietly. And almost scalded our skin in the bargain.

Oh my God! He is such a large grown-up baby. Who is going to believe that I saw an adult dragon cry?

Jokes apart, it felt like we were celebrating with family.

We were ready to leave and went to call Steve. He and Aurora were dancing on soft romantic music and the number was almost done. The two looked so much in love now. And I wondered about what that fortune teller predicted about Steve.

I beckoned him that we were headed back home.

Chapter 18
Gigantic Obstacles

That night I went out like a light, as soon as I hit my pillow. Thanks to Steve's abilities, we had beds and pillows in the cave for comfort. I was tired but felt content. There was a sense of satisfaction and achievement. And I slept very peacefully.

Soon after the break of dawn, however, I woke up to Archon's growls. I was trying to understand what was going on and saw that the others had woken up perturbed as well.

He was outside the lair, venting his anger. We rushed to ask him what happened. Aurora, looking terribly stressed, was there talking to him.

I hope this has nothing to do with Steve.

As soon as she saw us, Aurora started to retell what was going on. "Some giants just walked into the village a little while ago. Without so much as a word, they started to destroy everything we had made in the square. The Christmas tree, the shops, the stalls, the decorations…"

She quivered in fear as she spoke. "Everyone in the village was asleep when they entered. We woke up, with a start, when we heard their loud angry snarly voices, shouting threats."

Archon roared as she repeated the tale of their invasion.

"Everyone gathered in the square to see what was going on. But some of them ran back home to hide, out of fear. I saw the queen come out to handle the situation. My mother and father were there too.

"I took a chance and tried getting out unseen, to come and inform you. I'm worried that they will completely destroy the village."

I understood now why Archon sounded so furious. "Archon, please control your temper, so that you can see this in clear light," I tried to calm him down. "Let's go to the village and sort this out."

In a flash, Roy got us there.

The scene before us was very intimidating, to say the least. There were three giants there, going berserk, damaging everything in the square and hollering in their deep tone.

They were large enough to squish us like insects. They looked like enormous-sized humans with somewhat distorted features. I suddenly became conscious of how small we were.

Archon roared to get their attention. He breathed a raging jet of fierce flames that almost licked the skin off one of them. The giant stopped and turned around in painful wrath; the others too froze in response.

Yeah, the big guy had them listening when he spoke to them.

"Stop right there! What do you think you are doing? Why have you come here?"

One of the giants, who looked more morose and aggressive, spoke up, "These fairies are trying to take over the entire forest. Queen Titania wants to become the Empress of the forest."

He darted a look at her. "She has misled all the other communities into believing she is helping them. The truth is – she is after the 'power'. Let me tell you, no fairy is going to rule the giants. We will see to that."

"And we will make sure that the others don't follow or support them either," said the one who almost got seared.

"Are you threatening us?" Archon retorted with a deceiving calm, through which flickered the storm building up inside him.

"Take it as you wish," the third grunted, "you have seen what we can do. If they insist on continuing, they will pay dearly."

Archon was thoughtful for a few moments. "Continuing what, dear giants? The fairies have had no communication with you, good or bad," he now spoke with a more reasonable authority, replacing his fury.

"Neither have they tried to establish or assert their superiority over the other clans. It seems to me that you have been misguided. Misguided by none other than the evil sorceress, I'm sure."

The giant justified himself, "Selene has shown us the truth – the truth of the intentions of these fairies. They use their softness and sweet mischief as a weapon and manipulate everyone.

"But beware the power of the giants! No one can match the might that is housed in the Giant Kingdom."

Just as I feared, she had played her game.

Archon was in no mood to cow down. "Your king, Kronus, is too busy with the pleasures that weaken the spirit. The might, that you take so much pride in, has been compromised. That is why, you come here following the words of a wicked spellcaster."

The Giant was incensed. "Your insolence will be your undoing, Archon! Have you forgotten what happened to your clan at the hands of Balor?"

It was Archon's turn to show them their place. "You will, then, also remember what became of Balor."

The giants growled back at the slight and retreated. "Come on, our work here is done for now. But bear in mind, the next time will see the fairies crushed for good. Let this be a lesson for them to stay in their shoes."

They stomped off heavily, shaking the ground with every step.

The fairies were too scared to say or do anything, and quietly went back home. Queen Titania looked worried and asked us to join her in the castle. Just as we reached inside, we heard a commotion again from outside.

Her fairy guards informed that Lord Avery and the Imp Leader wanted to meet her. And just as they were informing her, the Dwarf Chief also arrived.

She instructed them to send in any leader who wished to see her. They walked in, all of them talking simultaneously about the giants that came and caused damage in their village.

"Please calm down. As you may have seen, our village has been vandalized too."

"What are we going to do? Have we made a mistake in antagonizing Selene?" said the Imp Chief. "We don't have the strength to fight off the giants."

Queen Titania replied pragmatically, "When we decided to stand up for ourselves, against Selene, we knew she is very powerful, and we may have repercussions. Yet we took the lead and got our families back. We have also managed to resurrect our faith and culture."

She went on, "The last few days have been testament that we are on the right track. In the same way, we have to continue to stay united and find a way to deal with the giants as well. As leaders, we owe our people a good life."

Soon the other leaders too walked in with the same anxiety and panic. It was time to find a permanent solution for this menace called Selene Kouris!

Chapter 19
The Beginning of the End?

As the other leaders joined us, each one fearfully related what happened in their domain. We had to pacify them every now and then, as they raised more concerns.

Primarily, it was the size of the giants that seemed to be the daunting factor. They felt inadequate against the enormous creatures.

So did I, to be honest. The ogres were large too, so they were perhaps not as intimidated, but they were still diminutive in comparison. They couldn't see themselves fighting the giants and emerging victorious. Only the dragons could match up to them.

It was very clear that our contribution would have to be strategy and unflinching support, as Archon and his tribe stayed on the frontline. I was wondering if it would be possible to have a peaceful dialogue, or we'd have to resort to other methods.

As we discussed the options, Archon didn't seem particularly optimistic about achieving our goals peacefully. But he was willing to try, if everyone was in agreement of what needs to be done.

Since all the foresters were so frightened of being overpowered easily, I felt it warranted an effort of that nature.

However, it was also clear that the peace talks need to be conducted on neutral ground. I suggested that we call King Kronus to the temple for a mediation. All agreed, but who was going to be the messenger to inform him?

Jim offered to go to the Giant Kingdom, along with Roy. Roy would be able to get the two of them out of there in case of trouble. I was still worried about both of them going there, without any security. But he was confident that he could handle it.

He opined that he was not a forest dweller and posed no threat, and hence, would be safe from their wrath. Their hostility was directed at the leaders, and Queen Titania in particular.

And it wasn't advisable for them to go in larger numbers, as the giants may believe it's a plan of some sort. Roy would be a safety net, just in case things did take a turn for the worse.

We had to agree. Archon said he would lead them to the kingdom. "That area is separated from the rest of the forest by a flowing river. Although the giants weren't ever friendly with any community, they didn't quite incite unnecessary aggression either. The last confrontation was the Balor episode with us. And again, don't forget, that too was instigated by Selene."

Everyone approved of the plan, and the three of them set out towards the kingdom. Archon was to take them across the river and leave them at the gates. The rest of us continued to wait at the fairy castle, nervously, for them to return.

It was a few hours before we saw Archon walk in again. I rushed to ask him and was grateful to see Jim and Roy follow him. Everyone was curious to know what happened.

Archon started, "I took them till the gates and informed the guard that they were there to give a message to King Kronus, on behalf of the rest of the forest. I also told him to make sure they come to no harm and that I'll wait for them outside."

Jim continued wryly, "The guard laughed that we're too puny for them to be bothered. I don't think he has heard 'the ant and the elephant' stories. Well, he'll know soon enough."

He continued giving a light smirk. "Anyway, we went unhindered up to the king and told him that that all the leaders want to have a peaceful negotiation in the temple. He laughed and said he doesn't need to come and negotiate peace. His intentions are clear, and if he wishes, he can destroy all the villages in one day. We appealed to him to give it a chance, and he reluctantly agreed."

We were all hanging on to Jim's every word as he ended, "King Kronus will be at the temple tomorrow by 12.00 pm. We shook hands with him on that note and guess what I realized. He has been hypnotized by Selene to do her bidding.

"At the moment, he's like her puppet, only without a string. Even agreeing to an arbitration, is not expected to be without an underhanded scheme. So, we will need to be prepared for the worst."

"Don't worry," Archon reassured the leaders. "I will keep my people on standby. One war cry will be enough to call them in. Meanwhile, I will have two of my friends stand guard outside the temple, when he comes. He has promised to come with just two guards."

All the leaders returned to their villages and waited in trepidation to see what events the following day would unfold. It was a long night, and we were unable to sleep. I asked Roy and Jim to tell us some more about the giants and their kingdom.

Roy started to describe the kingdom. "The gates were about twenty feet high. Everything about the place was enormous and vast. Even the common homes were huge. Imagine how we felt when we saw the palace. It had a humongous forty feet high entrance and was spread over an area that would be as huge as a golf course."

"And it was extremely grand!" he added. "The king may not be the best-looking guy, but he surely lives an extremely extravagant life. There were court dancers, and jesters keeping him entertained when we entered. But it did not look like a positive cultural scenario; it seemed more like he prefers to live in debauchery."

"Yes, that is exactly how he is," reiterated Archon. "It is probably why Selene must have chosen to hypnotize him. He isn't one to follow anyone's orders, and not easily convinced with reasonings."

"Was Selene there?" I asked.

"No, but it seemed as though he was listening to voices in his head," said Jim. "Maybe she has the power to hear him and communicate with him remotely, under the hypnosis. Because he appeared to be following what he was being told to do, when he agreed to come."

"Possibly!" I noted. "The point is, how do we un-hypnotize him."

Chapter 20
The Sage Oak

"There is a wise old oak tree in the forest. It can help you to work this out," Archon informed. When he saw our blank confused faces, he explained in detail.

"An ancient sage oak exists, that talks, and helps those in desperate need of advice. Seeking this oak will not be easy. No one knows the exact location, and it seems to be more of a legend now. The Sage Oak has not been approached in a long, long time.

"According to the legend, the last emperor, Leonardo Maximus – the lion head, often consulted a sage living in the forest, to make just decisions to run his empire. When this sage breathed his last, his soul found home in this oak tree.

"It is said, he did this so that he could continue to help the foresters always. Possibly, he foresaw the degradation of the Magus Forest, and considered it his duty to be available for consultation, whenever necessary."

"How will we know which oak tree is the one?" Roy enquired.

"Apparently, you have to approach the oak, and say, 'I need your guidance, O Wise One!' You will get an acknowledgement, if it is THE ONE. Not easy, by any means, to seek out every oak tree in the forest to check. It will be like looking for a needle in a haystack."

"So, you just go ahead and put forth your questions after that?" I asked.

He continued, "The Sage Oak will acknowledge with a series of questions. And you will have to answer all of them; if it senses any insincerity, it will become reticent again. If not, you can ask whatever you wish, and you will get your answers."

He paused for a bit, and reminded us, "But we're meeting King Kronus tomorrow. There's no time to scan the entire forest for the Sage Oak. However, I leave it to your discretion. I will support you, whatever you want to do."

I was thinking, in any case, we had no idea what we were going to do. So, it was worthwhile to try and get some help on how to handle the situation. I was ready to take the leap of faith and go all out. At the most, we would be losing a night's sleep in search of the mighty Sage Oak.

"I think I'm ready to look for the Oak. How about you guys?" I probed the Toon boys. They nodded in approval and Archon smiled in consent.

We got ready for a long night in the forest, as we flew off to the nearest forest area. Walking around looking for an oak tree for about half hour, it seemed like a futile exercise, as we saw none.

We moved onto another section of a thickly forested region, and finally saw one. But it wasn't the one we were looking for.

We had spent half the night, looking, and searching, asking for guidance to various oaks, with no success. I began to doubt if the legend had any veracity.

It is not uncommon that, with time, stories that become legends are laced with embellishments, that are improbable or just plain untrue. I was about to voice my doubts, when I had a thought.

Since we were already out in the woods, we could check if the grimoire we hid in the grand old oak near the hills, behind the temple, was in its place. In the dark of the night, we didn't risk being seen by anyone with the book. Besides, that is also an oak, so it was definitely worth a shot.

I told Archon to take us there, and it wasn't difficult to find 'our tree.' After looking at so many oak trees, I could honestly say there was something very distinctive about this one. It was really huge and magnificent.

I put my hand into the hole in the tree and rummaged around to feel the book. When my fingers felt the thick leather cover of the book, I smiled in relief. I stepped back and we asked the oak, "We need your guidance, O Wise One!"

The oak suddenly awoke and spoke slowly, in a very deep bass voice, "Are you the one who placed the book in my hollows?"

"Yes, I am," I said, feeling excited, relieved, and hopeful simultaneously. I looked around at the others and everyone was smiling. Archon beamed in disbelief, as though he was happily surprised that the legend turned out to be true. The grain of doubt he may have had was laid to rest.

"Are you a forest dweller?"

"No, I'm not. I'm a human from another realm."

"Are you trying to destroy the forest?"

"Not at all! I'm trying to help the foresters live in peace and harmony. You can check with Archon, the dragon here. We're friends."

"Why do you want to help them?"

"My friends and I were brought into this realm by deceit, and we saw that all the beings here are suffering. And it is very likely that our realms will suffer just as much, if we don't put a stop to it."

"What guidance do you seek?"

I had been holding my breath in nervousness and felt relieved when I got the 'go ahead' to ask my questions. "We are to meet the Giant King tomorrow, and he has been hypnotized by Selene, the sorceress. How do we undo the hypnosis? It's the only way, we can make him see reason. Under her spell, he is bent upon destroying every village."

In the very characteristic deep-throated tone, the Sage Oak replied, "Whenever the giant attempts to voice the thoughts of the sorceress, cut him short, and change the topic of conversation. Do this consistently each time, until you notice a change. You will have to be very sharp in your observations of his views and, also, his expressions. It will alter, and he will look more like himself. If he is in a trance, his eyes will be looking lifeless and stony."

"Is there any way to annihilate all powers of the sorceress?"

"No, that is an impossibility. But if her abode is demolished, it will render her helpless. Her powers are rooted in her home. It will be a long time before she can resurrect her strength to practice sorcery."

"Thank you, O Wise One, for your advice and direction. We shall take your leave."

The solution seemed simple enough and yet, not something we would have thought of on our own. I'd heard often from my parents, that the best solutions are always simple. It was now time to put it into practice.

Chapter 21
Meeting the Giant

We tried catching up on our sleep, for whatever was left of the night. Being tired wouldn't help, if we are to be alert to the giant's changing words or expressions. When I awoke, I was anticipating feeling anxious for the day's events. But, instead, I was excited and full of beans.

We reached the temple well ahead of time. Archon had informed the dragons to be vigilant for his calls. All the leaders arrived on time. But the giants were delayed. We were hoping they don't renege. After an hour of waiting, we heard the dragons on guard outside, inform us of their approach.

All of us went out to the courtyard to meet King Kronus. We decided to conduct our meeting in the courtyard. It would have been rather difficult accommodating the king and his two guards in the temple. Arrangements had been made with large stones serving as seating.

All of us gathered around them in our much tinier chairs. It must have looked like a scene from hell, very intimidating. A huge devil and his sidekicks presiding over and judging the fate of the lowly earthlings, after their death.

Or at best, we might have looked like a kindergarten class taught by Satan. It was up to us to turn it around and make it less unnerving or comical.

There was an awkward silence for a few moments, as we shifted in our chairs, wondering what to say.

Archon took the lead in opening the conversation. "King Kronus, you have affected heavy damage in the villages for no valid reason. This goes against the 'pact of harmony' between all of us in the Magus Forest. I ask you to refrain from such actions. It will only result in anarchy that will damage not just us, but you as well."

Kronus scowled. "In my opinion, it is the fairies that breached the pact. They have been methodically scheming—"

"Your Majesty, would you like to have some fruits?" I interrupted.

He was taken by surprise, and I ran in with Jim to get the large fruits we had arranged for the giants.

He continued, "I will not allow any of you to—"

"Please have some, they're delicious!" I broke in again and made sure they ate some.

He grunted, "It has been brought to my notice that you are all—"

"Did you like it?" It was Jim this time.

"Yes, it was good," he said, looking annoyed, and continued, "I will never allow the giant community to be—"

"Your palace is beautiful," Roy butted in.

"Thank you, can I continue?" He was looking exasperated now. We nodded and he went on, "Look, as far as I know, all of you are—"

"Can we get a tour of your kingdom? I'd love to see it." I was beginning to enjoy this.

If it was a TV show, this would've garnered a lot of laughs. But our constant interruption was making the other leaders nervous. They couldn't understand what was going on, or why we were risking angering the giants.

I looked at Kronus, and I sensed that instead getting angrier, he was looking a little more relaxed. Irritated, perhaps, but not infuriated.

I could see the ruse recommended by the Sage Oak was working. We had to continue until we were sure he was completely out of the hypnotic stupor.

"I've heard from my friends that it's a sight to behold. You know, you could hold tours for the rest of the foresters as entertainment. It would help bring more prosperity to the giants, and at the same time, improve relations with these communities," I theorized.

He replied, "Okay, I'll think about it. But first, I want all the communities to promise—"

"You are a powerful race, and I'm sure you can create a special place for yourselves in the positive development of the Magus Forest." Now I was trying to veer his mind towards a more productive viewpoint. I was also trying to placate his ego.

"Powerful we are." He sounded proud. "You are stating the obvious. That is why all of them should—"

"They would revere you for your contributions," I added.

He was silent for a few moments, before replying, "You make valid points."

Dhishhh! Cymbals clanged and crashed inside my head…! I could have screamed with joy! It did seem like he was speaking his own mind now. His eyes too didn't have that strange glassy look. I believed that we had done it!

I had to push a little harder on this line of conversation. None of the leaders had spoken up so far because of the strange route the discussion was taking. I could only tell that their anxiety was slowly spiking.

It was finally time for a proper exchange, and I had to address them, "How do you all of you feel about collaborating on various activities?"

The Ogre Chief spoke up first, "I think that's an excellent suggestion. It will make our lives more interesting, and there's a lot to learn from one another."

The Dwarf Chief voiced his agreement, followed by the Imp Leader and Gnome Chief.

Queen Titania addressed King Kronus directly, "Your Majesty, the fairies have no designs with regards to usurping anyone's powers or establishing our own supremacy. You were misinformed and mislead."

He was listening calmly, as she added, "I would be very happy to be able to collaborate and live in peace and harmony. In fact, if I may, I would like to make a proposal."

As everyone nodded their 'go-ahead,', the queen made her suggestion, "I have been considering various aspects of our lives. I firmly believe, it is time to make major changes. Mutual respect, peace and cultural exchange will enrich not just our lives, but our future generations as well."

Everyone murmured in agreement, as she continued, "For this, we need to consider returning to our roots, by crowning an able and just emperor to hold the forest together in unity. I propose that we choose Archon as our Emperor!"

Chapter 22
Emperor Archon

Lord Avery, of the elves, was the first to stand up and applaud. "I couldn't have thought of a better candidate. I fully approve."

I knew the four of us were totally for it. And I had discussed it with Queen Titania on Christmas Eve when the boys were busy with other activities. But as people from outside this realm, we could not sound our opinions. At least not until we had been specifically asked.

Everyone else started murmuring and discussing in low tones, and it seemed like they had reservations. King Kronus was quietly watching the proceedings, as he popped the fruits into his mouth.

The Imp Leader and Gnome Chief stood up. "We approve."

The Dwarf Chief questioned, "If you don't, mind I'd like to know why Archon was your choice? Did Archon ask for the position, or perhaps you are prejudiced in your choice?"

"Yes, you and Archon have been close. Maybe your choice is not objective enough," added the Ogre Chief.

"Not at all," the queen clarified, "I'm not prejudiced at all! Yes, we are close. But that closeness has shown me qualities in him which I see befitting that of an emperor. His quiet strength, his wisdom, his compassion for his people."

She allowed her words to sink in before she continued, "He is a dragon and, characteristically, given to aggression. He knows he can overpower most of his adversaries easily, and yet he avoids a fight. He looks for alternative solutions. He is honorable. What other qualities would you like to see in your emperor?

Archon, who had been listening silently, spoke up, "May I have a say in all of this?"

"Yes of course. We'd like to hear what you have to say," everyone goaded him in unison.

Archon cleared his throat. "I did not know what the queen had envisioned for me. And I feel deeply honored that she considers me suitable for such a huge responsibility. On my part, I see it as a blessing from God, if I am allowed to take care of my people. And for me, all of you have always been my people.

"But it is imperative that you trust me to do right by you. I leave it you to consider your welfare, and I will be accepting of any decision that you deem right."

Again, there was a round of murmuring. The low discussions had a more positive ring to it this time. In a few moments, all of them gave their approval.

King Kronus finally spoke up, "Now I shall add my opinion. The Giant Kingdom shall stay separate but friendly. I agree to joining hands with Archon for our common benefits. I have no problems with him becoming emperor."

Everyone was applauding the decision now. With that unanimous vote, all that was needed to be done was decide and arrange for the coronation ceremony! Archon humbly gave his acceptance speech.

"I, Archon, accept your title, love, responsibility with grace and humility. All communities shall retain their individuality and their leadership. I shall be there for whatever help is desired. King Kronus, your kingdom has always, through time immemorial, been strategically located to have a separate identity. I believe it serves the best purpose for your people. Our joint support is the best solution."

"HAIL EMPEROR ARCHON!" everyone called out.

King Kronus added, "After the crowning, we shall sit down to sign on the details how we may help each other."

"When and where shall we hold the coronation?" the Dwarf Chief enquired.

"Please, there is no need for any grand ceremony. I shall continue to live in my humble abode. My doors will be open to all." Archon was feeling embarrassed by the thought of excesses on account of him.

Queen Titania explained her stance. "Archie, you may continue to live your home. But you have to realize it is not easily accessible to many of the communities. They will always have to depend on someone's help to contact you. It is necessary to have at least a 'workplace' that is convenient for everyone to reach. And we can use the same grounds for the crowning ceremony as well.

"Again, a ceremony will be extremely important to establish the fact in the entire forest. We have lived a few generations without any sovereign and everyone needs to know and be present."

The Gnome Chief offered, "We will construct the grounds once any of you can decide on the location."

"Why not here, at the temple?" Archon suggested.

"No, the grounds have to be sufficiently large to be able to house the giants as well," Ogre Chief piped in. "We have to build with future activities in mind. It can be multipurpose. A place for you to attend your duties and convene with us and a space for the population to gather for any purpose. We will have to build it together. I think each of our clans has very characteristic skill sets."

Lord Avery and the Imp Leader agreed together, "Yes, exactly!"

This was working out just fine. But I had to bring up one more very important item on the agenda. "Respected leaders, we have one more thing to talk about."

They looked a bit confused. "We need to find a permanent solution for Selene Kouris. What do you propose we do?"

"Yes, she came to my palace unannounced one day and started to talk about the fairies' machinations for power. After that day, I knew what I was doing, but not quite in control of my actions. She had taken over my mind completely…until today," King Kronus said.

"I suddenly feel free of her commands. The solution is simple. Kill her! I can take care of it, if necessary."

"I think we should just set her mansion alight. That should render her powerless for a very long time," said Archon, "No one else can access her mansion easily. But for me the access from above and setting it alight, both will be easy. If she has no power, she can't do any harm, there would be no need for unnecessary bloodshed."

Queen Titania beamed proudly as she heard him out and supported his decision with a firm yes. All the others followed suit, and King Kronus also acknowledged that it was a better option.

We were finally ending the meeting and talking about how fruitful the day has been, when we heard loud angry war cries.

Chapter 23
Confronting the Giants

"Those are my people I hear." Archon sounded alarmed.

"And mine too." King Kronus was perplexed. "Let's go and find out what's going on."

They rushed towards the sounds of chaos with the rest of us trailing behind. Queen Titania flew along with Archon to see where the commotion was and returned solo to show us the way. She told us that the dragons and giants were fighting, like they were in a battle.

How did that happen?

My thoughts were running haywire. The meeting had been going very well. King Kronus was very supportive and keen to start a harmonious phase with the rest of the foresters.

If he had returned to his kingdom and backtracked on his word, he could have sent his men to start the fracas. But he hadn't returned…he had been with us all along. So we couldn't suspect his intentions.

Then why did the giants come in and start a fight? And he seemed just as surprised as we were.

By the time we reached the scene of the clash, it seemed that both the dragons and giants had stopped the physical altercation and were on a war with words. Archon was questioning the dragons, while Kronus spoke to his giants.

The dragons said they saw about half a dozen giants come in and randomly uproot trees and make noise. When the guarding dragons tried to stop them, they said it's going to get worse.

"Just wait till our king is done with the stupid meeting. We're going to wipe you out."

After a few more provocative statements, the exchange turned ugly and physical.

Archon turned to Kronus with an enquiring look. "Sir, we have been in conference over bringing positive changes in our lives and you have been in sync with us. How can you explain this?"

King Kronus looked disconcerted. "I have given no such instructions to my people." He turned to the giants half angry and half embarrassed. "On whose instructions did you come here? Why did you attempt to create discord?"

"Your highness," said one of them, "Selene Kouris came to the palace and informed us that you needed our help. She said that you wanted us to show these foresters who has the upper hand. We are here to help and support you in any way we can."

"Since when has Selene become my messenger?" the king bellowed. "You are to follow ONLY my command and not anyone else's."

He turned back to Archon, fuming at the audacity of the wicked witch. "I'm telling you she won't stop until she's dead. If she didn't live in the Dark Woods, I would've taken care of her in an instant."

"I'm not happy with what has happened here, but I can understand their point of view," Archon tried to pacify the king.

"They have seen you follow her bidding. You understand now that she had a magical hold over you, but they do not know that. They saw their king place faith in Selene and act on her say-so. In their eyes, you agree with her, and her words are akin to yours."

King Kronus grudgingly acknowledged the explanation by nodding his head. Archon pointed out, "You will now have to break that image and set it right in your kingdom."

"Don't worry, she is not going to set foot in my kingdom again. I'll make sure of that!" the king assured. He sternly ordered the giants to return to the kingdom with him. He shook hands with everyone and reiterated his allegiance.

Once they were gone, all the leaders expressed concern over the incident. "Do you think we can trust them?" was the common refrain. But Archon assured them, that the king was genuine in his support.

"It is my judgement that King Kronus has sincerely accepted our friendship. Please do understand, that trust is the basis on which we need to move forward. We will give shape to a more fruitful life, I am sure. And take care of Selene Kouris permanently!"

All the leaders accepted his encouraging declaration and returned home.

It had been an eventful day, and a stressful one. I wanted to relax my tired nerves. I thought it was the best time to visit that beautiful Lake Arcane and chill in the serene environment.

I informed Archon and the boys that I intended to go to the lake, and the boys decided to accompany me. Archon dropped us off at the beautiful pristine location and went on home.

Lake Arcane was picture perfect. The clear blue hues of the sky reflected in the still waters, which looked like a large mirror twinkling with diamonds. Reflections of the sun's rays shone on the blue surface like sequins adorning a beautiful blue dress. A light mist hovered over the surface like the veil of a bride.

The sight filled my heart with peace, and I wanted to fall asleep on the grass. I lay down to take in the surroundings along with the boys. The night in the forest searching for the Sage Oak had taken its toll, and soon we were asleep.

When we woke up, the skies had turned amber. The sun was low, and it seemed like another landscape poster was pulled up in front of us. Just as beautiful as the first. We were energized now and started to walk around. Roy wanted to swim in the waters, and all of us agreed that it would be relaxing and fun.

We were enjoying splashing around in the golden lake, when I remembered the remedial effects that the water is supposed to hold. I wanted to carry some of this water with me back home. Frankly, after our swim, we were all feeling like we had taken a dip in rejuvenating elixir. Maybe there's truth to the magic of these waters.

I was looking around for some appropriate container and asked the boys to help me out. Steve laughed. "Have you forgotten that I can materialize one for you?"

"Oh yes, of course! I would need some wooden bottles. I think wood is natural and appropriate to carry this water if it is magical and medicinal in property. The natural material will not interfere with the effects. Thanks Steve!" I was grateful.

In no time, we had filled up eight bottles. I had sparked interest in the boys too and all of us decided to carry two bottles each. The skies were a deep orange now, and it would be dark in no time. It was time to get back.

Just as we gathered our bottles to leave, there was a big swish in the lake that left the water rippling strongly. We looked at each other.

Was that a big fish?

Chapter 24
Narissa – The Mermaid

None of us was sure what we had seen, and we went closer to the lake to check it out. Nothing was visible other than the unstill water. I made a quick decision. "I think I'll swim and go under to see what I can find."

"Be careful, it could be dangerous," cautioned Jim. "Shall I come with you? I think I will."

"Let's all go in," added Roy, "It's a large lake, we'll go in different directions."

Just as we were about to step into the water, we again saw strong bubbling, and we instinctively took a step back. The mystery was mounting in slow motion, and we were getting restless. Finally, there was a big whoosh! Water splashed high and up came a mermaid.

That must be the mermaid Archon told us about – the one who made the water magical. It's true then, not just a legend. My goodness, she's beautiful!

She came up to the banks of the lake and gave us a piercing look. "You're taking the water from the lake? I need to know why."

"Hello, I'm Sid and these are my friends Jim, Steve and Roy," I made the introductions. "We'd heard that this water is remedial in property and wanted to keep some to take back to our realm. You are…?"

"I'm Narissa the mermaid, who lives in this lake. The water is indeed curative, but I do not appreciate anyone taking it for flippant reasons. You said you want to take it back to your realm. Are you not from here? How did you get here?"

"It's a long story," I replied, "We were tricked by Selene Kouris and brought here. We managed to escape with the help of some of the foresters. Since then, we have formed lasting relationships with some of them and are trying to help them with their problems."

Steve shared, "Things are now looking up for the Enchanted Forest. And we have started to wonder how we may go back to our homes. So far, we have no clue."

I spoke again, "As for the water, I was hoping it can help my father regain his health. He is very ill."

Jim also explained, "My mother is a healer, and I wanted to take it for her. She may be able to help some difficult cases."

"My sister," Roy added, "is autistic. I was hoping…would it help her?"

"I wanted to carry the water for my neighbor. He has always looked out for my welfare, and now he is dying and in a lot of pain," Steve told his story.

Narissa looked touched and spoke to Steve, "If he has terminal illness, he will not become completely okay. It's not a miracle solution you know. But it will relieve his pain and give him peace. That magic will surely help him."

"And your sister," she addressed Roy, "will show signs of improvement for sure. But don't expect a complete turn-around."

Both Steve and Roy looked hopeful with what she said. I hadn't known this side of them. I did find them very caring by nature, but we hadn't really talked to each other about our problems. Not as yet.

It was a revelation to know that each of us was struggling in our own way. It made me feel closer to all of them.

"You can take the water with you. I have no objections." Narissa just jumped right back into the lake and was gone in an instant.

We were stunned by the encounter. It seemed surreal, but it was also very reassuring. We quietly picked up our bottles and held hands to return back to the lair.

Back at the cave, we stacked our bottles with our Christmas gifts. And we started to discuss going back home.

"How on earth are we going to go back?" I wondered aloud.

Roy scratched and shook his head. Jim and Steve too just shrugged their shoulders. We were at a complete loss. Archon walked in and enquired about our time at the lake.

"It is a fantastic place," replied Jim, "so calm and peaceful. We had a lot of fun. We also met Narissa."

"Oh really! You are lucky then. She's sighted very rarely. I'm glad you had a good time." Archon nodded. "Let's have some special dinner. Queen Titania has sent some goodies for us, to mark the positive strides we have made today."

A scrumptious meal from the castle was always very welcome. We ate to our heart's content and got ready for the night's rest.

Everyone fell asleep quickly. For some reason, I stayed wide awake. And I couldn't help but think about Narissa.

She was so very beautiful! Her long dark hair cascaded down in waves, framing her ethereal glowing face. Her blue eyes shone like magnetic gems. Her body was covered with glistening scales. Having the lower body of a fish didn't at all take away from her beauty. She had the most captivating face I had ever seen.

I had to meet her again.

With that thought I drifted into dreamland.

I was walking along the shores of the lake, when I saw Narissa swim towards me. She held out her hand for me to hold. When I grasped her hand, she started to climb out of the water towards me.

She was dressed to kill. Blue flowing gown shimmering with crystals, complementing her deep blue eyes. It seemed almost as though she was wearing the waves.

What a gorgeous girl! I thought.

She came near me and whispered into my ear, "Can I have some laddoos?"

****

I woke up with a start.

What? Laddoos? What kind of dream is that?

I was annoyed with myself. I didn't want to wake up from such a fabulous dream. And all for some laddoos, even if they were my favorite. I tried my best to sleep and continue my dream, but it didn't work. Although I did eventually fall asleep again.

I woke up the next morning feeling edgy. All I could think of was going back to the lake. I had never felt so highly strung ever. It felt like I needed to know more about Narissa. I convinced myself she needed my help, though I didn't know whatever for.

Archon told us that he was going to do a recce of the Dark Woods and Selene's mansion. He needed to understand how to go about making her powerless.

"You boys enjoy yourselves," he told us as he left.

Chapter 25
Back at the Lake

Steve wanted to go to Fairyland to meet Aurora. Jim and Roy decided to join him. They had made some friends there and were happy to spend time with their fairy friends.

I would have joined them too, except, I couldn't get Narissa out of my mind. I told them I wanted to relax at the lake.

Roy offered to drop me off there, before they headed out to Fairyland. Thank goodness for Roy's instant travel, I didn't have to walk all the way. At that moment, patience wasn't exactly my strong point.

He left me there, hovered around for a bit to regain his power to teleport and left. I was finally alone and immediately felt very unsure of myself.

What should I do? Search for her or hang around and wait?

My brain had shut down. I sat on the shore and took in the beauty of the landscape, aimlessly throwing little pelts into the water. After a while, I decided to take a swim. I splashed around randomly looking out for Narissa till I started to tire out.

I thought of resting on the banks for a little while. As I lay on the grass, gazing at the sky and wondering how to locate her, I heard a little splash and a sweet voice, "You're here again?"

I turned around excited. "Narissa! I've been looking for you."

How does she come to know when someone's around?

"Why? Do you want my permission to take more water?" she questioned.

"Oh no! I wanted to – to talk to you."

I noticed her quizzical look, and quickly continued, trying hard not to sound desperate, "I like this place. It's very serene. And I was hoping to see you. Just to talk. You know I'm human – and this has all been very fascinating and I want to understand more. About you…" I trailed off.

I saw her face soften. "Do you know, I was human too?"

It was my turn to look baffled. "What!"

I saw her break into a soft smile. She looked even more beautiful. "About two decades ago, I was a regular teenager from Minnesota in the US."

"Oh wow! I'm from the U.S. too, from Brooklyn – New York," I ventured.

She continued, "I got interested in Wicca, but I wasn't following any sect. I was more of a solitary practitioner, not a very serious one though."

"You were into witchcraft?" I asked with surprise writ large on my face.

"Not exactly, but it's similar. You can utilize the craft for good or evil. My intentions were good. My parents fought a lot and were on the verge of splitting up. I was trying to learn a spell that would keep them together. There were a few other concerns too, but that was the main reason for trying to learn Wicca.

"During one of my practices, I accidentally opened a portal in my mirror and reached the enchanted forest. I was wandering in the forest, a little lost, and Selene Kouris saw me.

"I was very naïve back then and talked openly about myself. I shouldn't have placed so much faith in her. She took advantage of my interest and tried to get me to aid her in her despicable plans. It was the period when she had started scheming to take over the Magus Forest.

"She tried every possible method – sweet talk, playing victim, coercion. But I was a very clear-headed teen. I knew how to differentiate the good from the bad. I refused to take part in her evil schemes to start taking over the Temple of Faith.

"So, she tried to kill me. She clubbed me on the head and threw me into the lake with a rock tied around my waist.

"I gained consciousness after a while and realized what was happening. I managed to release the rock, all the while, repeating some chant I remembered. It was meant to help me, though I wasn't quite clear how.

"What I realized much later was that it took me almost an hour to release that rock. I was under water all that time and had, somehow, learnt to breathe in water. I would've surely died, but whatever little I had learnt about wiccan practices came to my rescue.

"After that incident, my amphibious characteristics continued to increase with time, and so did my healing powers. As I adapted to these waters, I gradually transformed into a mermaid.

"Selene did try to kill me again but failed as I could heal myself. After that, she just abandoned the thought and let me be. This lake became my home, and I never saw her again."

To say that I was stupefied, would be an understatement. I didn't know how to react to her story. I just about managed to ask her, "Didn't you try to go home?"

"At that time, I didn't understand how I opened up the portal, or how to find it again to go back. And as I had transformed into a mermaid, going back was not an option anymore. This realm had become my home," she replied wistfully.

"Do you miss it?" I asked.

"Not anymore." She smiled broadly. "I belong here now, and I'm able to help the sick with the healing water."

Wow, she looked ravishing when she smiled!

"Don't you feel lonely here all by yourself?" I couldn't imagine being in and around the lake all day with not a soul to share life with. All the other foresters lived in communities.

She gave me a thoughtful look. "How are you going to go back?"

"I don't know. She brought us here from the Toon World. If I could just go back there with the Toon boys, I'd be able to find my way to the same portal that transported me from my realm to the Toon World. But I don't know how to leave from here."

The helplessness of my last statement frightened me. I couldn't imagine never seeing my parents again.

"I can help you, but you can't tell anyone," She cautioned.

"You can send us back to the Toon World?" I felt a huge weight lift from my heart. "That would be the best thing ever! Don't worry, no one will know. Even the Toon boys will know only when we're ready."

I hesitated for a moment and then picked up courage to ask her. "Narissa…how can I meet you again, where do I look for you?"

"Just call out my name and I'll be with you. I will go now."

Was it that simple?

"Thank you so much. And – I…umm…want to meet you again – and again," I said bravely.

She smiled and jumped into the lake and swam away.

Chapter 26
Touching Emotional Cords

I watched her leave and felt like I was in a haze, on cloud nine. I couldn't think clearly. I was left with a sensation of her aura around me. I mindlessly started to walk to go back home.

I didn't give any thought to the fact that Archon's lair was a long way off. It would take a while to reach. But, for some reason, I was in no hurry to get back.

I was enjoying that feeling of nothingness that enveloped me. I wanted to revel in it. Nothing but electricity running through my body, while my mind stayed in the haze. It powered visions of her on replay.

I don't know how long it took me to reach the cliff. But when I reached, I realized I can't get to the lair without Roy or Archon. The pathway around the cliff was going to be too arduous.

It shook me out of my reverie. I figured the boys were still at Fairyland and I decided to go there. By the time I got there I was extremely tired.

Next time, I would have to make proper arrangements.

Dulcea saw me arrive and came to me with a refreshing drink of coconut water. I blessed her as I quenched my thirst. "Thank you, Dulcea. How did you know I'm thirsty?"

"Anyone who gets one look at you right now will understand you're tired, hungry, and thirsty." She smiled. "What were you up to?"

"Oh, I just walked a really long way," I explained.

"Ahh! It must have been a very important errand or reason to go wherever you went." She raised her eyebrows, partly questioning inquisitively.

I gave a cryptic smile and mumbled, "Hmm…Have you seen the boys?"

"Yes of course, they're with some of their men fairy friends in the park. You can join them and get something to eat," and strangely added, "By the way, if you want you can rub my horn for some luck. You may need it."

I was taken aback with that remark. "I would need luck for sure. But don't we all? So much has happened, and still expected to happen." I was trying hard not sound out my real thoughts but wondered what she saw in my expressions or aura to say that.

"You're right," she said half amused, "I wish you the best always. Now quickly rub my horn."

I did as she told and prayed that it should work. I found the boys bantering in the park and joined them. "I'm famished. Let's get something to eat." Their friends had arranged a picnic basket and said everything was ready.

Steve looked at me curiously. "Are you okay? You're looking lost and tired."

Oh my God! Can everyone see through me?

"Yeah! I just walked too much. Next time, I'll arrange with Roy," I explained. "I didn't realize it was so far away. Did you guys know I'd be coming here?"

"We did think you would. It would be hard for you to reach the lair on your own," added Jim.

I ate ravenously, much to the amusement of everyone. The chatter and the food refreshed me, and I was feeling more like myself again. We sat talking for a little while longer and got back to the lair.

We waited for Archon to come back and tell us about his day. I was in an emotional mood and wanted to know more about these wonderful Toon boys, whom I'd grown so close to in recent days. "Steve, were you always this quiet, or something happened in your past?"

His eyes softened as he spoke, "I had a girlfriend whom I loved dearly. I lost her in an earthquake. Some years ago, there was a severe one in Toon World where we live. That really shook me up and I found myself unable to make conversation with small talk after that. I started to feel it was irrelevant."

"I know it doesn't make sense, but that's how I coped with my loss. I'm fine now though; time is a great healer." He smiled.

"And so is love," added Jim. "Aurora had been good for you."

Steve nodded and I asked Jim to tell me more about his life.

Jim began to relate his story, "My father became severely ill when I was about 14 years old. My mother became a healer after I lost my father to the dreaded sickness. She became very spiritual and learned a lot about various natural remedies.

"Sad that she couldn't help your dad as a healer," I said.

"Oh, but she did," Jim informed me, "That's when she realized that she has a healing touch. She was able to give him peace and feel less pain."

He continued, "I have learnt from my parents how important it is to have a strong community. They were always on good terms with everyone. And it was due their good will that the community helped us so much in our times of need."

"Yes, support does help at such times," I thought aloud, "Unfortunately, large cities usually don't have very close-knit neighborhoods. And I was left to fend for myself. I grew up feeling very lonely. Thank goodness for the love and life I experienced in my early years, my sanity remained intact. I still hold on to that love and those memories."

"What about your parents?" asked Roy.

"My father has been paralyzed for several years, and my mother spends all her time after work, taking care of his needs – hygiene, feeding, administering medicine or whatever else is required. She still holds on to the hope that he will be well." I was lost in thought.

"My father was a performer, a clown, in the circus." Roy started talking about his life. "In those rings he was a star, he made everyone laugh. The audience applauded him, and he felt happy. But back home, he was bullied and made fun of by hoodlums living in the neighborhood."

Sadness took over his expressions as he told more. "He never responded or reacted aggressively. And that made matters worse, as other people also began to take him lightly and treated him like a loser.

"I know that he didn't let it bother him, because he was more concerned with my sister's wellbeing. Taking care of her was a priority for him. But it started to affect his self-respect with time. And I had to force my family to move out.

"When we shifted into the new home – near Steve and Jim – he started to recover his old self. And I found new friends. Life is good now," he ended on a positive note.

"And it's even better that we met!" I added happily.

"Yes!!!" all of them shouted in unison.

Just then Archon walked in.

Chapter 27
Something's Brewing

"How was your day, boys?"

"Oh, nice and relaxed, how was yours?" Jim counter questioned.

"Quite productive, I would say," Archon informed in a serious tone. "I think it will go as I had thought. Shouldn't be too difficult."

"Oh good!" exclaimed Roy, clapping, as you do when your favorite team wins a match.

"There's just one thing that's bothering me," Archon continued. "When the mansion is burning, she's going to try and escape. I think we should capture her as she comes out from the Dark Woods through the path. We need to keep her imprisoned, or there's no telling what she'll try next."

I nodded in agreement. "Yes, you're right. You can keep her in the dungeon in the rear side of the Temple of Faith. The same place she kept us. Since you'll be spending most of your time in that area at your new workplace, it will be easier to keep her under surveillance too. But who is going to capture her?"

"I've spoken to King Kronus about it. He too agrees with me, and he said he will personally be there with some of his people," he sounded confident. "I think they are the only ones who will be able to handle her."

"Sounds promising," said Roy.

"What about the coronation? Any news on the new construction site and the day you'll be crowned?" asked Steve.

"No, I haven't received any information about that as yet. They must be busy trying to work it out," Archon dismissed the topic.

He was very unassuming that way. His desire for the title was merely the happiness of being able to take care of the Magus Forest and its dwellers. To him it was an honor bestowed upon him by the foresters. It meant they trusted him enough to be able to protect them. The glory of the position and title eluded him.

Steve then turned to me. "Did you meet Narissa again?"

My face turned red, blue, and purple in embarrassment. I had no intention of discussing my time with Narissa. But I didn't know how to evade the topic. So, I simple nodded. "Yes."

"Oh! You went back to the lake?" Archon looked at me surprised.

"Yes, I really like the place," I replied, a tad sheepishly. "I feel like going there over and over again."

"Are you sure it's only the place that you like?" Roy added, teasing me.

I looked at him rolling my eyes, wanting him to stop. But Archon was quick on the uptake. He smiled and said, "Something's brewing, is it?"

"These guys are just fooling around. Don't take them seriously," I tried to brush it under the carpet.

Archon laughed lightly. "It's alright, Sid! Enjoy yourself. Do whatever you want."

Phew! I thought they wouldn't stop.

I veered the conversation to the nice picnic lunch that was arranged by the fairy friends of the Toon boys and how being at Fairyland was such a stress buster. All of them agreed that it was great fun spending time there.

Then, out of the blue, Steve looked thoughtful and reflected on the changes that had taken place. "Life is a lot happier now in the Enchanted Magus Forest, than it was when we first came here. Soon Archon will be Emperor and there will be new structure to look forward to and new developments."

He went on to point out exactly what was on my mind. "What are we going to do then? Shouldn't we think about ways to go back to our realms?"

"Yes Steve, I've been thinking about the same thing," I said somberly. "Need some time to get some ideas." I didn't tell them that Narissa offered to help. Maybe at the right time, I'd let them know.

Roy, however, offered a suggestion, "If we're going to imprison Selene, we could force her to send us back. After all, she's the one who brought us here."

"That idea may work, but it needs some thought," explained Archon. "She can't be trusted and may end up putting you in more trouble, just out of spite. Or use it as leverage to gain some benefit for herself. Either way, it's a big risk."

He paused for a bit. "Don't worry we'll find a way. You'll definitely get back home.

"In the meantime, I need to figure out a way to contact all the leaders at once. I want to keep them informed on all that I've gathered and the plan I have come up with. Right now, it takes us a while to get everyone together.

"Tomorrow I'll go to Queen Titania, and we'll work on getting the council together."

"Maybe you could install a huge gong or bell at the temple or at the new site, which could be rung and heard throughout the forest. This could be your signal," Jim suggested.

"Good idea," I agreed. "In fact, you could have codes for different things with the number of rings. For instance, one ring for council meeting, two for emergency, three for happy announcement, four for death. You get the idea, right?"

I'm lucky – we have mobile phones back home.

Archon agreed. "Thank you, boys! You are such a great help – always offering good suggestions. I'll speak to the council about it."

We sat together to eat and have random conversation before calling it a night. We were like family now, and the feeling healed my lonely heart. It washed away all the gloom I'd felt in the last 12 years of my life. I felt a renewed sense of energy to live.

I was also beginning to feel torn between my life back home and here. I wanted to go back to my life as it was and, yet, wanted to remain in touch with this new family too.

I wish I could travel through the realms at will. I would visit everyone whenever I wanted.

With that thought, I quickly drifted off to sleep.

Sunlight shone on my face, and I squinted my eyes as I awoke. I turned over to avoid the bright rays. I was in my room, on my bed.

When and how did I get back?

I could remember nothing. I rubbed my eyes and got up. After freshening up, I went to towards the kitchen to make myself some coffee. But…the aroma of freshly brewed coffee and breakfast wafted through. Smelled like parathas, the fried Indian flatbread.

Is that Mom?

I reached the kitchen. Waiting at the table, setting up breakfast, she smiled and said, "Just in time. Good morning!" It was Narissa!

****

"Sid, wake up! What do you want for breakfast?" Roy peered down at me with his characteristic goofy smile.

"Ooh…you party pooper!" I yawned, a little annoyed.

Chapter 28
Two Lonely Hearts

"We're joining Archon when he goes to Fairyland. Are you coming?" asked Roy.

"No, I'm going to the lake again. Please drop me and come to take me after a couple of hours," I requested.

With a sly knowing smile, he agreed. Gratefully, he didn't pester me with his retorts. Or they would all start teasing me again.

After everyone was ready to leave, Archon changed plans and said he'd drop me first. When we reached the lake, he looked around as if searching for something. Then asked me directly, "I don't see Narissa. You're here to meet her, aren't you?"

Oh no! Am I that obvious?

"Archon I enjoy the peace and quiet at this lake. That's why I come here. But…I'll be honest, having a little conversation with her is nice too." It was as inconspicuous as I could get without lying outright.

"All right! I'll leave you to enjoy your time here. Roy will come and get you later." He flew back towards Fairyland.

I ambled on towards the lake and sat at the banks, throwing little stones, and watching the ripples spread out. That was fast becoming my favorite activity while thinking or waiting for Narissa.

The hazy feeling of being with her started to envelop me again and I was lost in thought. I thought about how I was dreaming about her every day. This had never happened to me before.

I once had a crush on a girl in my class in high school, but I had never reacted like this. Never felt like this. We did date, but my lonely attitude, pushed her away. The relationship was very short lived. I reveled being on my lonesome ownsome.

On hindsight, I think I did it because I was feeling sorry for myself. I used to shut people out of my thoughts and life.

Being with Narissa, however, was very different. I wanted to enjoy my time with her. And then join others too for their company. I was feeling happier and more positive about life. I was more open to people now.

"Are you going to throw pebbles all day long, or did you intend to call out my name?"

It was Narissa! I lit up when I heard her voice. I didn't realize when she came up, so lost in thoughts was I.

"I was thinking about you Narissa!"

I thought I saw her eyes brighten up too; she was smiling. "You know I've come here just to meet you. I was thinking about you all day. Did you…" – I paused, unsure whether to ask her or not – "…miss me too?"

"Yes, I did," she said, very matter of fact.

My heart skipped a beat, and bells tinkled in my head. I felt like an Indian film protagonist ready to burst into a song and dance. And that's so characteristic about us Indians. Life is like one big musical! I'm sure I've inherited those genes, even if I was born on American soil.

She came and sat next to me. I felt like a magnet was drawing me to her. I held her hand, looked into her eyes, and confessed, "I like you. I like you a lot!"

'Like' you??? That's an extreme understatement!

I silenced my insolent thoughts and put my arm around her. She rested her head on my shoulder. "I enjoy your company too. I haven't spoken about myself to anyone in so long, it feels good to share. You've rekindled my human emotions. Your concern feels genuine."

She enjoys my company! I could just die right now.

"We've both been lonely. But your loneliness is far more intense compared to mine. I know how I felt all these years, and I can't even begin to imagine how you've lived your life for so long. And yet, you are so giving and caring enough to heal people." I was in awe of her.

In spite of all the challenges in her life, she was still positive. She exuded strength and had a compassionate heart.

We shared a comfortable silence for some time, as we held hands and sat there looking at our reflections in the water. I liked what I saw. Us – together.

I turned to her and asked, "Would you come back with me? I mean, I know you said you would help us reach our realms. What I would like is, for you to return with me to our realm. Your realm."

With a faraway look in her eyes, she said, "I don't belong there any more Sid. Look at me!"

My heart became heavy, as the realization dawned on me. I woke up to the fact that she wasn't a human anymore. Not a normal girl. She was right, she couldn't go back like this. I had to do something. Anything, to help her become a normal human again. But what could I do?

As I swallowed my emotions, I asked her desperately, "You were a wiccan, right? You must be knowing some magic or chant to go back to being what you were. You must've learnt something?"

She stared at me firmly. "No, I don't know any. I do have some powers now, which I honestly don't know how I gained. Maybe it just happened with the transformation.

"As a wiccan, I was a novice, an amateur, who was trying to learn the craft. And I didn't quite understand the repercussions of the practices. What I was trying to do didn't happen; instead, it started to bring about a change in me."

I listened with rapt attention as she continued. I felt if I listened carefully, I may get some inkling to the solution.

"It landed me here, and I just kept transforming without much knowledge of what was happening to me. And I don't know how to reverse it. But I did learn about 'my' powers here and how to use them in the right way. It's one of the reasons, I don't want anyone to know I can help you. I don't want Selene to learn of it and try to misuse it again."

I didn't want to consider it – the possibility that she couldn't return. Even if it was true. I didn't want to accept that I may lose her, never see her again. I blocked that negative thought from entering my head.

I leaned forward, locked my gaze with her icy pools of blue and kissed her lips with a fervor that said 'Stay with me.'.

She returned my kiss with love, and we hugged…holding on to each other for dear life, blending our souls, completing each other. In that moment, we bonded. Bonded in a way that was inextricable, inseparable. She touched my emotions like no one ever did.

It felt like a lifetime had passed in that bubble of bliss…

I think I'm in LOVE! Yes, I know I'm in LOVE!

Chapter 29
When Love Hurts

The realization that I loved her, hit me like a boulder. A boulder than showered me with soft fragrant rose petals. Sounds absurd I know.

It was a hard-hitting revelation as I comprehended my true feelings, that opened the doors of my closed heart to soft and tender emotions. It was heady mix and I reveled in that space.

Narissa, however, moved away from me after some time and had tears in her eyes. I was confused.

Did I do something to upset her?

She didn't say a word. She just jumped into the water and swam away. I was left wondering what happened. I didn't want this to end, and definitely not like this. I called out to her, but she didn't return.

My mind ran amuck with so many reasons for her sudden withdrawal, until I resigned myself to reality.

Maybe it was the hopelessness of the circumstances that distressed her. Yes, maybe that was it.

I felt sad that I couldn't do anything about it. Yet, upset as I was, strangely my whole being was filled with renewed energy and hope. The paradox that I found myself in was unsettling.

Just then, Roy appeared. He had come to pick me up. He sensed that something had happened and pestered me to tell him what was wrong.

I could just about muster the courage to say was that they were right about my interest in her – it was a truth I had just came to terms with. And that I, sort of, confessed my feelings to her as well. But she left without saying anything.

"Was she angry?" he asked.

"No. She left crying," I replied.

"I think she feels the same for you, but finds herself in a difficult situation," he hypothesized.

"It does seem like that. I want to know what's troubling her, and if I can do something to change it," I added.

"Don't worry, you'll know in good time. Give her some time to process her feelings." Saying that, he grabbed my hand and zapped us to join the rest of the boys at Fairyland.

Steve was with Aurora, and it seemed like they were having a serious conversation. Jim was hanging around with their fairy friends. I was told Archon was at the Fairy Castle in discussion with the leader council. I exchanged perfunctory greetings with the fairies, and they left soon after.

I took the opportunity to tell Jim and Roy that I had to talk about something important to all three of them. I waited with them in the park until Steve had joined us. As he walked towards us, after his meeting with Aurora, I noticed he looked sad.

I asked him what was bothering him.

"Sid, I've been thinking that it's time we tried to return to our homes. And that made me realize that Aurora and I would have to say 'goodbye' to each other. It wouldn't work."

I remembered the fortune teller's prediction, as he went on, "That is what we were discussing now. I feel low, but that's the reality. And Aurora is a strong girl; I know she can handle it."

Steve was right and I felt I had to accept the same. Maybe discussing it with Narissa would help because, at that point of time, I couldn't bring myself to face that fact. The fortune teller also predicted that I'd find my future here. I tried my best to hold on to hope.

"That's what I want to talk to you guys about," I started. "Narissa has offered to help us go back."

"Really? How will she do it?" Jim questioned.

"She hasn't told me how, but she says she can do it. And I believe she says what she means." I also warned, "We are not to talk about it to anyone. And I mean ANYONE! It's between the four of us. When the time is right, we'll know whom to inform."

I also told them about my situation with her. Jim voiced his doubts, "Do you think she will help us in that case?"

"I'm pretty sure she will. She's not fickle-minded. But I do need to talk to her and sort out other things. Going by the way she left, I'm not sure if she will see me tomorrow. And I can't wait a few days." I felt I would go out of my mind if she didn't talk to me.

We decided to check on Archon, and just as we neared the castle, we saw him emerging. His smile told us he had a fruitful morning.

"All done, my boys! Thank you for your suggestions. We are definitely going to work along those lines. The new site for the governing space has been picked out and construction has already started full swing. It had been finalized that a bell is going to be installed, and the coronation has been set up for next week."

Next week? Is that enough time to finish construction?

He had also informed the council about his observations and strategy to handle Selene. Everyone was ready to offer full support. All he needed to do was zero in on the day to put it into effect. I was sure he wasn't going to wait long.

Just as I was thinking it, he said it, "Tomorrow, I shall put an end to Selene's story. Let's go home."

We got back to the lair and sat down for a meal, when Archon made a request, "Could you please go to the new site and help out, boys? It will mean a lot to everyone, and you could oversee and give any more suggestions you see fit. I'll meet you there with King Kronus after we capture Selene."

It goes without saying that we agreed instantly. But I was nervous about seeing Selene again, and I wondered if the Toon boys felt the same. I asked and they concurred that seeing her was not exactly on their wish list.

Besides, after knowing Narissa's story, my indifference to Selene was quickly taking on the color of resentment.

SHE was responsible for Narissa's loneliness. SHE was responsible for Narissa's transformation. SHE was responsible for Narissa's pain. It was because of HER that I may never be able to share love with Narissa.

I wanted Selene locked up forever.

****

I waited at the lake, as I called out to Narissa. Soon she was beside me, her enchanting smile holding my attention. She stretched out her arms and I was ecstatic! She was not upset with me.

I held her hand and moved closer. In a flash, an unseen force dragged her away screaming. Selene's evil cackle echoed through the air.

I woke up drenched in sweat.

Chapter 30
The New Site

It was a bright and beautiful day, and very conducive to working outside. The Toon boys were quite gung-ho about putting in their energies at the new site.

Normally, I would have shared their enthusiasm. But my mind and heart were all knotted up with my personal sequence of events. I wanted to help and participate in setting up the new governing grounds. But at the same time, I wanted to go and meet Narissa and sort out our equation.

The location of the new office was behind the Temple of Faith, and we got ready to leave for the area. Meanwhile, Archon prepared himself to meet King Kronus at the Dark Woods. It was the eventful day that would spell the end of Selene's power and practices. No one would need to fear her again.

We left on our individual routes. The boys and I reached the temple region and saw the development on in full swing. The dwarfs and the ogres were the ones mainly doing the building work. Some gnomes helped carry the smaller building materials, while some stood as guards around the site.

The elves were setting up the detailing of doors, windows, and décor. Imps were taking care of the workers needs by giving them food and water as required. The fairies set up a community kitchen to cook for all the workers. There were a few designated fairies to oversee any medical needs.

All the communities had pooled in their labor forces. Everything looked well organized and moving as per plan. Jinzic, who was overseeing the guards, saw us and greeted us with a bear hug. It had been a while since we saw him, and it was a very pleasant feeling.

He led us to Gibel, who was supervising the construction of the main structure. Gibel was all smiles when he saw us. He welcomed us and showed us the plans with a lot of excitement. I have to admit the blueprint looked impressive.

From accommodating the imps to the giants, the plans included every possibility for the arena space. The office area too was apt for Archon and his tribe of guards. A gigantic rock was being chiseled to form the community bell that we suggested. Even the temple was going to be renovated with structural changes to be able to serve the diverse multitude of the foresters.

Their engineering skills were simplistic, yet no less a match for the kind of advanced world that I came from. In fact, it was more impressive that they envisioned such grandeur and executed it without the fancy machines that we have at our disposal.

Seeing the numbers that turned up to work, I understood how they anticipated to finish in a week's time to hold the coronation ceremony. I was also curious that the giants didn't figure in the workforce, and asked Gibel about it.

"Oh! They absolutely will be helping," he explained. "Once we are done with the basic work, we would need their help in installing the huge pieces of rock that are to form the walls. Or the bell even."

We discussed with him some more minor details pertaining to the large arena where the coronation was to take place and asked him to delegate some work to us. One by one, he showed us where we might make ourselves useful.

We got busy with the work, and I started enjoying what I was doing. Even though my anxiety remained at the back of my mind, the positivity of lending a hand to such an important event brought joy. I prayed that this joy would spread and color my prospects with Narissa. This joy made me hopeful.

Just then we saw Aurora come towards the site with a group of 50 to 60 female foresters from the various communities. Steve instinctively rushed to greet her and find out if all was okay. She informed that she had mobilized some active female members to form a society called Community Support of Kinship (CSK).

The group had come to the site to offer their help among the all-male labor that was working there. It was normal for only males to engage in hard labor at the Magus Forest. But Aurora was trying to bring in some change in the mindsets of their society.

Gibel and some of the other seniors spoke to them about their objectives and intentions. The group had been formed to offer assistance to any individual or event when needed. It was a welfare club and the idea appealed to the managers.

They whole-heartedly approved their inclusion. The go-ahead from the seniors quashed any dissension among some of the male workers. They grumbled under their breath but accepted the female services. Besides, they would need all the hands they could get to complete this construction in time for the coronation.

Steve felt proud of Aurora's initiative and brave steps to bring about positive changes. He had no doubt that she would achieve what she set out to do.

Work was progressing at a satisfactory rate, when a giant rushed towards the site to inform that Selene had escaped. The news hit like a bolt of lightning. Everyone was shocked and dropped whatever they were doing to know what exactly was going on.

The giant informed that Archon and King Kronus were at the Dark Forest with some more giants and dragons. Archon had managed to blow her mansion up in flames, but Selene did not emerge from there as expected.

The crowd of workers started chattering nervously among themselves. A sense of fear was gripping them. Some of them rushed back to their homes to protect their families from any unexpected attack from her. The others returned to inform their village chiefs. We decided to rush to the Dark Woods to see what we could do.

Suddenly, the site wore a deserted look as everyone was advised to stay home until their leaders addressed them. Roy zapped us to the Dark Woods.

We reached there to see huge red flames glowing ominously and licking the blue skies. Thick black smoke moved with the wind and dominated the atmosphere like dark clouds trying to envelop the earth.

The large imposing home looked like a devil screaming, with several glowering red eyes and mouth. The mansion was alit, but the forest around it remained magically untouched. It was a strange and curious phenomenon.

One major change we saw was that the thick fog covering the path was gone. It was as clear as day, and the view of the blazing mansion was uninterrupted. There was no way that Selene could have escaped without getting noticed now.

The dragons and the giants stood there in a line, forming an obstruction that would be impossible to penetrate without getting caught.

What happened? Where is she?

Chapter 31
The Witch Is Missing

As soon as Archon and King Kronus saw us, they relaxed their stance enough to talk and tell us what was going on.

"Everything was going according to plan. I flew over the mansion and breathed enough fire to light it up like a gigantic bonfire. King Kronus took position here with the others to capture her. But she never came out," ranted Archon.

King Kronus continued, "You know, as the house burned, the fog started to clear. I think the hocus-pocus that kept the path hidden had its base in the house. We thought this was a positive development for us, since we'd be able to catch her easily. But..." He shrugged exasperatedly.

"How long has it been? Maybe she's hiding behind the house, knowing you all are here," I ventured an explanation.

Archon negated my rationale. "I don't think so. We've been waiting an hour or more. Surely, she couldn't hide that long around that blaze. Do you think she died in there? We'll just have to wait till the fire subsides, to check."

"How come the woods around it didn't catch the flames?" Roy was curious, as he looked around at the untouched greenery.

"That could be because of the curse of the Dark Woods," King Kronus opined. "The ghouls and fiends reside there, and it must be their power that kept it protected."

Steve had another valid question. "Would Selene also be in danger in the woods, or can she control the spirits?"

Both Archon and the king shook their heads. "We don't know if she has any hold over them. Perhaps she does, she's a witch after all! And for all you know, that's where she may be hiding."

We decided to wait with them to check what happens eventually. In any case, work at the new site had halted.

It was almost nightfall, until the building was reduced to dying embers. There was still no sign of the wretched witch. Finally, we decided to check the burned building to verify if she had indeed got caught in the fire and perished.

Carefully, we approached the charred abode and did a thorough check. There was no sign of a body or ashes of a living being. We were perplexed and came up with the theory that maybe she wasn't in her home at the time. This meant that she was out there somewhere.

Steve reminded that with the mansion burnt to ashes, she would be powerless. There was no need to worry too much, and we could try and figure out what to do next morning.

Oh yeah! That's what the Sage Oak had advised.

In any case, all the clans were told to take precautions and stay home, not to venture out until the situation was resolved. The giants also returned to their kingdom and agreed to come again the following day.

Once home, we told Archon we were impressed with all aspects of the new site and were happy to be a part of this historic period of the forest. We informed him of Aurora's brave initiative and couldn't but notice Archon smile, in spite of his concern over the day's conclusion.

"She's going to become an important part of our lives soon," he prophesied. "I hope Selene's disappearance will not set us back with the site. I can't wait for tomorrow morning to work on whatever is happening. It's going to be a long night."

It definitely is going to be a long night. I miss you, Narissa!

Sleep eluded me that night as my mind was in a sort of frenzy with all kinds of thoughts. Selene, Narissa, home, coronation…everything seemed to be in a disarray. I eventually slept only out of sheer exhaustion.

By daybreak, all of us were up quickly. I guess everyone had a sleepless night. We first returned to inspect the blackened carcass of Selene's mansion. Once again, we were assured that she was indeed alive and in hiding somewhere.

We decided to take a quick look at the construction site before congregating with the councilors.

Another shock awaited us…as we saw the site in fading flames! The witch had taken her revenge at night apparently. And what we saw before us was a large area of blackened remains. Our hearts sank, as we took in the devastation of the labor of love.

With a heavy heart, we went to inform Queen Titania. She sent her messengers flying out immediately to summon all the leaders and site supervisors to gather at the destroyed site. An aura of gloom descended, as all of them collected to take stock of the devastation.

The supervisors walked around assessing the damage. After they were done, they approached the council. "No doubt there is extensive damage. We have lost a lot of our work. But some of the walls that were erected were rocks and still stand. The rest we will have to start from scratch. Luckily, we have our plans with us intact. We may be set back by a few days, that's all."

"But now, we shall have to finish with Selene Kouris before we restart the work," said Archon determinedly. "We can't give her the chance to do this again."

Lord Avery of the elves sounded his apprehension, "What if we can't find her and get rid of her? In this huge forest, how are we going to find where she is hiding?"

King Kronus boomed in his characteristic aggression, "We can't stop working or living in fear of her! Everyone will continue their duties here, and the site will be guarded morning, noon, and night. We shall keep all the villages guarded as well while the daily work is attended to.

Everyone agreed it made sense to do that, as he added, "We will create schedules to inform everyone who will keep vigil and when. This singular witch cannot defeat our united spirits!"

And with that monologue, he managed to lift the veil of gloom. Everyone was feeling hopeful again. Archon agreed and asked everyone to first start making rosters for the guards. Every village entrance and the Giant Kingdom was to be manned 24 hours.

The imps who did not have a walled village, sounded out their fears. King Kronus assured them safety by offering to, temporarily, move them to a small, wooded area in the Giant Kingdom. "There is no need to fear the giants. I will keep you guarded there as well from any frivolous mischief. And you will get food delivered to you."

The imps were grateful for the offer. Again, the work started and within a few hours, things were back to normal. The day began to look busy again.

It was a good time to check in on Narissa now…

Chapter 32
The Power of Love

I requested Roy to take me to Lake Arcane. In a few moments, we were there, and he promised to come back for me. They were going to continue working at the site along with Archon.

He urged me to be cautious. "Be careful! This is an isolated spot and with Selene on the loose, there's no telling where we will encounter her. I'd like to say hello to Narissa as well. I'll wait till she's here."

I called out to her a few times and was worried that she may not show up. After the way she left the last time, I was afraid she would never see me again. When we finally saw her wade through the waters, I heaved a sigh of relief.

As she sprung up to sit on the banks, Roy and I gave out a collective gasp. She had changed. Narissa had metamorphosed!

Her scaly skin had given way to the normal, smooth, fair as milk skin of humans. Her modesty was now covered with interspersed leaves sewn together, like the nests of tailorbirds. We walked towards her with our eyes widened in amazement.

As we reached closer, we were stunned once again. She got out of the water and stood on two normal human legs! Gone was the fishy tail fin.

She looked like a woman. A normal human woman. And she appeared even more angelic than ever.

How did this happen???

She saw us gawking at her and smiled broadly. "How are you, Roy?"

Roy, after taking a few moments to find his voice, answered, "I'm doing great! You look great! What – how – when…?"

She laughed. "Your friend here is responsible for this." She gave me a meaningful look. "With his loving touch, he unknowingly broke a hidden spell that had bound me to the lake and caused me to become a mermaid."

Roy gave me a naughty smile and hugged me tight. "You frog, you have turned into her prince!" And he laughed out loudly. "I'll leave you two together and come back later. We'll talk more another time."

After he left, Narissa came close to me and held me in a long, soulful embrace. My world just stopped for those moments. I could feel electricity course through me as we stayed lost in each other.

"Thank you," she whispered in my ear.

I spoke to her softly, "I can't tell you how happy I am to see you like this. When you just upped and left the other day, without saying a word, I thought I had displeased you. Made you unhappy somehow."

I looked skywards holding back happy tears. "You gave me sleepless nights, girl!"

"I left because I was feeling too emotional. I felt unable to handle it or share it. It seems like forever since I felt any deep emotion at all. And I didn't know, no clue whatsoever, that a genuine human touch would change me back into my original form."

Her actions and words were giving me courage to face my own feelings.

"Over the course of that day," she continued, "my body slowly started to alter. I was uneasy and uncomfortable, until I realized that I was modifying back into the human form. Then I started to feel exhilarated."

I was encouraged now to talk about how I was feeling about her. I searched for appropriate words as I didn't want to see her disappearing again. But I just couldn't hold it in.

"I'm in love with you," I blurted out.

There, I said it.

And I became tense immediately. She moved away in shock, her blue eyes widening with uncertainty. She looked at me, staring into my eyes as if looking for some answers.

"I-I don't know what to say," she hesitated. "I'm not sure how I feel. I only know I like being with you. And I'm very happy that it was your kiss that made me a woman again."

Yes, I can deal with that!

"It's okay Narissa. You don't have to say anything. I had to let you know of my deep love for you. I sense your affection. And that more than makes me happy right now." I was on cloud nine!

I could see her relax. Her million-dollar smile lit up her face and my heart, and she held my hand. We strolled around the area, talking about whatever she remembered of her childhood.

She spoke of her happy life with her parents and when and how they started to fight. She talked about how the breakdown of their relationship affected her, and how she turned towards Wicca looking to change things around.

I wanted to let her know she wasn't alone. I related some of my life's trials, "I understand how you must have felt then and how you may feel now. The sense of isolation that one is left with, is something we both share. But I'm with you now. And not just me, you will soon see that you have many friends."

"You know I haven't taken a walk like that in ages. It does feel good," she admitted and then changed the topic. "How do you like my new outfit?"

I couldn't help but laugh at her child-like joy. "It's very innovative. How did you manage to do that out here?"

She giggled at her own resourcefulness. "I found some abandoned bird nests that I felt I could put together and use."

"Narissa, do you still have your powers?" It suddenly struck me that her retransformation to a human may have taken away her gifts.

"Yes, I do," she replied. "Only I can't live in the water all the time, unlike before. I can still breathe under water. But I need to come out to land every once in a while, as this skin now is not suitable for permanent aquatic habitation."

A fleeting thought crossed my mind. I wanted to ask her. "Do you remember you said you can help us go back to our homes?" I wanted to say more…but changed my mind. "I've told the boys about it. And don't worry, we haven't let anyone else know."

She nodded in affirmation. "Yes, of course, I haven't forgotten. When do you wish to go?"

I was going to tell her about the new developments in the forest, when I saw Archon arrive with the toon boys. I was surprised to see all of them come here. I sensed Narissa get tense when she saw Archon.

"That's the new Emperor of the Magus Forest, Narissa! And a very able and compassionate one. Archon is the one taking care of us. You have nothing to worry about," I calmed her apprehensions and held her hand reassuringly. "Wait here, I'll bring them over."

I walked up to them. "What brings all of you here? I thought only Roy was coming?"

Jim spoke up, "Roy told us about how Narissa had changed. We wanted to see it for ourselves and give her our best wishes."

Archon added, "You haven't introduced me to her as yet. I have wanted to meet Narissa as well for some time, and—"

A shrill scream cut through the air.

Chapter 33
Selene Strikes Again

We turned to look and saw Selene trying to overpower Narissa. It looked like she had stealthily moved in from behind, coming through the woods. That's why we didn't notice her earlier.

She put her arm around Narissa's neck and pushed her down to the ground. She had her pinned with one hand, and with the other she was trying to turn Narissa's face towards herself.

Narissa struggled to push her away, as she was taken by surprise. We rushed in and swooped like a large pile on the old hag. We tried pulling her away, but she was really strong.

How does a scrawny old woman become so strong?

She managed to throw us off. I realized from the way she was trying to get Narissa to look her, that she was trying to hypnotize her by making eye contact. I shouted out to Narissa to close her eyes. Meanwhile Archon came closer and aimed some heat towards the witch with his fire breath.

That worked and she screamed out and loosened her grip. Narissa pushed her away, got up and ran towards us. If it wasn't such a serious situation, and with the girl I love, I would've burst out laughing. It was quite comical to see Archon almost grilling Selene's backside.

We again tried to get a hold of her. But all of us together were still not strong enough to capture her. Archon stuck to his guns about not killing her; otherwise, he could have easily used this opportunity to burn her to ashes.

She threw us off like nine pins and extricated herself from our hold. Archon again tried to stop her from escaping by creating a circle of fire around her. She tried to jump through the flames but saw that the blaze was too high to go through without getting seriously singed.

"You can't hold me back. You'll never be able to catch me," she screeched in a grating high-pitched voice. "Aaaahhhh!" She kicked the ground as she sounded out her frustration at not being able to get out of that circle.

Suddenly, she started to wave her arms around in a studied manner. Her beady green eyes squinting into a tiny slit.

An indescribable light started to form in front of her. Like an orb. And it grew bigger and bigger into a blinding luminescence. In a few moments, it became big enough to engulf her and drag her in. And just as suddenly, it closed up and she was gone!

We stared open-mouthed at what just happened in front of us.

"Where did she go?" asked Jim, perplexed.

"She has left the realm, Jim," Narissa informed us. That is one of her primary powers. She can open portals at whim.

"How come she's so strong?" I asked.

Archon explained, "It is believed that Selene is a descendant of Aegeiros, the nymph who married the last emperor of Magus Forest. Even though Aegeiros was banished to the mansion in the Dark Forest, she used her black magic to sire offspring."

No wonder she's so evil.

"Maybe she wanted to have heirs to her powers so she could maintain her dominance, even though it was in the Dark Forest. And the same black magic was used to continue the line of descendants. No one knows anything about the partners through which these descendants were sired."

"So that's why the evil continued to grow in that part of the woods," Roy observed.

"I remember Flora mentioned it too; that Selene was a descendant to Aegeiros," I mentioned.

"Yes, and Aegeiros was a dryad, a tree nymph. Emperor Leonardo had met her in the forests. One of her powers was enhanced strength and durability, like a tree. Selene seems to have inherited that strength."

"But aren't the nymphs bound to their homes, which in her case would be the trees?" Narissa was curious. "How did she live with the emperor, or in that mansion?"

"Again, I think it was with the help of her black magic," Archon answered. "She must have gained some extra abilities through it."

Veering the conversation back to Selene, Steve asked, "Is Selene going to return here at all now?"

"She can return any time she wants. There is no guarantee on what she will do," Narissa informed.

"Yes, that's true. But I don't think she'll come any time soon. She has no home, and no support here right now," Archon surmised.

He turned to Narissa. "I think she attacked you to use your powers and also hold you to ransom. She saw the two of you together. She must have felt that she can get her way with us by keeping you captive."

Tension was rife with all the action. But now that she was gone, it started to feel lighter. Yet, I was not going to take chances again by leaving Narissa alone. "You will stay with us now, please. I can't leave you here by yourself."

Archon seconded my thoughts, and she accepted. We quietly headed back to the lair. Archon welcomed her into the home and told us to take care of her for the day. "Forget about work for today. Make her feel at home."

He turned to Narissa and comforted her with genuine care, "You have nothing to fear here. I know you are very strong and have taken care of yourself for a very long time. But now, you can consider us family. And this family will be with you always."

After reassuring her, he left again for the site.

Narissa looked overcome with emotion. I had never seen her like that. Even when she was affected by my kiss, she had left so that I wouldn't see the sentimental side of her. But now, she was being open with her feelings.

We huddled around her and gave a group hug to cheer her up. "You have all deeply touched a chord within me," she said, almost gratefully. "I couldn't ask for better friends…or family." She returned the hug individually and smiled happily with tears streaking her glowing cheeks.

"Let's get something to eat," Jim suggested.

"Yes, but let's go eat at Fairyland," Roy butt in.

"Good Idea! I'll introduce you to Aurora, Narissa. I'm sure you two will get along," added Steve.

"I'm in," I said in agreement. "Narissa, you'll enjoy this for sure. You're going to have many new experiences. It's now time to change your life!"

Chapter 34
Learning to Live Again

After making necessary arrangements and space in the cave keeping Narissa in mind, we took off to Fairyland. We noticed that the gates to the village were manned. That means the rosters for the vigilantes were in place and put into practice.

I truly appreciated that the foresters didn't waste any time getting their systems in order. That's why it was very believable that the site construction would be completed on time as planned.

As soon as we entered, we saw Dulcea. She skipped over, smiling, and started checking out Narissa. She gave me a look and cheekily commented, "I told you rubbing my horn is lucky." I was terribly embarrassed, and she started to giggle.

I made the introductions, and Dulcea gave her a warm welcome. "Enjoy yourself my dear, we're all friends here. Whatever you need, feel free to ask."

Narissa thanked her and appreciated the village, "It's a beautiful village. It's strange that I've been in the forest for years; yet never got to see much of it other than the lake. Of course, it's because I was bound to the lake. And you are all so wonderful. Thank you!"

We gave her a quick tour of the village and decided to eat from one of the eateries at the square. Their food was delectable.

When we entered, I noticed that Narissa was looking a little uneasy. Even though she was born and raised human, it's been years since she lived that life. And it may take a little time for her to get used to the community life again.

I figured it would be better to pack our food and eat it in the park. The open grounds and greenery would be easier on her. As we sat down to eat, I saw Narissa picking on salads.

"Aren't you hungry?" I asked her.

"I can't eat those meats. I'm used to the greens or sea food," she said.

Of course! Living in water what else would she eat.

I quickly went back to get her some fish. She smiled and started to eat. Then she grimaced. "It's cooked."

We laughed at her expressions, and I urged her to finish her food. "Narissa, you have to get used to this now. Please eat or you'll compromise your health."

She nodded and ate; although she looked like a little girl being forced to finish her meals.

She is so adorable.

We relished our meal and Steve went to call Aurora.

Her interaction with Aurora went very well. She looked very comfortable. Aurora met her with a big hug and showered her with love and compassion. She informed Narissa about her CSK group and told her to get in touch whenever she needed help.

Narissa was impressed. She appreciated the group efforts and expressed her desire to join them once she found her footing in her new life. Aurora was elated that Narissa was interested. She offered to help put a few clothes and shoes together for her, and Narissa agreed. They traipsed off to Aurora's house chatting like girls do.

It was endearing to see her like this – like a normal girl. As a mermaid, she was beautiful and that's when I fell in love with her. But as a human woman, she was shedding her defenses bit by bit and was not shy about showing the emotional side of her. The side that she had forgotten.

She had been dealing with so many dangers that Selene put her through and the loneliness that came with her changed being. She had put up a large wall to hide her true self.

I suggested to the boys we should meet Queen Titania before we make the final decision to go back to our homes. They agreed and we went to see the queen, while Narissa was busy with Aurora.

"My favorite boys!" she smiled and welcomed us. "How come you aren't working at the site?"

"We didn't go today. Narissa – the mermaid – is now going to live with us and we had to make her comfortable. We came to give you some news." With a brief pause, I continued, "As soon as the coronation is done, we will be leaving the Magus Forest."

With a look of surprise and disappointment, she said, "Where are you going?"

"We will be returning to our realms. We have loved being here, in spite of the fact that we were tricked and brought here. The love and support we have received from you is a treasure we will cherish. Thank you!" I said, a lump forming in my throat.

"I will miss you. We will all miss you. I understand that you boys have to return to your homes and families. But, if possible, do visit us from time to time. How are you going to go back?" she asked.

"Your majesty, do you know Selene has escaped from the forest and left the realm? She had tried to overpower Narissa, but we managed to avoid any untoward incident. When she was cornered, she escaped." Queen Titania was astounded to learn of the goings on.

"Now that she's not here, it's safe to tell that Narissa is going to help us go back. But I don't know if we will be able to return to the forest," I informed.

She looked pensive for a few moments and called for her royal staff. With the staff, she blessed each one of us, touching the crystal on our heads. "May the almighty take care of you and your loved ones and keep you safe always."

She hugged us and continued, eyes gleaming with care like the crystal on her staff, "If you cannot come, I will come to visit you and also bring you with me to meet the others. My royal staff will bring me to you." She brandished her impressive black and gold staff in the air.

Oh wow! I didn't know the queen can also jump portals.

It was exciting to think we could keep our relationships alive by visiting each other. What an interesting prospect! It would be great to explore the possibilities.

"Sid, when you first suggested to me the idea of voting for Archon as emperor, I was not sure how it would go. But I soon observed that you were indeed right, and that's why I brought it up in front of the council. And today, I am very happy with that decision. Thank you, boys, for all your help in improving our lives!" she ended fondly.

We went back to the park and saw that Narissa was already there with Flora and Aurora. Flora greeted us a huge smile and affectionate embrace. Narissa was excited to show us her make over. She was wearing a frock similar to what the girls in Fairyland wore.

She looks absolutely gorgeous and alluring!

"Flora has sewn this for me herself," she said excitedly. "There are a few more from Aurora's closet, and another one in the making."

She sounded so typically like a young girl enthusiastic after her shopping expedition and happily displaying everything she has bought.

"Flora, we didn't know you had sewing skills too," I complimented her. "In the future, you will get orders for our wives and daughters too."

Everyone laughed at the teasing remark.

Chapter 35
Back to Routine

We returned home and waited for Archon. Narissa was now looking a lot more relaxed and at ease. She was getting along with the Toon boys too.

She noticed a waterfall nearby and was happy to freshen up there and feel the water on her skin. Water had been her home for so many years; it was as necessary for her to immerse herself in it, as important as breathing air.

I noticed that the environment in the lair had changed since she arrived. It seemed more homely – cozy and sedate. Maybe it was the presence of a female that made it so. We boys were not as rambunctious as we normally used to be.

We were discussing going back to work the next day and Narissa wanted to join us. I thought it was wonderful that she was taking a step towards keeping herself busy.

Archon returned from work, and we updated him with the day's news. He was happy with Narissa's intention to join the construction site, though he allowed her the comfort of resting at home. Narissa showed that she's made of tough material, when she refused to stay back.

He too had informed everyone at the site that Selene had left the forest. While everyone rejoiced, he also cautioned them that she could return any time. It was imperative that the plans they had put in place was followed diligently, so that she would not be able to do any more damage if and when she returned.

Two weeks passed quickly with the routine of going to work, meeting our friends in Fairyland, enjoying each other's company, and me stealing glances of Narissa whenever I got the opportunity. The last one I turned into an art, no one ever noticed.

With every passing day, my respect for Narissa grew, as she displayed her strength of character, her compassion for everyone and her dedication to work. I was already in love with her and with the increasing admiration, I began to envision a life with her.

I felt antsy that I couldn't convey my feelings. But I didn't want to frighten her or make her feel like she owed me her presence in my life. It would defeat the relationship if she didn't feel the way I did. So, I watched and waited.

I did, however, sense her growing leaning on me for emotional support. She was also more open to asking for help when necessary. And I was loving it. The earlier Narissa was distant, and this Narissa was growing closer. She didn't shy away from sharing her views and thoughts.

All of us sat down to dinner and discussion every day after work. An easy camaraderie and connection had formed. One more member had been added to this 'family'.

On a personal level, she was growing more comfortable with community life. She had also started trying out different foods and was appreciating them 'cooked' too. She was not feeling claustrophobic in closed spaces anymore. We even sat in the very eatery she avoided earlier and enjoyed an easy, fun evening for a weekend dinner.

She left no doubt that she was coping well with becoming human again. Although that shouldn't have raised doubts at all, considering she coped so fabulously becoming a mermaid. At least, she knew what it was to be human for the initial years of her life.

At work, she was helping out with Aurora's CSK group and also doubling up as the medical support. Her healing powers were put to good use when anyone hurt themselves or fell ill. She received a lot of acclaim for her efforts, and I often saw pride in Archon's eyes. I felt proud of her myself!

We were at work, two weeks after Narissa joined us, when Archon announced that the community bell had been installed. He clanged the heavy stone bell amid applause and cheering. The leaders' council had come in to see the site as it had almost reached completion.

They also had an announcement to make – the coronation had been fixed for two days later. In these two weeks, not only had the plans been followed, but they had been upgraded. The complex was now better than expected.

The Temple of Faith had been renovated. It was bigger and the inner sanctum was arranged beautifully. The clerestory windows shone lots of sunlight into the room. The room itself had been extended as well. It was bright and exuded positivity and hope, unlike what we had first seen there.

Large ornate gem encrusted candle stands were placed on either side of a cross, that was beautifully carved into the stone wall and polished. The earlier cross that we had placed there was relocated on an upper level, between the windows. The stone altar was engraved with intricate design and covered with luxurious bright fabric.

Other walls were also engraved with beautiful designs and religious scriptures. Elaborate arches adorned the inner sanctum and the outer courts. The dungeon at the back had been separated from the temple and attached to the governing grounds. The bell was placed between the temple and the governing office.

The office was large and high to accommodate Archon and the other large dwellers. It also housed a resting space. Behind the office was the humongous arena for public gatherings. That is where the coronation would be taking place.

The work was a sight to behold!

No wonder we have ancient beauties of architecture still standing, while new buildings often crumble to adulterated material.

Excitement was rife, as everyone worked towards the last and finer details. It heralded a new phase of life that seemed full of hope and promise. The news was received with a lot of happiness.

That evening when we returned home, we celebrated with a special meal and toast to the new Emperor Archon. We informed Archon of our desire to return to our realms after the coronation was done.

His expressions of cheerfulness dimmed as he spoke, "I know, and I understand that you have to leave. So, I will not stop you. But I still must tell you that I don't quite like how I feel about it."

We huddled close to him like little pets and expressed our love. Narissa also wore a disturbed expression, and she asked us, "Can't you stay a little longer?"

I couldn't bear to leave her behind, and I finally asked, "Narissa, would you come with me?"

Chapter 36
She Said 'Yes!'

Narissa was taken by surprise and took a few moments to gather her thoughts. But not very long though, she seemed to be more in touch with her emotions now. She held my hand. "I want to. But I don't know if my parents are in the same place now, or even together. I don't know if I can go back to them."

"No, I meant I want you to be with me. Live with me and I will help you find your parents too," I asserted.

She smiled slowly, and softly said, "Yes."

My heart was doing cartwheels and my head was in the air with butterflies everywhere!

"That would be wonderful, Sid. If she has you by her side, I think she'd best go back to the human world," said Archon. "Otherwise, Narissa, you always have a home here. You can stay with me. You are all like my children. And you are familiar with life in the forest."

Narissa was overwhelmed with the love shown by Archon and rushed to give him a hug. Even though, literally speaking, our 'hug' only managed to encompass his leg.

"My home will become empty without all of you." Archon sighed, looking mushy for the first time.

"Queen Titania says she will bring us here for visits every once in a while," Jim gave him hope.

"Oh! You've informed her about your plans already?" he asked. "That's good. I had mentioned to her too the incidents that led to Narissa living with us. The queen really does think of everything, doesn't she?" He smiled. "That would make me very, very happy."

Roy added, "Besides, if Narissa can get us out of here, she can get us back too, right? You are definitely going to be seeing us again."

Archon nodded and patted our heads with his forelimb, as a blessing.

That night, I dreamt of my grandparents. It was a happy dream. The cherubic smile of my grandpa and the loving countenance of my grandma engulfed me with a peace that had been missing for some time. I dreamt that I was vacationing with them along with my parents. And with us was Narissa!

It felt like they were also blessing us – Narissa and me. I took that as a good omen.

Early next morning, as we prepared to go to the site, a fairy from the queen's palace came to let us know that we were all invited for a royal lunch. That was always something to look forward to. I guess this was our farewell lunch.

We went to work thrilled, in anticipation of the day's lunch. Roy updated Narissa on the grandeur of this invitation. And she was excited to experience it. She had met the queen on one or two occasions, when the lake's water was required to heal some fairies. But she didn't get to know her much.

The day went by quickly. Everything was being wrapped up for the coronation the following day. And while others took their lunch break at the site, we hopped onto Archon and headed for Fairyland.

Just like us, Narissa too was in raptures over the aerial view of the forest that we had witnessed, being airborne the first time. She couldn't stop gushing. We reached the village and entered the castle to a heartwarming welcome as usual.

Narissa was floored. She couldn't believe the warmth being showered, that too from a queen. The grandeur was intimidating for her, but the affection given made her feel at ease. Honestly, she echoed our emotions when we experienced the same initially.

Queen Titania was a very compassionate and loving soul. I could imagine how Archon must love her, given that she had been the mother figure in his life. It was so easy to see how effortlessly she took on that role.

We were led into a living room next to the dining area and seated down for some conversation. A delicious welcome drink made of fresh fruits was served.

Queen Titania first addressed Narissa to make her feel welcome, "You look wonderful Narissa! How are you coping with the changes? Archon has told me all that happened, including the confrontation with Selene. You are brave."

She waved her hand toward us, saying, "…And really blessed that you have all of them with you."

"Absolutely! I can't thank my stars enough that I have received so much care and concern from everybody. Including you." She smiled. "I feel special with your welcome. It is all the love I have received that has helped me cope very well with everything that has happened."

With a benign smile, Queen Titania asked, "The boys told me that you're helping them go back home. And what are you going to do after that? You can live in Fairyland. I'll arrange for a small home for you."

Narissa was silent for a few moments and her eyes shone with tears held back. "I'm so lucky! Archon has given me a home, and you wish to do the same for me. Everything that was missing for so many years, has come to me all at once."

She paused and collected herself. "And I'm even luckier that Sid is here. I'm going back with him," she ended softly.

"That's excellent! Nothing could be better," the queen remarked, giving me an approving nod. "You take good care of her, Sid."

"Definitely, your majesty! Nothing would give me greater pleasure," I agreed, gazing at Narissa with a deep look.

In your eyes, I see my life.

In your arms, I will live my life.

I was turning into a poet! If there was a meter, at that moment, to measure my feelings on a scale of 1 to 10, I would have blasted it and crossed the mark. I was feeling a little goofy suddenly.

She spoke some more about our departure, giving us advice about how to take care of ourselves, and then we proceeded towards the dining hall.

As usual, the table was decorated with an array of dishes. I noticed that any remarks we had made on earlier occasions, about our favorite dishes, were prepared for us. The Toon boys and I had enjoyed the food immensely during our last meal at the castle. And we happily spoke of our individual favorites.

The special spread of desserts was even more impressive and drool worthy.

Our meal was laced with fun and laughter. And not once did the queen treat us like we were going for good. She spoke like we'd meet again, and that our connection was not to be forgotten.

When we finished, she ordered her staff to get something. They walked in with gifts that she said was a farewell memento. She gave each of us, the Toon boys and me, a beautifully wrapped box.

She turned to Narissa. "I didn't know you were going too. But I have something special for you." She removed her bracelet and put it on Narissa. She whispered to her lady-in-waiting and turned back to us.

Narissa was dumbstruck with her gift. A bracelet from the queen herself! And if that wasn't enough, the lady-in-waiting walked in with an exquisite royal gown for her. "If you like this gown, I'll have it packed for you," said Queen Titania.

Narissa was at a loss for words. "I…I do…it's gorgeous! But your majesty, you don't need to—"

"It's yours," insisted Queen Titania. "It's a token of my love."

Chapter 37
Coronation Day

Back at the lair, Narissa couldn't stop looking up her gown again and again. She couldn't believe that she owned a royal ensemble fit for a queen with a bracelet to go with it. After checking it out for the umpteenth time, she finally spoke, "Can I take this with me, Sid?"

"Of course!" I replied. "You can take all that Flora and Aurora have given you as well. We're all going to carry whatever we've collected to take back to our homes. We got gifts from Archon, Flora, and the queen."

I showed her our small boxes where we kept the keepsakes. "Although yours is going to be more voluminous. Lucky that we don't have flight rules to follow!" I laughed. "Actually, it makes me wonder, is it possible to jump portals with baggage?"

"I can manage that." She grinned. I almost fainted hearing her little laugh. I was falling hook, line, and sinker.

"What did you boys get?" she was curious.

We realized we hadn't opened our gifts and starting unwrapping. Each of us got an exquisitely embossed silver wine goblet encrusted with gems. It had a fairy queen designed on one side and a dragon emperor on the other.

This surely had to be the most thoughtful gift ever. A beautiful reminder of Queen Titania and Archon. Kind of like a family photo, that might become an heirloom. We kept it in the box with the other things we had. I also showed her all the other gifts we had received.

We were all set for our departure now. The coronation was the next day and after that we were going home!

"Are you prepared for tomorrow, Archon?" Jim asked him. He had been pacing back and forth for some time.

"I'm nervous," he said.

"What?" Steve asked surprised. "You get nervous too?" Everyone was laughing. Our laughter made Archon laugh out too and he accidentally almost scorched us.

"Too much laughter is dangerous around me," he said sheepishly. And we laughed again uproariously.

The next day was a bright and pleasant one. And full of excitement for us. Archon was going to be crowned EMPEROR! He's family…

Hmm! Does that make us royalty too?

I was wondering about that, when Queen Titania came to the lair with some courtiers. They were armed with some packages. She called out to Archon and told him he ought to look like an emperor today.

She opened a wooden box with a royal insignia engraved on it. Inside on red velvet rested a long thick leather cord carrying a large gold pendant shaped like a crown. She draped his neck with the impressive neckpiece, that instantly made him look sovereign.

Once she was satisfied with his look, she beckoned us. "The emperor's family has to dress for the occasion too."

The courtiers came forward one by one with the other boxes. They contained silk cloaks with golden lace trimmings. One each for all five of us, which we were made to don. "Now you are ready for the coronation." The queen gave us a look of satisfaction.

I was feeling a bit awkward. I never had the propensity to dress up in flamboyant clothes, let alone something that looked like a drama costume.

If I had a turban, I'd look like an Indian magician.

We reached the arena earlier than the crowd was expected to gather. The leader council had assembled before time, to discuss the procedures and protocol to be followed. We didn't have to participate much, but we were required to be on the dais beside him. We represented 'his family.'

I guess we were royalty after all.

I was smiling my most dignified smile; all awkwardness dissipated. All of us felt immense pride.

The arena walls were decorated with colorful flags swaying in the breeze. The dais had a huge, gilded arch that represented Archon's throne. Under it was a carpet of flowers. On either side were stone seats for the Council and next to them were seats for the family.

The foresters started to trickle in after some time, and within an hour the arena was packed to capacity. There were separate areas marked for all the different clans, depending on their size. It seemed pretty much like our stadium concerts with a noisy, cheering crowd.

A gong was sounded thrice to silence the audience. King Kronus was the first to address the assembly. He easily got their attention as his voice boomed across.

"People of the Magus Forest, I welcome you to this historical congregation that marks the beginning of a new era. As leaders of our respective clans, we have formed a Council that unites us in an effort to refine our lives."

Applause and cheers followed. He held up his hand to quieten them and continued, "We have decided to take this unity to a new level and have elected an Emperor to guide and govern us. Please welcome with open hearts and minds, our new Emperor, ARCHON!"

The crowd went wild. He silenced them again and spoke, "I, King Kronus, of the giant community pledge that we shall extend every help to integrate all the races and exchange our cultures for advancement and betterment. I shall now call Queen Titania to share her thoughts."

Thunderous applause followed as Queen Titania had her say and interspersed all the leaders' speeches. One by one, all of them addressed the public, mainly to reach out to their subjects and promote the idea of unity.

Finally, the moment arrived when Gibel was summoned to bring up the crown. Gibel rolled onto the dais a wooden cart carrying a huge, majestic gold crown, set with different colored jewels.

Queen Titania was preening like a proud parent and went forward to lift the ceremonial headdress. She soon realized that it was too heavy for her. We started giggling under our breath. She then called upon King Kronus to do the honors.

The king lifted the royal crown waved it to show the people with a flourish and placed it upon the head of a beaming Archon. Whistling and clapping reverberated in the air. The deafening sounds took a while to die down.

Archon waved to the happy assembly and stepped forward to say a few words.

"You are all my people, and I undertake an oath to protect and support all of you. No community, no individual is too small to approach me. Whatever troubles you, I implore you, please seek help from me, or anyone around you in a position to assist."

After the imperial statement, we took turns to pay obeisance to the new Emperor, as did the Council members. An announcement was made for the people to accept the celebratory drink being offered and the ceremony was drawn to a close.

We headed back to the lair, on the back of the new Emperor, feeling as high as the altitude we were at.

Chapter 38
Time to Go

We had to celebrate the day with Archon – one, because he was crowned and, two, it was our last day with him. I told Roy to get some delectable bakes from Fairyland. Steve went along with him, deciding we should have a delicious meal too.

The euphoria of the day had not died down. And Archon asked us if we'd like a quick tour of the forest before we left. We agreed. Before that, we thoroughly enjoyed our lip-smacking lunch and dessert, with fun and laughter being the prime ingredients. Then, we headed out for our grand tour as Archon promised.

We flew over to the hills where we first hid, when we escaped the clutches of Selene. We pointed out the dwarf village to Narissa. We saw the Sage Oak, Lake Arcane, and also all the other villages. It was a trip through nostalgia lane.

The imps were still living in the Giant Kingdom under the watchful eyes of King Kronus. We went up to the Kingsfair river, the river that separated the forest from the Giant Kingdom. It gave us a fair aerial view of the kingdom. Narissa was terribly impressed with the grandeur of the kingdom.

I sounded out an observation to Archon. "You know, the imps could go back to their home if their entire area is enclosed in a metallic net, that extends above the trees and covers overhead as well. That would protect them from any invader."

"You're right. It's a bit of a task, but it's possible. I'll mention it to Alaris, their leader and see how he feels about it."

Finally, Archon flew over the Dark Woods. The fog still covered the forest canopy there, but the path was clear, and the charred remains of Selene's mansion were also visible.

"Hey! Who's that?" Jim spoke abruptly, as I related our experience at the woods to Narissa. He felt he saw movement around the mansion. But there was no one when we looked.

Roy looked down straining his eyes. "I don't see anyone or anything. Are you sure you saw someone there?"

"I'm quite sure I saw someone. Could it be Selene?"

Archon did not look very much perturbed. "Although I don't see anything, I don't doubt what you may have seen. No one from the forest would have anything to do there. If at all, it could only be Selene. We have no control over her movements. But there's no need to worry. Our defenses are in place."

"She might have hidden herself when she saw you flying above. What would she be rummaging for from her burnt mansion?" I wondered aloud.

"Not important to us now," said Archon and headed back home.

"Archon, should I take the hidden grimoire with me? I don't want to take any chance of her finding it again." I was worried she would try to get back her powers.

"Not at all," Archon assured. "She doesn't know where it is. And it is very safe with the Sage Oak. She might come after you, if she ever gets an inkling that you have it. And there's no telling what tricks she'll resort to, to get it."

I nodded in understanding and left it at that.

We reached home and kept our things ready for the next day. Narissa had told us we need to be at the lake to go back. Archon had decided to accompany us and make sure there was no trouble. We retired early, reflecting on the past couple of months that we had spent in the Enchanted Magus Forest.

So much had changed in our lives.

I thought about how excited I had been reaching the Toon World, hoping for an adventure that brought my childhood dreams to life. I didn't stay there long enough, but I definitely got my adventure – in another realm. An adventure that healed my soul, an adventure that brought me so much love, an adventure that taught me to be a fighter.

I was sad to leave and yet happy to go back. I'd see my parents again. Seems like forever that I spent time with them. I wanted to be with them and also introduce Narissa to them. What would they say?

****

"Mom, how are you?" I had phoned her as soon as I got home.

"Where have you been? I tried to reach you so many times. But—" She broke off and started crying.

"Mom, Mom... Please stop crying. I'm coming right now."

"That won't be necessary." She sounded terse and my blood pressure was rising.

Just then, the doorbell rang. I ran to answer, but Narissa opened the door. My mom and dad stood before me smiling.

****

"Wake up, sleepy head." It was Jim. "You're smiling again. Another happy dream?"

"Yeah! The best," I answered cheerily. "Time to go home."

The day seemed brighter than usual. And it wasn't just me. The Toon boys looked excited as well. The chirpiness in the air was infectious and even Archon was looking vibrant. Our regal Emperor was in his element.

"You haven't gotten rid of me just yet. I will come and surprise you some day," he threatened in jest.

"Wouldn't we love that!" Narissa smiled. Everyone agreed.

He laughed and said, "Except, I won't fit into your homes." Everyone was laughing.

We had a hearty breakfast and were soon ready to leave. We had decided that Roy would zap us there with our baggage, much against Archon's insistence to fly us there. Although the Archon Airways was tempting, with the fabulous view and all. We certainly didn't want the emperor of the forest to become our porter!

He insisted on reaching the lake first. Even though we weren't sure if Jim had actually seen someone or he was mistaken, Archon didn't want to take chances of Selene being there. We waited about fifteen minutes after he left, after which Roy took us there.

Archon was there, flashing the 'all clear' look and we exchanged our final hugs. Narissa summoned the waters with the power of her mind and a wave of her hands. The lake swelled up and rose in a high wave. It extended towards us, moving like a remote-controlled surge of water. And right before us, it stood still forming a vertical whirlpool.

"Come on boys, we just have to step in, and the waters will recede," Narissa instructed.

"Will we be able to breathe?" I asked.

"Yes, don't worry, it will be fine."

Hmm…I suppose this is how I'd feel if I were in a washing machine.

We walked into the sparkling blue whirling tunnel of water. As soon as we were all in, it rose up into a cyclonic spiral and started to recede into the lake.

Chapter 39
The Apollyon Abode

We could see Archon until the water rose up and after that everything became a blur. I felt like we got sucked into the whirlpool, but we didn't get drenched. We spun around into the vortex with alarming speed, and the next thing I knew, we were being spat out onto the banks of a lake.

We were all disoriented for a few minutes, after which I noticed that we were in the Toon World. Everyone was smiling from ear to ear. The Toon boys almost screamed in unison, "We're home!"

"C'mon, pick up your stuff and lock arms," Roy commanded. He quickly zapped us into their neighborhood. "That's my house, right there." He was pointing towards a modest home with a small yard. "You have to meet my family."

We walked into his house to an uproar of delighted greetings and hugs. His family, very loudly and volubly, expressed their happiness on their son's return. Roy introduced Narissa and me. Greetings done they started bombarding him with questions of his whereabouts for the last couple of months.

He alleviated their concerns by saying he had had the adventure of a lifetime and that he will tell them the whole story later. After a few more minutes of cheerful banter, Roy said he'd be back in a while after meeting the families of Jim and Steve.

"Leave your stuff here Sid and Narissa. No need to carry it around. Once you've met everyone, you can take it before you leave for your home."

We went on to meet Steve's family and then Jim's mother. All of them were so welcoming and warm, it was a pleasure. With the pleasantries over, I told the boys I'd like to see their neighborhood.

I really hadn't had the chance of experiencing the Toon World much, because Selene had abducted us. I was hoping I could see some fun stuff – like those we see in our cartoons or animation movies.

We trotted off to the nearest park for a walk. As we ambled on across the greensward making small talk, we saw a small group of people huddled together in a mysterious manner. They were dressed in black robes with hoods covering their heads.

"What's going on there?" I asked curiously.

"Looks like some cult meeting," assumed Jim. "We have some of those here too."

We continued to walk past them, though I threw a glance at the group out of curiosity. I saw one person turn to watch us, but I couldn't see the face clearly, with the hood casting shadows. We strolled on, brushing it off as inconsequential, and continued to chat.

We were caught unawares, when from behind, some people started to grapple with us and tried to bag our heads with a dark cloth. The action was quick and unexpected, and we were unsuccessful in escaping their clutches.

The next thing we knew, we were being bound by rope and pushed into a vehicle. We could see nothing because of the bags that covered our heads.

After a blind car ride, with none of our questions or objections being answered, the vehicle came to a stop. We were pulled out and shoved forward. We walked a few steps and heard a squeaky door open. We walked into some place and were prodded to continue walking some more.

"Bring them here," a surly bass voice echoed.

We're in a big hall or auditorium, I think.

We stopped, and the bags covering our heads were removed. We squinted as the glare from a couple of spotlights from the side shone into our eyes. We were in a large empty enclosure, like a warehouse.

A tall man in a black robe stood before us. It seemed to be the same cult group that we saw at the park. We couldn't clearly see his face as a hood almost covered his eyes. All that was visible was a mustachioed lower face and angular jawline.

"Why have you brought us here? We don't even know you," I said, sounding tired and frustrated. I was no mood for more stress. I wanted to go home and start living a somewhat staid existence, a normal life.

"You are in the Apollyon Abode. Consider yourself lucky to be here. You and your friends are going to be of good use to us in our rituals. It is our goal to enlighten the universe to the power of fearlessness towards constrictions and restrictive laws."

Does he seriously believe we're lucky to be pawns of a cult?

"Our doctrine advocates fearlessness as a key to attaining supremacy. For that we make live sacrifices to appease our God, so that he may grant us that attitude in abundance."

"You're crazy if you think you can become 'fearless' by killing somebody," Steve retorted.

"Hush!" the man bellowed. "You are not invited to start a discussion. You are to bow before my commands. I am Daemon Dickens, the commander of the Apollyon Abode. I have been anointed by Lucifer to spread his words. And in this family, my order is to be carried out not challenged."

Oh no! One more Selene. How are we going to get out of this now?

"Walter." He turned to one of the heavyset guys from the group that captured us. "Can you call her out?" The man exited through another door to do his bidding.

Call 'her' out? Who is this lady he's calling?

"You won't get away with this," I made a weak attempt at a threat to change his mind.

"Quiet!" he yelled at me harshly. "Are these the same people?" He was speaking to someone behind us.

We turned around and, to our horror, he was talking to Selene!

"Hello again!" she cackled, after she nodded an affirmation to the tall man. Her infuriating, vile, high-pitched laughter resonated in the empty space.

Chapter 40
Cult Commotion

"Thank you, Daemon!" she addressed the cult leader. "You're a worthy confrere. I am happy to become associated with your Apollyon family."

She walked across to the Daemon and explained, "That girl there is going to help me reclaim my supremacy in the Magus Forest. The pesky human, I believe, would serve well as your sacrificial offering. The other boys can join your devotees and help grow your tribe."

"You speak my mind, dear sister Selene." He nodded in reverence to her. "Walter, lock them up while I prepare for the ceremonial offering."

Walter tied our hands behind us and walked us through a hidden door ensconced behind a large tool shelf. The door opened into a small corridor that led into a small commune complex. The warehouse was just a façade to camouflage a secret cult domain.

We went through the empty passageway padded with soundproofing material. It acted as a wall, forfending intruders, and buffering the sounds of their everyday life. It led us onto a small courtyard surrounded by a single level housing densely covered by foliage. The courtyard seemed open with bright sunlight but was actually covered by a glass roof to drown out sounds.

Another cover-up, I thought, looking at the foliage.

I peeked into the rooms as we walked past. They looked like living quarters assigned to the members. After about 6–7 rooms, we were pushed into one similar to the others and locked up. But Narissa wasn't locked in with us. She was taken somewhere else, and this worried me.

"Now what?" I asked, as I gave everyone an exasperated look. "It looks like I'm going to become toast and Narissa is going to become Selene's puppet. You guys get to wear robes and sing that guy's glory, I guess," I ended, rolling my eyes.

"Hey, you're forgetting we have Roy with us." Jim sounded calm and collected. "He just has to zap us back home."

"That's right!" Roy added. "We'll just have to huddle together and lock our legs. These nincompoops have tied our hands."

Oh yeah, I hadn't thought of that!

After a moment's relief, my optimism nosedived as I had an upsetting realization. "But they have Narissa. We have to get to her before Selene does. And we don't know where they've kept her. If we get out of this room, they can easily spot us. The place has a very simple layout. We can't hide."

"Hmm…" Roy was deliberating. "I'll go and find out where they've kept her first. But I should wear one of those cloaks. Is there any way you can free my hands?"

We started to search the room for a sharp object that might help cut the rope that tied our hands. We struggled to look through drawers, the wardrobe, and any place we thought might have something, but there was nothing.

"We haven't checked the bathroom," Steve reminded.

I quickly went in to look and found a razor. Adjusting our positions, back-to-back, we attempted to cut open the ties. I somehow managed to sever part of the rope, when the door opened, and a guy threw us some cloaks to change into, for the ceremony later that evening.

Just what we need.

When he was gone, we continued to work on the ropes. In a few minutes, Roy's hands were free. He quickly he cut open the ropes binding the rest of us as well. All of us wore the cloaks.

We had now decided, since we all had cloaks, we could leave together without being recognized. In a quick moment, we were outside the room and we decided to break up to search for Narissa. We picked a hand gesture, an inconsequential thumbs-up, as a code to know one another.

Keeping our heads down, we split up to go in different directions. We looked, as inconspicuously as possible, through windows of closed rooms. I had no success in my direction and walked back to where Jim was to search. He shook his head too. I looked out where Steve was to check. After confirming our identities, Steve too answered in the negative.

I was beginning to feel a little desperate now. Roy was the only one left. I looked around to see if I could find anything we were missing. We had covered most of the area. Just the last few rooms were left. And where was Roy? I could sort of guess from the body language if it was one of us. But I couldn't see anyone that even vaguely resembled Roy.

Luckily, there weren't too many people to dodge from being noticed. I guess most of them were out during the day, giving shape to their nefarious activities. We sauntered around the remaining rooms, trying to look out for Roy.

After about ten minutes of loitering around the area, I saw someone emerge from one of the quarters hunched over, head lowered. I instinctively did the 'thumbs up' and got the same response. Roy gestured to follow him in and shut the door. There was no one there.

In a low voice, almost whispering, he said, "There's a door through the wardrobe here. I just saw someone walk in. I followed and it was a very short corridor leading to another room. I didn't go further, but I could hear Selene's voice. I'm sure that's where Narissa is too."

"What are we waiting for then, let's go in." I was impatient.

"No," Jim disagreed. "Have you forgotten how strong she is? If she knows we're free, she might hurt Narissa. We have to wait for them to leave."

I saw sense in what he said, and agreed, although every muscle in my body urged me to rush in. Jim and Steve decided to wait it out in the en suite bathroom. I hid under the bed and Roy behind the large dresser. If any one of us was in danger of being found, the others would pounce in.

And we waited. It seemed like time was moving at a snail's pace, as my impatience grew. After about half hour we heard voices. Selene, Daemon and one more member came out from the concealed room.

"She resists strongly." It was Daemon, sounding impressed with Narissa's strength.

"That's one of the many reasons she is useful to me, her strength," Selene said. "But it's very difficult to get through to her. I will have to try something else. Coercion will not work."

Chapter 41
The Narrow Escape

Selene and the others left the room. We quickly got out from hiding and went to the secret room. Narissa was on a very basic hospital style bed and had her hands tied up to the railing at the head. She looked drained of energy.

As soon as she saw us, she perked up and a smile sparkled in her eyes. "Thank God you're here. She was trying her best to break me down to follow her back to the enchanted forest. I'm not sure what she's going to try next, but I would rather not be around to find out."

We untied her, grabbed an extra cloak from the wardrobe for her and got out of the secret room. "What next?" Steve wondered as we reached the first room.

As soon as he uttered those words, Daemon and gang returned. Before we could react, he had half a dozen of his disciples restrain us with a chokehold. Now all of us were led into the same secret space and tied up in different corners.

That put an end to our escape plans for sure. They walked out asking a couple of them to stay in the outside chamber and keep an eye. Not that it would've mattered. Being tied up didn't help at all.

"If we had another five minutes, I would've zapped us out of here," said Roy ruefully. "Now we're all tied up so far from each other, it's impossible to do that."

If anything, it speeded up their preparations. Instead of waiting for the evening, they returned in about an hour or so, to start their major yagna-style worship. And I was to be the sacrificial lamb.

God, please help me out of this, I promise I'll try to become vegetarian.

I was beseeching God in my mind, while we were taken to the courtyard, where they had set up a large pentagram with stones. A circle was formed in the center of the pentagram, where they kept some tinder and kindling, finally placing wooden logs around it to form a rectangular stool of sorts.

Daemon was seated near the pentagram with the other members behind him. Selene was by his side. Narissa and the boys were also made to sit next to them. They ensured that Narissa and the Toons would be close to them, so they couldn't escape.

Also, Selene intended for Narissa to 'watch' my sacrifice to break down her resolve and resistance. The Toon boys were to understand how joining the 'family' was for their own good. It was meant to intimidate them into submission.

I was taken to Daemon, who got up and anointed my forehead and arms with some potent hallucinogenic emollient. All the while, he was rattling off some ritualistic chant. There was a small table next to him, on which was placed the bottle of the emollient, a Saracen scimitar (a sword with a broad curved blade), several cups and a big abalone bowl.

He turned to look at his disciples and explained, "I will slice the wrist and collect the blood in this bowl. This man, our oblation to our Supreme deity, will be placed on the pyre. We will torch the pyre and sing our praises to the deity, asking for the power of 'fearlessness' to be imbued in us. After the worship is complete, we will all sip the libation drink that will be infused with 'his powers'."

The followers hailed Daemon in excitement and expressed their happiness. All the while, I was visualizing every gory description he made, in excruciating detail, to the point that I almost felt the pain in my wrist and the heat in my body. I was totally freaking out in my head but held a resigned calm. The ointment had started to take effect.

"Can I get some water please?" I asked softly.

Daemon looked a bit annoyed but asked his favorite henchman Walter to get some for me. Once the water was poured out, I took a big sip and set it on the table. I darted a quick look at Narissa. She had her eyes closed in concentration, like she was praying. I wanted to see her eyes…

I want you to be the last person I see, I thought with dramatic emotion.

Just then, there was a light rumbling sound could be heard, that seemed to be gradually growing. Everyone looked around, but there was nothing. Until Daemon noticed the table next to him.

The glass of water that I had set down was shaking. As we watched, the vibrations started to get violent, and the water rose upwards and magically swelled in volume. It pushed out of the glass and like a gigantic wave, splashed and flooded the commune.

Everyone was taken aback and started to run helter-skelter. The flooding was only knee deep but the sheer impact of the splash and the suddenness of it all had them reeling.

Narissa got a hold of the boys and ran towards me. Roy caught me by the wrist and POOF! We were in the boys' neighborhood. I heaved a sigh of relief, and was half laughing and half crying, out of exasperation.

I almost shouted, "I thought, for a minute, you froze there!"

I was talking to Narissa. It's what I had felt when I saw her eyes closed. When we were tied up in the room with no way out, we had started to discuss our options. That's when Narissa, came up with the idea that we play along with their schedule.

All she said was, "Ask for a glass of water before he starts. And leave the rest to me. Boys stay prepared."

We may have escaped the commune, but they knew where the Toon boys lived for sure. That's how they were in the neighboring park. Selene must've somehow followed us through the portal. It was clear now that she was targeting Narissa and wanted me out of the way.

I told Narissa, "Let's get back to our world as soon as possible, so we can leave her behind. Let's quickly pick up our stuff from Roy's house and leave before she reaches us again."

Roy took us back to the lake and Narissa opened up the portal back to our dimension.

Chapter 42
Our Homecoming

The cyclonic whirlpool veered onto the shores of a lake and spat us out. I looked around a little dazed from the whirling vortex. But I was happy to be back, and with Narissa by my side.

Where are we?

It seemed quiet and isolated. I was thankful for that though, or we'd have people treating us like aliens. We walked around a little until we saw a group of people enjoying a picnic. I walked up to them and asked them where we were.

They looked at me like I was high on some hallucinogenic substance and laughed. We must have looked strange to be honest.

We were carrying boxes, unaware of where we were. Narissa was wearing clothes that looked like they belonged to another era. Fairy fashion wasn't quite in sync with modern day styles in our universe. To top it, it was cold, and we weren't wearing anything warm.

"This is the Prospect Park Lake," one girl finally answered.

I thanked her and we walked on. But I could hear them still jeering at us.

This place was about a half hour drive from my parent's home, the one I grew up in. The lake was manmade and a part of the Prospect Park, which was an urban public park in Brooklyn.

"Narissa, how did you know where we should come?" I asked her curiously.

I mean what are the chances that we reached the lake that was close to my childhood home. All I knew is it would be a lake. What if the lake was in another country, or at least in some other city?

She grinned and replied, "I remembered you had mentioned Brooklyn to me when we first started talking. I have to focus with the place in my mind. We could, of course, have landed on any other lake in Brooklyn if there are."

"No, this is the only one."

Now we had to reach some transport. Roy wasn't there to give us the free ride. I had quite gotten used to that. I had lived the fantasies one finds in story books or sees recreated in amusement parks for entertainment. But back to reality, and we now need money to commute.

I had realized from the reaction of the picnickers that we would need to concoct a plausible story in order to get help. We continued to walk for a good twenty minutes till we saw some cyclists. I shouted out to get their attention. This area had more people around.

The cyclists stopped and gave us a curious look-over. I told them we had come with some friends to rehearse a play but, somehow, managed to lose sight of them and lost our way. It wasn't possible to get back home since we didn't have any money on us.

They were kind enough to give us a pillion ride to the nearest subway station. I was grateful for any help that we could get. We reached the station, approached the security, and managed to get a ride to my apartment building.

Narissa was in awe of the neighborhood. The last that she had seen of this world was her own home, which was in a rural area. She had never seen the skyscrapers. The fancy elevator, with automatic doors was an amazing machine for her.

It was curious how our roles had reversed. I had returned from a fantasy, and she was now experiencing one.

There was a sweet old lady who lived next door to my apartment, whom I had given a spare key just in case of an emergency. I rang the bell on my neighbor's door. The door opened and Mrs. Stewart flashed her trademark warm smile.

"Sid, where have you been? I haven't seen you for a couple of months. Were you on a vacation? Didn't you let your mother know? She dropped by about a month ago to visit and was disappointed that you weren't there. Worried too. And you're not wearing warm clothes; it's freezing outside."

"I'm sorry Mrs. Stewart, something came up suddenly and I just had to leave. I didn't have time to inform anyone. I'll speak to my mom immediately. Thank you for letting me know." I smiled back. "Can I have my keys? I lost my own set."

"Sure." She quickly fished out the spare keys from a drawer nearby. Handing them over to me, she saw Narissa. "Pretty girl, your girlfriend?"

I gave a sheepish grin in response and nodded. "I'll speak to you later, thanks."

I walked into my apartment and immediately felt at home. Yet there was something missing. I had gotten used to life at the enchanted forest with Archon and the boys. The feeling of living with family. I decided I'm going to try and live that kind of life now.

I guided Narissa to the spare room and rearranged some of my stuff, so she had her own space. And it was freezing, so I found some warm sweaters for both of us.

Once she had put her stuff in place, I checked on grandpa's CRT television that accidentally became the portal into another universe. The portal had closed, and it was again just a memory that I had preserved.

I called up my mother on the mobile, and she wouldn't stop talking as soon as she identified my number. She had a million questions on my disappearance, which I promised I would answer soon.

For now, I wanted to know how my dad was doing. She perked up saying he had improved. I promised to visit her the next day and I could almost hear the happiness in her voice.

It was late evening, and I ordered some pizza for us. We had to rest out our stressful adventures and rejuvenate to prepare ourselves for a more regular life. I had to make sure that Narissa didn't look out of place in our world.

I made a mental note of our to-do list – shopping for Narissa, visiting my parents, calling up my office and research for Narissa's parents.

The day was going to be busy. And soon we were ready to hit the bed.

Chapter 43
Back to Reality

Having the comfort of my own bed after so long was a treat. I woke up feeling well rested and ready to tick off my activity list one by one. Narissa was up before me and was lounging around in the living room staring out of the huge French windows.

"Good morning!" I greeted cheerfully. "You're up early. Were you uncomfortable at night?"

She turned around, her big blue eyes gleaming, her bewitching smile brightening up the moment even more. "Hi! Yes, I did have a little trouble. But I'll get used to it. Seems like forever since I slept on a proper bed."

Luckily, I had a two-bedroom home. I had intentionally taken up a spacious apartment, so I could get my mom to spend time with me occasionally. But that hardly ever happened, since Dad's condition required her to be around him.

The only time she came over for a weekend was when Dad had to undergo a barrage of tests. Occasionally, I would get a friend from work over for company on weekends, when I felt too lonely.

"Shall I get you some coffee?" I asked, even though I knew she didn't have tea or coffee. "Maybe you'd like to try it out."

"I'll take a sip out of yours first. Otherwise, I think I'll drink some milk," she replied unsure. "I was looking at the streets. Everything looks so small from up here. It's like flying on Archon's back, except we aren't moving. Life has really changed since I left!"

"It has! But then you were from a rural region, so even if there were a few skyscrapers, you wouldn't have got the opportunity to see it. I'll make us some breakfast." I quickly rustled up some eggs and toast, with a glass of milk for her and coffee for me.

I had to call up my office...I was assuming I still had a job! I phoned and asked the secretary for my boss with some apprehension. Although I was lucky to have a boss that treated me like a friend and not a subordinate.

"Mike, how've you been?" I enquired after him.

"Sid!" He added a string of cuss words after that, before he continued a little angrily, "Where the hell have you been? I've had a hard time covering for you."

I knew he was truly worried about me and must have sincerely tried to justify my actions. "I'm really sorry I disappeared without informing you. Something came up during the Christmas holidays and I had to leave immediately. Unfortunately, there was no way I could inform you. Am I still working for you?"

"You are for now...but if this happens again, I won't be able to hold your position," he forewarned a little more calmly. "When are you coming in?"

"I'll be there tomorrow morning. I'll explain everything to you." With that I hung up and started to wonder how I was going to explain all that happened. Most people would think of it as a fictionalized excuse of a story. But I owed him the honest truth...that's the kind of relationship I had with him.

"Aren't you going to finish your breakfast?" Narissa got me out of my reverie.

"Do you want to try the coffee?" I asked.

"I did. I can't handle it just yet." Both of us laughed.

"Okay, let's get ready and head for some shopping," I told her.

The sweet Mrs. Stewart dropped by to give us some fresh homemade cookies and ask if we needed anything. The aroma of the fresh baked cookies reminded me of Fairyland at Christmas time. She was kind of like my Queen Titania here.

We headed to the nearest mall. It felt funny when I had to guide Narissa through the revolving door and the escalator. I couldn't get over the fact that this Braveheart of a girl needed help through these mundane issues. I did understand it though, and I found it so cute when she looked exasperated trying to get through.

Shopping with her was fun. I had never shopped for a woman before, and I was as lost as she was, trying to pick and choose the outfits. The sales lady was a great help though. And I think Narissa began to understand a little better what works for her.

We bought some comfortable and casual clothing and shoes that immediately changed her personality to a trendy beauty. There was enough to last a couple of months, and I asked her to wear one outfit right away.

Satisfied, we headed over to meet my parents. I called my mom, and she was at the hospital, so that's where we headed directly. Seeing my mother became a very emotional moment for me. I could see in her eyes how happy she was. Her hug was tight and unrelenting. She held me for several minutes before she looked up at me.

Holding my face in her palms, she teared up, and cried, "Don't ever go away without telling us. You have no idea what was going on in my mind. I was so worried that I filed a case with the police."

"The police? Oh no. Okay no problem, we'll call them and tell them I'm back and I'm fine," I reassured my mom. She nodded and led me to my dad's room.

Dad's eyes lit up when he saw me. "How're you doing, Dad?" I asked, holding his hand.

"I'm much better now," he smiled and replied slowly.

I cannot explain the rush of happiness that coursed through me when I heard him speak.

How many years had it been since I heard him speak intelligibly?

I looked at Mom and she was smiling widely. I held him close and firm, trying to be careful that I didn't hurt him in any way.

"If I had known you'll get better when I'm gone, I would've gone earlier," I made light of the situation.

Laughing softly, he said, "Please don't go away like that." And I hugged him again.

Mom noticed Narissa behind me. "Who is this with you?"

Chapter 44
Introducing Narissa

"Mom… Dad… This is a dear friend of mine, Narissa. She's a healer. I wanted you guys to meet her." I nudged Narissa forward gently.

Narissa greeted and shook hands with both of them. "I'm very happy to meet you. I've seen how much Sid cares about his parents."

She turned to Dad. "Sir, Mr. Rajan, may I hold your hand?"

As my dad nodded, she sat down on the seat next to his bed and took his hand into hers. She closed her eyes and concentrated quietly for a good five minutes. Then she poured out a glass of water from the table on the side, held it for a minute and asked him to drink.

"You're already out of the woods, and you'll only get better," she assured him with a gentle touch on the shoulder. "Once you start to move around a little, please take your therapy very seriously."

My mom was smiling with hope. "He'll get better? You're sure."

"I'm sure." She fueled the hope with confidence.

"Thank you, my dear, it's so nice to see you." My mom hugged her with a warmth of gratitude. She then shot me a look. "Now would you tell us, where did you go?"

"Mom, it's a long story. I'll definitely explain, but some other day. Now I just want us to have lunch together and then I have to go and meet my boss."

I hugged my dad again before leaving. "Dad, I'll see you again soon. Please take care of yourself. Mom let's go the café at the corner and eat something. I see that you haven't been good to yourself."

The three of us ordered some quick sandwiches and juice. I made sure my mom ate well. She had looked pale and tired, though she was looking alright now…more relaxed, and happy. And what gave me real peace was seeing her smile. She had forgotten how to smile.

After I promised to see her again very soon, we left for my office. I was on tenterhooks about meeting Mike and explaining what happened. I felt taking Narissa along would help him understand that this wasn't a flamboyant and fictitious excuse for disappearing.

We reached the office building and headed towards Mike's cabin. His secretary politely greeted and enquired after me. After informing him on the intercom, she ushered me in. I asked Narissa to sit and wait till I was ready to call her in.

"Hey Mike! Happy to see me?" I tried to joke.

"What the heck…? I'm glad to see you looking well though." He got up and came to give me a friendly hug. "You are looking very…umm…happy. What's the secret? In the many years that I've known you, you've never gone away…let alone, gone away without informing. What's going on?"

"You need to sit down and hear me out." I motioned towards the sofa. I told him what happened in a quick highlights-kind-of version, and watched his expressions turn from 'interested' to 'incredulous' to 'alarmed'. Maybe he thought I was losing my mind.

"Sid, I've never known you to be a fibber or one who concocts hyperbolic tales. Yet, what you're telling me is hard to swallow. I want to believe you, but—"

"Wait, Mike, I want you to meet someone." I got up to call Narissa inside. "This is Narissa," I introduced her. They shook hands and I told him, "Narissa can jump portals. That's how I'm back home."

He stared blankly at her, and she smiled and spoke, "I know it's hard to believe, but it's true. I'll show you something."

She looked at his glass of water set on the desk, closed her eyes and in a few minutes the water rose up in a spiral, circled the room and went back into the glass. He almost jumped up from his seat in disbelief.

"Are you sure, that was not some fancy illusion, a magic trick?" He was still trying to hold on to his sense of logic.

"I would've felt the same way, Mike. But believe me, it's all true. And we had a wicked witch on our tail that we managed to shake off," I ended the narration.

"I want to get back to work now and back to normal life. But I may need to take a few days off, if I get any clues on her parents' current whereabouts. If you come home sometime, I'll show you my souvenirs from the enchanted forest." I was hoping that I had gotten through to him convincingly.

He stayed quiet assimilating all the information, and then said, "Okay Sid, I believe you. I still can't get my head around it, but I know you're not lying. I won't be able to give you time off immediately. We need to get some projects complete before I can give you a few days."

"Thanks so much, for having my back." I was truly grateful to have him as my senior. "You know how important this job is to me. This industry is an extension of my personality. I would hate to lose it. I'll come in regularly from tomorrow."

We left feeling satisfied. I could see that Narissa was getting as involved in my life as I was in hers. It felt fulfilling and I was grateful for her presence. We headed to the subway station to return home.

I guided her through the crowd, shopping bags in our hands. The day's mission was complete. Once we got home, we could start thinking about tracking her parents. We got onto the train and waited for our destination.

Twenty minutes later, we alighted at our station and headed towards the exit. Without warning, Narissa stood rooted to the spot.

"What's the matter, why aren't you…"

I followed her gaze and froze. Selene was entering the station and headed towards the trains. But she didn't seem to notice us.

She was wearing a long green dress, not her usual black robe. It changed her persona from the archetypical witch to a more regular senior citizen. Her features bore the same mean, beady-eyed looks though.

How come she didn't notice us?

Chapter 45
Narissa's Roots

She walked right past us. I found it impossible to believe that she didn't see us.

Was she pretending? But why?

I grabbed Narissa's hand and pulled her to follow. We were almost running to keep Selene in sight among the crowd but with a safe distance. As soon as we saw her board an incoming train, we too entered the same car from the next gate. I didn't want to lose sight of her at any cost. I was grateful for the people's traffic to keep us hidden from her view.

We alighted at the Bergen Street Station in about ten minutes and followed her all the way as she walked towards some old brick row houses and rang the doorbell to one in particular. The door was answered by an elderly man with a long white beard.

We waited for about half an hour, but Selene did not leave the house. Eventually, we decided to continue our surveillance another time. We returned home exhausted from the day's events.

After resting for a while, it was time to get a little organized at home. I went to the neighborhood grocery store to pick up some food and other supplies. I explained to Narissa where everything was stocked, so she wouldn't have trouble being on her own when I went to work.

I asked her to join me in preparing dinner, so she could learn to cook something for herself when I wasn't around.

"Did you ever cook when you lived with your parents?" I asked.

"I did make some basic food," she replied. "But I can't seem to remember much now."

"I'm sure it'll come back to you once you start doing it again," I encouraged. "For starters, you can do sandwiches. You just have to assemble the ingredients.

And I'm going to make some pasta for us now. I'll show you how that's done. Tomorrow we'll make breakfast together as well."

Once dinner was ready and we had satiated our appetite, I tried to teach her how to search for her hometown on the internet. After spending a futile hour on it, we sat down to relax and watch some TV. But she seemed a little preoccupied.

I tried to decipher from her expressions what was upsetting her, and finally asked, "Are you upset because you couldn't find your home on the map?"

She nodded.

"Don't worry, you'll work it out soon enough. It's a tedious process; it'll take time." I paused for a while, and spoke again, "I hope you're not regretting coming back with me."

"Oh no, not at all! It's just that I had my hopes up too soon, I guess. Being with you has only been a boon for me." She gave me a look that almost stopped my heartbeat.

"And I was also thinking about Selene. For someone, who has single-mindedly targeted us, she seemed too oblivious to the fact that we were following her."

I agreed, "Yes, I had the same doubts. I don't understand. But we'll find out soon enough. We'll go back to that house in a couple of days. Right now, there are other things to sort out. You need to be more at ease with your life here."

Our day ended on a pleasant note. We laughed watching the comedy shows, exchanged some casual conversation and I felt lighter than I ever felt before.

The next day was a routine that is followed by most people. But I hadn't ever realized how much that routine would be desirable one day. I actually enjoyed the banal practice of preparing breakfast, going to work, and coming back home to staid activities. Especially since I was returning home to see the girl that made my heart flutter.

Work was exciting, as Mike and I brainstormed on ideas for the next project. He was always happy with my inputs, but he seemed to be more impressed now. He opined that my adventurous experience had given me new wings.

When I got back home, it was pleasant surprise. Just one day on her own, and Narissa was already exuding more confidence. She had some soft instrumental music playing in the living room. I could smell the aroma of something cooking.

She brought me coffee as if on cue and joined me with a glass of juice for herself. Her smile was wide and open as she enquired about my day. I asked her about her day, and she said, "Productive!"

"What did you do?" I prodded.

"Well, dinner is ready." She laughed. "I know how to use the map now and have found my hometown too! And…I've learned how to look up a recipe to cook. Mrs. Stewart helped me."

I hugged her in appreciation. "That's amazing! I'm so proud of you. Thank you for the coffee, and also the dinner, in advance." I laughed back.

After freshening up, I checked out her search for her hometown. She had zeroed in on Ely, a city in Saint Louis County, Minnesota. It was located on the Vermilion Range.

She said their home was a small cabin near the Miner's Lake and was surrounded by wilderness. Her grandfather had been a miner and so was her father. But after the mines closed down, he took to drinking.

Narissa spoke about her parents, "My father felt mining defined him. The very typical manly job gave him a kick. Losing it meant losing his identity. He became an alcoholic and my mother started working to keep the home fires burning."

"What did your mom do?" I asked.

"An International Wolf Center had been newly opened by a wolf biologist. Mom, being the wildlife enthusiast that she was, joined as an intern and later got a proper job there, caring for the wolves. It hurt Dad's ego, that she was providing, and their relationship began to crumble."

"Were you studying or working at that time?" I wanted to know all about her.

"I did complete my school and joined college too. I had a deal with the wilderness camp, where I joined the environmental education programs without charge, in exchange for helping the staff set up the programs. I was an ace swimmer even then."

"You were a born mermaid!" I exclaimed, and we laughed.

"Come on." She got me up and directed me to the dining table. "Time to eat some rice and fish. I hope you like it."

Chapter 46
Return to Ely

Dinner was actually quite nice, but more than the food I enjoyed her company. We exchanged easy conversation with our childhood anecdotes. I couldn't stop smiling.

I could easily get used to this.

I asked her, when we sat down to relax after dinner, if she would be comfortable going to Ely by herself to find out about her parents. I assumed she may want some space to herself since she was going to be returning after a very long time.

"I'd be fine Sid, but I want you to be there with me. I want to share my experiences with you, whatever they maybe. If I find my parents, I want to share that happy moment. And if I get disappointed, I want you right beside me."

Her statement took me by surprise but made me extremely happy as well. I was elated that I meant so much to her. Her down-to-earth, unassuming, and candid expression of emotion touched my heart.

"I need to give a little time to the office and then we'll take out a few days to find your parents. I'll inform Mike, so we can speed up on the work," I reassured her. "In the meantime, check online if you can get any telephone numbers where you might get some information about them. We can make some calls from here."

"Yes, good idea! I think we should be able to connect with the Wolf Center," she said optimistically. She became quiet for some time with a lost look in her eyes, as though her mind was racing through flashback sequences.

After a little silence, she continued her story, "You know, I was nineteen and was one of the wilderness campers participating in a survival trip, in the summer program. There I chanced upon a small group of people in the woods.

"I thought it was part of the program, which teaches you to take any help you can get in order to survive the wild. But I got to know later that it was a Wiccan group that met occasionally in the isolated woods.

"I was introduced to the possibilities of changing circumstances around you, and also mindsets, with the practices. And my naïve mind was drawn to that chance of improving the relationship between my parents."

"Did it work? I mean did your parents get along after that?" I was curious.

Narissa elaborated, "Initially I did see some positive changes. But it didn't last long. Dad went back to his drinking habits and verbal abuse. Then, I wanted to try something stronger and that's when I accidentally opened up the portal and reached the Magus Forest.

"I was new to it. One of the ladies in the group was from Ely and she was teaching me some of the magic and spells. She used to consult a higher, more powerful medium to teach me. I never met that person though."

There was something else that I was curious about and had wanted to ask her. "How come you still look like a teenager, is that because of the wiccan magic?"

She laughed out, before explaining, "No, I wasn't interested in using the magic for those reasons. Mermaids do not age in appearance – that's the secret. Now that I'm human, I will most likely start to age more naturally."

"At least, your parents will have no trouble recognizing you." I winked, and she giggled once more.

"I miss Archon, he is so caring; like a parent," she suddenly remembered.

I nodded and sighed. "I do too." And we called it a night.

The following week was strictly routine. I managed to get a few days off from Mike after I put in extra hours to complete the project. Narissa was now more comfortable living the regular human life in an urban environment.

We met my parents one more time before we fixed our plans for Ely. This time I told them that I'd be travelling for a few days. My father was improving every day and my mother was more the person I preferred to remember from my early childhood. She smiled a lot more now.

I wondered if the lake water had worked for the Toon boys as well as it did for my dad. I'm sure it had.

I discussed travel arrangements with Narissa, and she reminded me that we didn't need to consider the time required to reach Ely, with her around. Her teleporting powers through lakes would help.

She had also called the Wolf Center to enquire about her mother and was told that she still worked there. Narissa was elated and terribly excited but refrained from connecting over the phone. She wanted to meet her in person for the first time, after so many years.

It had been about twenty years. The moment would be special. And she wanted to capture it in her mind forever. The surprise on her mom's face, the tears of love and happiness, the feel of a much-longed-for hug…

It had to be seen and experienced in the flesh.

The day arrived and we packed our backpacks for a few days. Narissa had been on pins and needles ever since she got to know that her mom is still living in Ely. But that day, her emotions could hardly be contained. She laughed and cried at the same time at the slightest stimulation.

We headed to the Prospect Lake and found a quiet isolated spot. Narissa activated the cyclonic whirl, and, within moments, we found ourselves on the banks of the Miner's Lake. Her excitement knew no bounds as she took deep breaths of the air in the place, she had once called home.

Her eyes scanned the beauty of the landscape as she tried to recollect her memories. After several moments of contemplation, she looked at me with hope in her eyes. She interlocked her arms in mine and pulled me move forward.

"Come, I want to show you my home," she said. We walked through a small, wooded area that led to a cleared patch of land. A small wooden cabin stood there, alongside a larger home.

"That small cabin, that's where I grew up," she pointed out. "The larger one wasn't there then."

As we reached the cabin, a woman came out from the larger home. "This is private property. You can't come here."

"Oh! Sorry!" Narissa stopped. "I used to live in this small one. I didn't know it belongs to someone else."

The woman was now scrutinizing Narissa closely. "Are you Nora's little girl?"

Chapter 47
Narissa's Reunion

Narissa's eyes shone as she asked, "You know my mom?"

The lady's face softened, and she intuitively came forward and embraced Narissa. "I'm Laura Miller. Yes, we've been friends from the time your mom started work at the Wolf Center.

"After you disappeared, your father blamed your mother 'coz you went missing. He accused her of being careless. And the fights became a little violent. Eventually they got divorced. He threw her out of the house and, luckily, she was provided staff quarters in the Wolf Center premises."

"Does she still live on the Center's grounds?" Narissa asked impatiently.

"Oh no! She has a house now. Your father was so steeped in alcohol all the time, he became extremely ill and died soon after. After his death, we got to know that the house actually belonged to your mother. She didn't have the heart to contest him on occupancy, because she knew he would be on the streets."

The news brought tears to Narissa's eyes. Her father wasn't a bad guy, just lost, in his life. She had spent some good years with him. He was a doting dad and had been a caring husband at one time…until alcohol started to fill up the emptiness that he felt from losing his mining job.

"I want to meet my mom," she beseeched Mrs. Miller. "And why didn't she continue to live here after Dad?"

Mrs. Miller now invited us into her home, the larger cabin. She offered us some juice and continued to tell Narissa about her mother, "Your mom didn't want to live here anymore. She couldn't face the hurtful memories all alone. You had gone missing, and she was devastated by it."

She added with questions in her eyes, "She sold the house to me and bought a new one closer to work. My husband and I built this bigger home as our family grew but we wanted to keep the original cabin for our guests. Now tell me, what happened to you, where did you go?"

Narissa didn't want to or know how to explain the events that led to her disappearance and simply said that she'd been kidnapped. "I was trapped in a faraway place for many years. Recently, I managed to escape and here I am. This is a very dear friend of mine, Sid, who helped me."

Mrs. Miller nodded at me in acknowledgment and exclaimed, "Your mother will be ecstatic to see you again. And you look beautiful. You haven't aged at all!"

We laughed lightly, and Mrs. Miller allowed us to look around the old home – the little cabin. Narissa walked around the familiar space, touching the walls and feeling the vibes that took her down memory lane.

She shared little anecdotes attached to every corner. I could almost see her fill up her soul with lost emotions. Emotions that stayed locked up for years, as she battled a solitary existence, as her strength formed the walls of a fortress around her heart.

When she felt satiated, we went back to Mrs. Miller. "Thank you for being so welcoming. I want to go and see my mother now; would you give me her address?"

The warm friend extended her support by offering to take us to her mother's new abode. "I want to see Nora's happy face. God knows she deserves every bit of it. Your mother is such a loving woman."

She drove us to a residential area with a row of cabins. We stopped at a pretty little one with a small well-kept garden in front. It wasn't very large but did not look sparse like the old home. We rang the doorbell and waited in excitement.

The door was opened by a cheerful looking elderly man dressed comfortably in khaki pants and plaid shirt. He greeted Mrs. Miller.

"Laura, how are you this morning? How can I help you?" He turned inwards and called out, "Nora, Laura is here."

"I've come to give Nora a pleasant surprise." Mrs. Miller smiled with a cryptic note in her voice.

"Can I stay for the party?" He laughed good-naturedly. "Come on, in."

"Sure, you can Paul." She laughed back. "Please meet Narissa and Sid – the surprise."

Just then, Nora joined the group. "Laura, nice to see you. How…"

She saw Narissa standing in the doorway and her face changed a thousand expressions. She stayed rooted to the spot in shock. Narissa gathered courage and walked forward. "Hi Mom!"

A stream of tears flowed from her mother's eyes, and Narissa squeezed her mother in a tight embrace, with every ounce of emotion she had gathered that day. Nora held her tight and broke into uncontrolled sobs.

The two ladies stood there crying and holding on to each other for a while, until Paul interrupted, "Everyone please sit down."

We were led into the living room. The house was modest but comfortable and neat. It exuded a sense of well-being and happiness. Narissa sat next to her mother.

Laura broke the uncomfortable silence by introducing us. "Paul, this is Narissa, Nora's daughter. And Sid is her friend. And this is Paul, Nora's husband."

It was his turn to be surprised.

"Oh my God! That's amazing. I knew about you" – he looked at Narissa – "but it's been so long, I never imagined I would ever meet you. We've been married sixteen years now and she often spoke about you."

"She was kidnapped and held captive for a long time, and Sid helped her escape recently," Laura explained, sparing the overwrought mother-daughter the need to go into details.

His eyes widened. "Have you gone to the police?"

Finally, Narissa gathered herself and spoke, "No I don't want to report anything. I just want to go on with my life. They can't reach me now," she tried to put off the topic. "I wanted to meet Mom and let her know I'm fine."

Her mother was an elegant lady dressed in simple trousers and woolen top, with grey-black hair tied up neatly. Narissa resembled her mom, which told me that her mom must have been just as beautiful in her youth. She was still beautiful, aged with grace, as they say.

"I missed you so much my darling," Nora spoke tearfully. "You have no idea. But I'm so grateful to God for his beautiful morning. Thank you, Sid for bringing my little girl back to me."

"This calls for a celebration!" Paul got up with a flourish.

Chapter 48
Celebrations and Revelations

The day was a happy mix of tears and smiles, memories of the past and gratitude for reuniting. Narissa met her half siblings as well. There were two of them; both were married – Adam and Amanda. Both of them were called by Paul to meet Narissa. They seemed nice too and met her with warmth. Of course, it would take a while for them to feel like family.

Nevertheless, the gathering was pleasant and emanated positive emotions. They planned a picnic in the woods for the next day. I was keen to try out canoeing, which Ely was best known for now. And we fit that into our list of activities.

We were not allowed to stay in a hotel. Nora insisted we stay at the house. It was a two-bedroom cabin and one bedroom remained unoccupied as Paul's children were both grown up and married.

There was a bunk bed near the window, and they had some extra mattresses, in case either sibling visited with their spouse and kids. It was clear that there were heartfelt attachments between all the family members.

Both Paul and Nora made every effort to make our stay comfortable and memorable. It was heartening to see the wonderful couple share such a good relationship, especially after knowing the hard time Nora faced with John, Narissa's dad.

The picnic was interesting for me. I had never gone out picnicking in the wilderness. Conversation flowed easily and it was great to see Narissa re-bonding with her mother. Her mother had packed some delicious food.

Adam and Amanda returned to their homes after the fun picnic, and we insisted that Paul and Nora go back and rest too. Narissa and I had decided to explore the wilderness, after we were done canoeing.

We gathered our prepared backpacks and headed to the canoe outfitters. Having been provided with all the necessary gear and information, we started out. I was very excited, as I had always wanted some adventure in my life but did not have the right company to explore it. Narissa looked like she fit right in, and she kept my nerves under control too.

"Relax," she said, "You'll love it."

We paddled towards the direction recommended by the outfitters, and once we were farther into the lake, the peace and serenity of the environment started to seep into my being. The views were breathtaking. The landscape looked like a beautiful painting in motion – changing from distant hills to a vast expanse of forests to the calm stillness of the glassy lake.

For someone like me, who spent all of his life in the concrete jungle of an urban city, seeing nature in all its glory was like manna to my soul.

My first taste of living with nature was the enchanted forest. And it was memorable. But the experience was full of trials and tribulations, and it didn't quite satisfy my spiritual quest.

It was only after spending some beautiful moments at Arcane Lake with Narissa, that I drank in the artistry of God's creation. Now, here, again I felt that tranquility that seems to transform me into a more content person.

And I also realized that paddling was great exercise.

"I'm definitely going to have bigger biceps by the end of the day," I said, flexing my muscles at Narissa.

"Maybe you need to do this more often," she joked and continued to paddle.

"Look!" She pointed towards the forest. "There's a bear."

A bear was drinking water from the lake. Soon it was joined by a little cub as well. It felt like going on a Safari. I quickly captured the moment on my mobile phone and took pictures of the wondrous view around me as well.

I wanted to share these sights with my mom. I had also captured the family moments at the picnic for Narissa. Once we returned, it would help her relive the joy.

We decided to dock the canoe near the forest and explore on foot for a while. The outfitters had outlined the spots where we could do so. Narissa expertly rowed toward the sandy shore, pulled up the canoe and secured it.

She's the yin to my yang.

I looked at her impressed and possibly wearing an unabashed 'fan' look. We walked into the forest and she chalk-marked trees as we moved along, so we could return. Our conversation was educational for me, as she explained all that she had learnt from her childhood encounters.

We looked out for the different species of flora and fauna as we walked. We saw a deer and a nesting bald eagle. We also heard a pack of wolves howling from a distance. I didn't have the heart to get any closer to them.

It was almost sunset time, when we chanced upon a small group of people sitting around in a circle. Narissa motioned for me to stop and keep silent. They seemed to be engrossed in some kind of bonfire activity.

Narissa whispered, "This is similar to the group I saw as a kid, the wiccans."

We remained quiet and hidden, when one of them got up and stood in the center, addressing the rest of the group. The person in the center wore a long black coat and had their back to us. The others were in dark clothes as well.

"We need more recruits," a woman's voice stated. The one in the center was a lady.

"We have to increase our numbers to have more power. Bring in more youngsters from your vicinity. The inherent energy of young people can have a higher reach. I will continue to guide you on how to initiate them and harness their intrinsic potential."

Narissa whispered again, "I think it's a similar group. Looks like they're looking for more kids to induct into their clan. The same way that I got lured."

"It's better we turn around and go back then. It's going to be dark soon. And we may not be able to deal with it, if we get caught in the middle of something unpleasant," I whispered back.

"You're right," Narissa agreed. We were about to make a move, when the main lady in the center turned around.

My jaw dropped and I forgot to breathe. It was our arch nemesis again – Selene Kouris! But her voice was different. Not the grating, evil cackle that we knew. Do doppelgangers actually exist?

Chapter 49
The Wiccans

I quickly clicked a picture on my phone to confirm later that I wasn't mistaken. Narissa and I exchanged flabbergasted looks and decided to shadow her.

We hung around hoping the group would disperse soon, and we could follow Selene. Thankfully, their meeting didn't last too long. In about ten minutes, they were ready to leave.

Selene (or was it her lookalike?) was exchanging words with each member before they left. When there were only two members remaining, we got another jolt! She was talking to Amanda, Narissa's half-sister.

Amanda did not leave. She waited till Selene finished talking with the last man waiting. All three of them left together. We followed them surreptitiously, till they reached a clearing with a narrow path. There was a small car parked, in which all of them drove away.

We turned back to where they had congregated, so we could return to our canoe.

"Amanda is into all of this as well?" Narissa said, looking worried. "I should try and talk her out of it. All it helps to do is mess up lives."

"I'm wondering about Selene," I voiced my doubts. "Or if that is Selene. I know she looks like her. But she sounded different. Do you remember, she didn't notice us at the subway station? She looks like an identical twin but a little younger. Doppelganger."

"What are the chances," Narissa spoke slowly and thoughtfully, "that another person who looks exactly like us, is into the same activities? Doesn't seem likely." She looked at me theorizing. "And knowing Selene and her powers…this lady could be a clone, an unscientific one."

My mind was reeling.

This woman is not a real human?

"Do you mean using a spell to create a clone of herself?" I asked for confirmation.

"Yes, that's exactly what I mean." She seemed surer of her deductions now.

I continued to try and make some sense of it, "But I have her grimoire. Her spell would have become ineffective if that were the case."

"Hmm…" she paused to think. "Maybe she got someone else to do it for her then."

That did seem plausible. Although we couldn't put much sense to why she may have wanted to do it. We just assumed that she was trying to create a wider network for herself in her quest to take over the universe.

So, does she control the mind of her clone? My guess is, she does.

It was dark by now, and we used our flashlights to find Narissa's markings to take us back to our canoe. Inside the woods, we were enveloped in black. But once we reached the shore of the lake, where we had docked our canoe, it was a little brighter. The moon and starlit sky and their reflections created a beautiful ambience.

It was easier to wield our way out with the reflections. Silently we were paddling back the same route we came, when the atmosphere brightened unexpectedly. We looked up at the sky and saw a dazzling river of green, purple, and red forming, flickering, and pulsating through the expanse.

The Aurora lights!

I couldn't believe my luck. I was really witnessing the northern lights! The magical phenomenon of psychedelic colors in the sky was something that had to be seen to be believed. Nothing I had read about it prepared me for the glorious sight.

Click! Click! Click!

I couldn't stop taking pictures. This kind of magic I welcomed wholeheartedly. I was ready to be hypnotized by it.

We sat there in our canoe in the middle of the lake, taking in the beauty that unfurled in the sky and drenched us in its myriad shades. We watched wonderstruck for several minutes. Narissa came closer and put her hand over mine. She was looking up at the sky and then straight into my eyes.

"I love you, Sid!"

The magnetizing aurora spread its electricity around us…into us…igniting in my heart sparks of color I had never known before. I was awash with a wave of emotion that threatened to unsettle me. And yet I felt calmer than I ever felt before.

The magic of the sky and the earth around me had just permeated into my life. I wanted to hold this moment still forever!

I leaned forward to kiss my Narissa. We submitted ourselves to the beauty of the universe as it engulfed us and enriched us. It was the most beautiful night of my life.

When we finally reached Nora and Paul's home, they looked worried because we were late. I told them we stopped at the lake to enjoy the Aurora lights. That put them at ease.

Paul explained his worry, "I lost my late wife, Audrey – Adam and Amanda's mother, to a wolf attack there, in the forest."

"A wolf-attack?" I implored him to continue.

"She used to have a regular meet up with a group of friends there. She was late returning one evening. I got help from the Forest Services' offices and went in search of her. We finally found her mangled by a beast." His speech was laced with emotion as he recapped the hurtful memory.

"I'm sorry." I patted his hand with concern. "That must've been hard. I understand why you worry. We'll try not to be late again. I truly appreciate your concern."

Next morning, Narissa decided to visit Amanda. I thought it prudent not to accompany her. My presence could be perceived as intrusive.

I stayed back and helped Paul in the garden and Nora in the kitchen. They looked happy that I made an effort to spend time with them and help. We were bonding.

By lunch time, Narissa was back. From her expressions, I reckoned that there was some new development. Or something new that she learnt about this whole quagmire. I had to summon a heavy dose of patience to go through the motions of eating, appreciating Nora's cooking and making pleasant conversation at the table.

After we helped clear the dishes, we retired to our room to relax. I quickly shut the door, and prodded Narissa to relate the details of her meeting with Amanda.

Narissa too had been trying hard to keep a straight face all through the lunch. Now in our privacy, with a wide-eyed look, she informed, "Audrey, Amanda's mother, was the same lady who was teaching me wiccan practices!"

Chapter 50
Audrey's Death

"How did you get to know about her mom?" I asked.

"I saw her picture on the mantelpiece and recognized her instantly. When I enquired, Amanda told me it was her mother." Narissa was bubbling with information.

"It was a cue, that I don't need to tread on eggshells to talk to her about the issue. I brought out my concerns very directly after that. I also told her Wicca didn't have positive effects and completely disoriented my life. I didn't tell her about the enchanted forest though."

"Continue…" I urged her to go on.

"She told me she's not into Wicca because she believes in it. She doesn't, not anymore. She's only trying to get to the truth of her mother's death. Do you know, the man who was with them in the forest is her husband?

My eyebrows jumped up in surprise.

"Last three-four years she's had doubts about how her mother died. When she had gone for one of these meetings, she overheard something. That's when she asked her husband to join as well. Her father knows nothing about it."

"What about Selene?" I asked. "Did she give any information on her?"

"Well, yes, she did. The truth gets more and more curious by the day," she spoke with a startled look.

"Selene Kouris was the High Priestess, so to speak, in the days I was being groomed. Do you remember, I told you my 'coach', which was Audrey, was getting instructions from a higher power?"

I nodded a yes.

"Amanda had seen her mother with Selene as a teenager. A few years later, after her mother's death, this younger version of Selene, took over. Her name is Sybil Kouris, and she is her sister."

"Her sister?" It was my turn to be wide-eyed. "Then our clone theory does not hold. But no one in the enchanted forest ever mentioned her sister. I think there's more to it. Why did Amanda develop suspicions about her mother's death?"

Narissa continued, "Audrey was a wolf care specialist at the Wolf Center. She knew how to deal with wolves. It was unlikely that she would put herself in a position to get mauled by them. She had gone for a wiccan meet in the forest that day. Something might have happened."

Hmm…There's definitely something amiss.

"Amanda was approached to join after Audrey's death, and she went along, because she wanted to be a part of her mother's activities. At that point, she had no suspicions. Slowly she got genuinely involved in the wiccan practices. Until a few years ago when she overheard Sybil's phone conversation with a sorcerer."

My eyebrows danced in surprise again.

A sorcerer? What else are we going to find out?

"They talked of Audrey's death and mumbled something about Amanda finding out the truth. That's when her niggling logic that Audrey couldn't have been mauled, took the shape of suspicion."

The scenario was beginning to look like a conspiracy now. Was it a coincidence or a well thought out plan that Narissa ended up in the enchanted forest?

"That means Amanda too knows a thing or two about spells and magic," I concluded.

"Yes, she does," Narissa concurred. "But she hasn't used it for nefarious purposes. Mostly she was asked to train newbies, like her mom, after she picked up simple magic. She says she has consciously avoided the dark use of this knowledge."

"I guess she continues to be a part of it only to get to the truth of her mother's death," I concluded.

"Yes, that is what she told me. There is another meeting set up for tomorrow, and this time the sorcerer is paying them a visit. This has to do with their latest instructions of getting more young people to join the group."

"Hmm…" I was thinking about a possible course of action. "Should we join? Neither Sybil nor that sorcerer know anything about us. We could find out a few things too being on the inside."

Narissa agreed but reminded me that it was risky. I pointed out that we were four now, with Amanda and her husband on our side. We could look out for each other. I called Amanda and spoke to both husband and wife about our intentions.

They were all gung-ho!

The evening was spent giving quality time to Narissa and her mother's togetherness. And we informed them that we were going out with Amanda and husband for lunch the following day. Both Paul and Nora were happy to see the children get on well together.

The next day Amanda and her husband, Jacob came over to pick us up. We all had breakfast together, before leaving for our forest tryst with the pishogue practitioners.

Ideally, I would have put all this magic business behind me for good, but it seemed to have inter-twined itself in Narissa's life in more ways than one. And I couldn't leave her, and her family, tangled in the mess.

And it would also help my adoptive family in the enchanted forest, if we could see the end of this devilry. All of them were a very important part of my life now.

With great trepidation, we met the other wiccans at the coven. There were five other youngsters who had accompanied them for the initiation. We waited quietly till Sybil arrived with the sorcerer.

It was the same elderly man we had seen Sybil visit, when we followed her to his (or was it hers) home in Brooklyn, near the Bergen Street station. Maybe they are all related, this man and the witchy sisters.

Sybil greeted, "Good afternoon, fellow wiccans! Please welcome our High Priest, Oscar Blaise."

A mature, tall, fair man with a long white beard, he was thin and had sharp penetrating eyes, and a broad nose on a thin, long face. He raised his hand in acknowledgement. "Please come forward, all initiates, and relate your purpose to join our community."

One by one, all of us went forward, bowed to Oscar, and spoke of our reasons for joining. Narissa and I had earlier decided on our corroborated stories. Each one was assigned their coach, which was the person who brought them.

Sybil and Oscar both gave a little talk on what was expected of us and how our dedication would decide the time of our formal initiation. They addressed the wiccans on how to groom their rookies.

After the general address, they told us, the newbies to leave. They spoke one by one to each wiccan again before they were allowed to disperse. We went and sat in the car.

We could see the gathering and waited for Amanda and Jacob. Moments later, our hearts started to race as we saw the dreaded Selene join the group.

We quickly ducked to avoid being seen and prayed that Selene wouldn't want to meet the new people.

Chapter 51
What's Going On?

We heard footsteps approaching and we held our breath. We had hidden at the back behind the seats of the car. The lock flipped open, and we heard Amanda's voice, "Sid, Narissa, are you there?"

We slowly peeked out and, both Jacob and she sat in the front seats.

"Why were you hiding?" Jacob asked.

"We saw Selene," Narissa replied. "She's the one who had kidnapped me."

"Oh my God! Really?" Amanda was surprised. "Then I'm not wrong in doubting these people."

"You're definitely on the right track," I concurred. "She's dangerous. By the way, why was she here?"

"Oh, she was just saying the same thing they told us – to train the rookies well. And to follow their dictates to the 'T'. She said it's important that we grow our tribe and assert our significance," Amanda repeated verbatim.

"Other than that, I think they wanted to have their private discussions and we were excused."

Just as Jacob powered the ignition, I thought aloud, "I wish we could eavesdrop on them."

Jacob warned, "That would be extremely risky. Besides, if they see our car still parked out here, they're definitely going to get suspicious." He went into reverse gear to take the car out.

"How about we park the car somewhere else and come back on foot?" I adjured subtly.

"They may be gone by then. Besides how can four of us hide without being found out. There are no big walls around here or bushes. We can't all fit behind a tree or two."

I considered the consequences as he started to drive back to the house and gave in to his good sense. I was so keen to wrap up Selene's shenanigans, I was getting impatient.

"You're right. We know where the sorcerer lives anyway. He's from Brooklyn. We once followed Sybil assuming her to be Selene, all the way to his house. We can try to get something from there. Are you willing to join us?"

"Definitely!" Amanda piped up. "It's taken us so many years to try and get something on them. Thanks to you, we have a chance at finding out."

"Great! We're leaving tomorrow. You guys make your arrangements and come as soon as possible," I finalized the plan.

I gave them my address and invited them to stay at my place. It would be much simpler to do our sleuthing that way. It would also give a chance for the sisters to bond.

The following day we got ready to leave and Nora was in tears. "Why can't you live with me?" she beseeched her daughter.

Narissa was emotional too. Holding her in a loving embrace, she quietened her and reassured her. "Now that I've returned, I'll keep visiting, Mom. You're not going to lose me again." A single tear streaked her rosy cheeks.

God, she's truly strong!

She never failed to impress me with her handling of tough situations. Paul insisted that we come for every holiday, and I told him we'll try to visit as much as possible. With warm goodbyes, we left for the lake and returned to Brooklyn.

Back home, I went to meet my own mom. I shared with her the pictures of the beautiful place I had just visited and the mesmerizing Aurora lights. She was ecstatic. She was secretly worried that I may disappear again. But meeting me allayed her fears.

Dad was in good spirits and had gotten better even in the couple of days that we were gone. He was recovering at a good pace now.

Mike, at work, was also relieved to see me. It seemed like everyone was doubting my return. I related to him the events involving Selene. He found the coincidence disconcerting. He felt that Selene was up to some major rascality, and I agreed.

He offered his help in any way possible. I was grateful for his support and told him I'd let him know if I needed anything.

When I returned home that day, I had a pleasant surprise waiting for me. Queen Titania was sitting in the living room talking to Narissa. I couldn't be happier. Her visit was like a gift. I animatedly expressed my joy and enquired about Archon.

"Emperor Archon is making us all proud." She beamed. "He misses all of you. I met the Toon boys as well, you know, and they are doing very well too. They remember you a lot."

My smile widened till it touched my eyes. I felt a warm glow in my heart as I reminisced our days in the Magus Forest.

"How did you know where to find us," I asked curiously.

The queen mischievously brandished her grand royal staff and said, "This is my tracking device."

"What? How?" I was confused.

She clarified, "When I bless you with my staff, it absorbs your aura and helps me find you whenever I want and teleport me to your location."

"I'm so glad you decided to visit us," Narissa expressed happily. "Now I have the opportunity to make you some dinner." She got up to go into the kitchen and prepare a meal.

"Oh, I would love that!" the queen motivated her.

Meanwhile, I updated her with our experiences with Selene in the Toon world and at Ely.

She furrowed her brows thoughtfully, before adding, "Actually, she's been seen a few times in the forest as well. She wasn't able to do any damage like the last time, because we have good security in place now.

"But she did try to abduct Aurora when she was in the woods. Luckily, some of Aurora's CSK group ladies were around and heard her cries for help. They managed to thwart Selene's attempts."

Dinner was ready, and the queen relished and commended Narissa's chicken and rice like it was a gourmet meal. It was delicious no doubt, but a humble meal by royal standards. That's what is so special about Queen Titania – her caring heart.

At the dinner table, I brought her up to speed with our upcoming plans to find out more about Sybil and Oscar. She insisted on joining us. I informed her we had help from Amanda and Jacob. But she refused to be left out.

"In fact," she suggested, "I think I'll bring the Toon boys here as well."

My eyes lit up with the thought of meeting them once again.

Chapter 52
The Recce

This was beginning to sound like a party! There was one logistical issue though – where would everyone stay? I spoke my thoughts and Narissa suggested renting a house. Queen Titania agreed readily.

Really? Would a queen stay in a small house with so many people?

I was unsure that she would be comfortable. "Are you sure, Your Majesty? You may not feel comfortable with the constraints of the space."

"My dear boy, you have no idea what I've seen in my lifetime. I'm sure I can deal with it." She was very confident.

I have a lot to learn from life.

I thought about Mike and his offer to help, and immediately called him. I asked him about renting a house to accommodate about ten people. He was very forthcoming with a generous proposal. Without a moment's hesitation, he said he had a weekend home near the Prospect Lake, which we could use.

I was floored with his generosity. He was like my older brother, always looking out for me. I realized how fortunate I was with the people in my life.

I gave the good news to the queen and Narissa. "Do you think we should stay in that house too while everyone is here?"

Queen Titania got excited. "Oh yes please! The more, the merrier. And I think it will save all of us a lot of trouble if we can be together while dealing with this. One thing bothers me though…no one in the enchanted forest knows anything about Selene having a sister."

"I had thought about the same thing. I feel there's more than meets the eye." Meanwhile, I had already started thinking of what may be necessary to put this together. "Tomorrow I will look into arranging for food to be delivered when we're there."

I spruced up my room for the queen to rest for the night and got comfortable on the couch. I figured it may be a week before Amanda and Jacob join us. I would have to let the queen know when to bring the Toon boys.

The next morning was bright and chirpy with Her Majesty regaling us with anecdotes of her youth. Queen Titania had an easy charm, apart from her beautiful heart. She was a wonderful conversationalist.

We agreed on when to meet again and she left us just as suddenly as she had arrived. I told Narissa we could, during the week, nose around the sorcerer, Oscar's house and see what we could find out, before everyone got together.

I went to work and discussed a project with Mike that would have elements of my adventure. He thought it was a brilliant idea. And I was given the permission to pursue our snooping as part of the job!

I left early for home, and both Narissa and I, reached the same Bergen Street home. We hung around outside for a little while to be sure we wouldn't bump into any one of them.

After a few minutes, I covertly peeked into the window. All seemed quiet. I tried to pry the window open, but it was locked. I gestured to Narissa to come and then tried to open the door. Again, without luck.

I told her I'd try to go around the back and see if I can find an open window, or open back door. Narissa started to check out the crevices around the entrance and picked up the mat. Voila! The key was under the mat!

"How did you know?" I whispered curiously.

"I didn't. I was just looking," she whispered back. "When I was young, my mom would leave the keys hidden under the mat before leaving for work. She did this so I could enter after returning from school. Dad was hardly ever around to let me in, even though he wasn't working."

I nodded with empathy, and we quietly entered the house. We stood in a tastefully done up living room. Nothing about it spoke of their witchery.

Carefully, we looked around. There was a dining room, kitchen, washroom and small storeroom. Nothing of significance. After ensuring that there was no sound, we climbed the staircase to the check the rooms upstairs.

We had come at the right time. There was no one at home. I checked the time; it may help if we want to do this again. There were three bedrooms. All three were open. There was one more room which was shut.

My instinct told me that's the room we need to see. But it was locked. We took a quick peek at the bedrooms.

One had a couple of wall hangings of occult nature. Another didn't have anything unusual. The third had candles placed in various corners, a witchy gothic tapestry, an optical illusion artwork, and a metal pentagram on the nightstand.

I checked the closet of the third room and there were women's clothes. Rummaging through the drawers, I found a small grimoire. Judging by the clothes, this was definitely Sybil's room.

The second room had black robes in the closet, so it looked like a temporary stay for Selene. I assumed temporary because she seemed to be jumping realms and didn't add a personal touch to the room.

The first room with some robes and men's clothing was obviously Oscar's. In the closet, there was also a large, decorative wooden staff with a quartz head shaped like a flame. In his bedside drawer, I found a key. I was hoping it was the key to the locked room.

Quickly, we inserted it into the keyhole of the mystery room and turned. It unlocked!

How lucky are we!

In front of us was a room that reeked of demonic practices. It wasn't much different from the darkness prevalent in the inner sanctum of the Black Temple when I first saw it.

The pentagram was etched out on the floor and skulls were placed at strategic points. A red glow emanated from lamps in the corners, heightening the eeriness.

Ensconced on a low table in the corner was a large grimoire. It was a thick book with a black leather cover, with the legendary basilisk etched in gold. I opened it and the first instructions were how to make the staff.

I recalled the staff in the closet and continued to read.

"It says," I read and informed Narissa, "the staff is to be made of ash wood with a unicorn hair in the core and a head of clear quartz to heighten its power. There is also an incantation written down, which is to be used while making it."

I showed her the incantation and she drew in a long breath. "That's a very dangerous, powerful staff. It's made using dark magic."

"Shall we take the book?" I asked.

"No, they will get suspicious. We have to leave now. We can't get caught, we're no match by ourselves." She rushed me out of the room and out of the house. We made sure we put everything back in its place, including the house key.

Chapter 53
Amanda and Jacob Arrive

We just about managed to cross the street when we saw the three diabolists walking towards the house.

Phew! Just in time.

We went back home feeling like we need to find out a lot more about the evil trio. But we did get to know that Oscar's magic staff was very powerful, and we need to keep that in mind when dealing with them.

I wished we had the grimoires of Oscar and Sybil. "Narissa, why did you stop me from taking the grimoires. It would have nullified any spells that may have been cast."

"No Sid, it may nullify their spells, but we wouldn't get our answers. What happened to Amanda's mother…who is Sybil, exactly…" Narissa reminded me.

I acceded, "You're right. Amanda has been in this for years just to know the truth about her mother's death."

Narissa continued, "We need the answers to these questions first. Besides, they may continue to garner support from like-minded spell casters. And this would never end. We have to root them out completely."

I hadn't thought of it that way. I had always considered dealing with the problem at hand. She was right. We needed to bring an end to Selene's evil machinations. I was quite sure that all her actions were a step towards her ambitions of ruling the world.

In our realm, we could involve the police to bring them to book. But there needs to be some proof of wrongdoing. If they had anything to do with Amanda's mother's death, we could go to the police.

I realized this was enough sleuthing until the rest of the gang arrived. It could get dangerous if we tried breaking in again. Also, we might end up in jail if someone sees us trespassing.

With Roy's help we can go in and out unnoticed. We'll have to wait for them to come.

The week passed slowly, and our patience was wearing thin. Often, we sat down and discussed possible strategies to break them, but it didn't amount to much.

I continued my routine of going to work. I checked in more often with my parents and my relationship with them became healthier and more like the olden days, when I felt secure.

I also took Narissa with me again. They were really welcoming towards her and that really warmed my heart. My dad tried to walk and that was a big step for him. Narissa encouraged him and gave him some healing water again.

Narissa too kept in touch with her mom. The family ties were flourishing.

And then Amanda called to confirm their arrival. We got ready to welcome them into our home. In a couple of days, we went to receive them at the airport.

We had arranged for them to stay in Narissa's room. I gave my room to Narissa, while I decided to use the couch. But Amanda wanted to share the room with Narissa. Jacob said he was fine to use my room with me, so no one was on the couch.

It reminded me of my childhood vacations in India. Cousins would pop over for a slumber party. And we would all fall asleep on the same bed.

We told the couple about our investigative day in Oscar's home, and they didn't seem surprised.

"Nothing unusual about it, Sid," Amanda stated. "After all, they are witches and sorcerers. But it's helpful to understand that they're not in this in a positive way. The witchcraft they employ can be dangerous. Our defense should be in order before we challenge them."

I thought it was the right time to tell them about the other realms, and the others who would be joining us in our fight with the evil trio.

This time our account astounded them. Their expressions changed from curious to shock to utter disbelief.

"Is this for real?" Jacob was having trouble believing the truth. "Did all this really happen? I used to think Amanda's group was like a cult group indulging in hocus-pocus to satisfy their quirks. High grade magic tricks at best."

Even though Amanda believed in the power of witches and sorcerers, Jacob still had his reservations about how effective they can be. He became a part of it only to uncover the truth of Audrey's death, to help his wife.

Narissa affirmed to him, "You're going to meet the others soon. You'll see this isn't a fairy tale. In fact, Selene isn't fully human. She is the descendant of a nymph."

Jacob was reeling with the disclosure, but Amanda was just as amazed. She had never imagined fantastic beings from other realms were a reality. We had still not disclosed that Narissa had become a mermaid; there was no need for that.

Narissa stated plainly, "I didn't believe either, but that's where I was taken after I had been kidnapped all those years ago. And Sid reached the Toon World when a portal opened accidentally. He too was kidnapped and taken to the enchanted forest."

I pitched in, "Selene has been plotting a universal takeover for years. We managed to disentangle her hold over the enchanted forest. And she'll stop at nothing to harm us. That's why I now feel we need to quash her completely."

Both husband and wife were startled. The scheming takeover information rattled them.

"Are we capable of dealing with them?" Amanda was concerned.

"That's why we have the others joining us." I smiled as positively as I could. "No doubt it is extremely risky. But it is something we have to do."

As an afterthought I added, "Oh, and please don't tell anything to Nora and Paul. It would disturb them unnecessarily. They may not be able to deal with the insecurities."

"Of course, of course!" Jacob spoke up. "They can't know anything about this dangerous mission."

Once we had brought them up to date on the real situation, I lightened the ambience by starting a karaoke party. We sang songs, laughed and ordered in some food.

Over the next two days, the sisters became close and spoke to their parents to share the bonding. We also checked out Mike's holiday home near the lake and made necessary arrangements for everyone.

After the enjoyable couple of days, we had just finished our morning breakfast when Queen Titania arrived with the Toon boys. "Good morning, everyone!"

Chapter 54
Friends Inc.

The pleasure I felt when I saw them cannot be put into words. There had become like my brothers. Lots of greetings and hugs were exchanged. The cheerfulness was palpable.

Amanda and Jacob almost had their mouths open. It was hilarious to see their expressions, even though they were told about it. I have to admit it was strange to see the boys in our environment.

I wondered how the couple would react if Archon had come and laughed at the thought.

Narissa enquired about Roy's sister and if the healing water had helped.

"She's so much better Narissa! I am amazed with her progress. She doesn't throw wild tantrums anymore and is trying to do some things on her own." Roy sounded grateful.

Narissa turned to Steve and Jim. "What about your neighbor Steve? And Jim, has your mother benefitted from it when she's healing people?"

"My neighbor has got some comfort now. Thanks for asking," Steve said.

Jim smiled and added, "Yes it has helped her patients too."

I introduced the Ely couple to the queen and the Toon boys and announced to everyone that we have a house ready for all of us to stay as long as necessary.

"This sounds more like a vacation than a mission." Roy chuckled.

I retorted, "Who says we can't mix business with pleasure?"

After the laughter died down, I continued, "I think we should avoid all of you being seen by humans. It will attract too much unwanted attention and make our investigation difficult."

"What do you suggest?" the queen asked.

"The four of us," I said pointing to the couple, Narissa and myself, "will reach there. Your majesty can then track us to the house with your staff. Till then please make yourselves comfortable. It should take no more than half an hour."

We arranged breakfast for everyone and left for Mike's house. In about an hour's time, all of them had joined us there. It was a nice home with all basic amenities in place. Queen Titania was given the master bedroom. The rest of us distributed ourselves in the remaining three bedrooms in the house.

The location had a beautiful view of the lake on one side and lush, green expanse on the other. The spot was isolated as it was in the middle of private property. That made it safe for the others to be outside around the house and get some fresh air, without being seen.

I suggested we enjoy the day before starting our courtship with danger. We sat together having a cheerful conversation and talked about our findings in our earlier visit to Oscar's house. Our food arrived and the ambience turned party-like.

Music was playing, laughter rang in the home and good-humored jibes were thrown about. We even danced. It was fabulous afternoon and brought alive our good times in the enchanted forest. When it started to get dark, we went to sit outside and enjoy some fresh air.

Slowly the sky turned purple and twinkled with stars. It looked like a velvet sheet strewn with crystals. The weather had been perfect. The moonlight shone in the lake, and everyone decided to go for a swim.

It was fulfilling day, and much needed to make the Ely couple comfortable with the rest of the gang. In any case, the gang was so open-hearted. It didn't take long to break the ice.

The next morning, we started to discuss how to begin our investigations. I suggested we again get into the house, but this time with Queen Titania and Roy. Both would be able to get us in and out without detection once they see the place. Plus, the queen would be able to understand more about their powers.

We would go at the same time as our last probe, when they, most likely, are not around. Again, Narissa and I reached that home using the subway and the queen tracked us there. Roy zapped us into the house, and we quickly took them through the rooms.

The queen got a good look at both the grimoires. The little one in Sybil's room and the large one in the ritual room. And then she brought us back to Mike's house. Everyone was waiting in anticipation to hear what she had to say.

"It was exactly as you both had described earlier Sid. Your deductions were all correct. Sybil is also a witch; but she is not Selene's sister."

Everyone was confused with her hypothesis.

"Then how do you explain the likeness?" I asked.

She took a deep breath. "Sybil is a clone of Selene, and she has been created by Oscar using black magic and witchcraft."

The confused look was now accompanied by a collective gasp.

"The procedure was detailed in the large grimoire. I had my doubts even earlier, because no one in the forest had ever heard of any sibling. Also, Sybil's room had a hypnotizing wall hanging."

She looked at me and continued, "The artwork of optical illusion? That's the one. It keeps her mind under Selene's control. And the pentagram on her bedside is meant to keep her under Oscar's control, as he's the one who created her."

"Our clone theory was right after all," Narissa thought aloud. "So, to get rid of Sybil will be easy. If we destroy the large grimoire, she will disintegrate into thin air. But the reckoning forces are Selene and Oscar. How do we put a stop to them?"

I made my suggestions. "We need to tail Oscar and get something on him that's criminal. Then we just find a way to veer the police towards him. He's human, as far as I know. Once he's behind bars, there's not much he will be able to do."

"Also," Jim spoke up, "With the grimoire destroyed he won't be able to cast spells."

"We'll have to destroy his powerful staff too," Steve reminded.

Amanda who had been listening intently so far, finally pitched in, "Yes, that's right. And what do we do about Selene? If she can jump portals at will, how do we pin her down and destroy her?"

That's a million-dollar question!

Chapter 55
Working on Strategy

Narissa suddenly remembered our cult experience in the Toon World. "Jim, Steve, Roy...did any of you encounter any more problems with that cult leader, Daemon Dickens?"

"None of us had a problem," Jim answered. "But we've heard that the cult is growing. A lot of people have started talking about them there."

"Wouldn't that become dangerous?" Jacob reasoned.

"That's exactly what I was thinking and mentioning to the boys," Steve said. "My gut feeling says that Selene is behind that push for growth. From the very beginning, she has been trying to garner support for her intention of absolutism. Power has been her ultimate aim."

Amanda nodded. "Looks like she's preparing her army."

"Which means," Roy added, "We have to weaken the Apollyon Abode and Daemon too. It will be easier to destroy Selene when she's alone."

I agreed. "She has already lost her hold in the enchanted forest. We'll work on Oscar and Sybil for now. Then move onto Daemon."

"Our next move has to be to eavesdrop on their conversations," said Queen Titania. "This time Amanda and Jacob will come with me. They've been in touch with the gang over the years and will be able to make more sense of what they're saying."

"Definitely, Your Majesty! Finally, I have a chance to get the information I seek." Amanda was relieved that she could go.

Unexpectedly the queen stood up and addressed everyone in a serious tone, "All of you...no more Your Majesty, Highness...or any of those formal titles. Please! I want you to call me Aunty Tee." And she flashed a big smile.

Everyone broke into peals of laughter and shouted in unison, "Yes Aunty Tee!!!"

As decided, the three of them swooshed off to do their snooping. The rest of us were catching up on lost time when out of the blue, Aunty Tee appeared and spoke in a rush, "All of you, follow Oscar. He's about the leave the house."

Just as suddenly, she disappeared again. Quickly, we gathered, and Roy flashed us into a street corner outside the house. Oscar was walking out. Keeping a safe distance, we started shadowing him.

I had given some of my real time clothes and hats to the Toon boys to avoid being too noticeable as animation people. Narissa and I wore hats as well to avoid easy recognition, just in case he noticed us.

We followed him into a café where we saw him meet a man with an intimidating personality. Burly, tough looking guy. They pretended to enjoy coffee together while having a serious conversation.

They were seated next to the window and we were two tables behind them. Steve quickly drew two cups attached by a string that passed through a long hollow stick.

I was amazed with his presence of mind. That's the kind of stuff we used to do as kids, to listen in on conversations from behind a wall or door.

Very surreptitiously, he pushed the cup from the low windowsill till it reached their table. There was no way they would see that, because it was below their table. The other cup was plugged to his ear.

Every few minutes each of us took turns to listen in. We saw the man hand Oscar a bulky envelope and Jim who was listening to them at that moment, quickly gestured to leave the café.

We walked out and hid in an alley waiting to tail him again. We followed him back to his house and then Roy zapped us back to our place. We saw that Aunty Tee was also back with her team.

Aunty Tee – that has cute ring to it actually!

I was smiling to myself when I noticed Amanda's crestfallen face. Jacob had a protective arm around her, and it seemed like he was consoling her.

"What happened?" I asked.

Jacob answered on her behalf, "The trio was in the living room, when we found ourselves in the kitchen there. It was easy to hide and listen to them. They were discussing expanding their network and how it was time to take some serious steps."

Aunty Tee continued the narrative, "Selene asked about the different recruiters and what they were doing. Then she mentioned Amanda. She showed concern that Amanda may not go along with them just like her mother, Audrey."

"Audrey didn't go along with them?" Narissa was taken aback at this revelation.

"No, she said Audrey became a troublemaker when she was asked to hypnotize recruits in Selene's favor. She threatened to alert authorities and end the group and walked off one of their meetings in the woods."

Jacob added, "Selene was gloating that she had to cast a spell on a pack of wolves to stop her; they mauled her to death. Sybil was defending Amanda, saying she hadn't seen any signs of dissent so far."

"That's when Oscar said he has an appointment with someone nearby and will be back soon," interjected Aunty Tee. "And I came to inform the rest of you. We continued to listen to Selene and Sybil discuss controlling the newbies to give shape to their plans."

"I think we kind of expected that they had a hand in it, right?" I looked at Narissa. "But it's so comforting to know that Audrey was against their evil machinations."

We tried to console Amanda and make her feel loved. After some time, she gathered herself and said half crying and half smiling, "Thank you all for your concern. I've not only gained a sister, recently, I've made some new friends and have an aunt too. And my pride in my mother as a good human is intact. So many blessings."

"What did you gather?" asked Aunty Tee of our team.

"Oscar is in collusion with the underworld. He uses his black magic to make them powerful and gets paid for it," Jim explained.

"Do you mean," she said, sounding a little alarmed and confused, "that he helps Satan?"

"Oh no." I laughed. "Underworld also refers to the world of organized crime. They're called mafia as well, or 'Cosa Nostra' as they call themselves. We have to check out his connections to this. It will help us put him behind bars."

We had his weak spot figured out.

Chapter 56
Cosa Nostra

It was clear now that all of them followed criminal means to achieve their goals. But it wasn't going to be possible to get them incriminated in the eyes of the law, without proof or some solid information that could be passed on to the police.

Audrey's murder was too old a case and it was impossible to prove their hand in it. We would have to find a strong lead that we can give the law enforcement. Oscar's links to the mafia would surely give us something tangible.

We definitely had to follow him more closely. And we had to be as covert as possible. That would be more effective in achieving our mission and shattering their quest for power. It was also the best bet in keeping everyone safe from backlash, just in case things did not go as planned.

As the next day dawned, I decided all of us would take turns to keep Oscar under continuous surveillance, keeping vigil outside his home, two or three at a time. We would inform the rest of any movements that needed more help using the cell phone.

I had arranged two extra phones for the Toon boys and Aunty Tee. I even gave them tutorials on how to use it. Once we sorted the logistics, I went with Jacob and Jim for the first round. Nothing much happened. By noon, we had returned, after which Narissa, Amanda and Roy took over.

Aunty Tee was all set to cover round three with Steve, when Amanda called to say that they were in a cab, following all of them to an unknown destination, after a car came to pick up the trio.

My intuition told me that Oscar was going to involve the witches in his deal with the mafia. Just how their complicity was going to shape up, was a mystery to me.

I told Amanda to let us know when they reached the destination. The rest of us waited in anticipation to join them as soon as she called again.

She called again to say they had lost them.

"How?" I was upset. "What happened?"

Sounding disappointed, she said, "They entered a private gated property with a lot of security. We can't follow them in there."

"Stay right where you are, but in a hidden area," I told her and hung up. "C'mon everyone, time to go. Aunty Tee, wave your staff."

In a moment, we were all outside the property behind a cluster of trees with our Team Two that followed the villains.

"Amanda, you're forgetting security can't keep us out." I smiled devilishly, making her grin in understanding. "Roy, can you climb the tree and look for a good hidden area that we can get into. I don't want us to be zapped on the grounds in full view."

Roy scanned the grounds and finally climbed down. We huddled together, Roy worked his magic and we found ourselves in a toolshed inside the gated property.

Looking out the window, we saw huge beautifully landscaped grounds surrounding an impressive luxurious looking mansion. There were smaller simpler homes about fifteen minutes walking distance away. And other small, roofed areas close to the mansion.

As we discussed and contemplated our next move, we heard a car drive in. A bright yellow convertible, driven by a beautiful well-dressed woman, headed to one of the low-roofed enclosures. She parked inside and walked towards the mansion.

"That area must be the garage," remarked Jacob.

"The car that we followed must be parked in there too. That's why we don't see it outside. They must all be inside the mansion," Amanda pointed out.

"Then we should be inside too," said Aunty Tee and before any of us could remark, we were inside the mansion in the corridor on the first floor! We heard voices getting louder and we rushed into the nearest room.

"That was close," whispered Jim.

We heard the voices getting louder and froze, thinking they are going to enter the room. There was no way eight of us could stay hidden, even if it was a large room. Then we heard another door creak open and shut.

We heaved a sigh of relief, until we heard the lower voices come from the next room. With a finger on my lips, I gestured to all to stay silent. They were right next door.

"How do we listen to what they're saying? Actually, I want to record their conversation on my phone for proof," I whispered and looked at everyone one by one, to see if anyone had a solution.

Everyone drew a blank.

The silence was disconcerting, and everyone was thinking hard, when we heard a soft whisper from behind, "I'll do it for you."

It was that pretty lady in the yellow convertible! She emerged from the en suite bathroom, wiping her wet face with a napkin.

Oh no! What do we do now?

"I'll do it for you," she repeated. "You want a recording of their conversation, isn't it?"

I nodded, unsure of her offer.

But why is she helping us? Is she trying to trap us?

"I'm not trying to trap you," she said, as though reading my mind. "I have my grievances with Santino. He treats me like dirt." She proceeded to show us some scars on her left leg, in the area of her collar bone and a finger that wouldn't bend. She even had a deep, fresh scratch on her cheek.

Looking at her more closely, I realized there was extreme sadness emanating from her eyes.

"I'm his wife," she answered before we asked. "Wait here quietly. I'll sit in on the meeting and get you what you need." She picked up her phone, and Jim caught her hand.

She darted a look at him, and he dropped his hold and apologized in a whisper, "Sorry, I'm not sure we can trust you."

She showed him her recording app, set it up to record and went into the room next door.

"How can we believe her?" Jacob voiced his incredulity.

"She's telling the truth," said Jim. "I read her."

Jacob looked puzzled and I gave him a reassuring nod. "I'll explain later."

Chapter 57
The Don's Wife

We waited with bated breath for the boss man's wife to return. Just to calm Jacob and anyone else who had doubts, I whispered an exit plan, "We'll abort the mission and zoom out if things go wrong."

They nodded in agreement.

We sat waiting for more than an hour, until we finally heard their door squeak open. Their voices were loud in the corridor and all of us almost forgot to breathe with the anxiety. They walked past and their voices gradually became more distant.

The lady did not return. We soon heard a car ignition turn on outside. As we peeked through the window, we saw the diabolical trio leave. Narissa recognized the car in which they had arrived at this mansion.

In a few minutes, the woman came back into the room. "You can speak a little bit now. Santino has gone to the pool area outside. And I've got something for you." She smiled, leaving us confused.

"I told you how he treats me. I may be the wife of a powerful man, but I don't have any freedom. I don't even have the freedom to walk out of the marriage. He threatens me if I talk of divorce, and we all know he can actualize his threat."

The girls took a deep breath, trying to figure out why any woman would want to marry a man like that in the first place.

She saw their expressions and related her tale. "Santino Acierno can be very charming when he wants to be. I was very young and naïve. He wooed me in style, and I fell for it. It was only after marriage that I got to know about his business…and his character."

Amanda looked deeply affected and perplexed. "But your life is…you drive a fancy car, wear fancy clothes, have a gorgeous home."

"That's my compensation for living with the demon." She stared back with deadpan eyes.

"What's your name, dear?" Aunty Tee asked with some compassion. "What would you gain by helping us?"

"I'm Sophia. I was a nurse and we met when he was a patient. He was hurt in a car accident. As I understand him now, it was probably some rival gang that tried to kill him. If I can help you get him into trouble, I will be able to get my life back." She paused and asked, "Are you from another gang?"

"Oh no!" Narissa said. "We're actually trying to get the police involved. We need something substantial to give the authorities to set them on their tail. We're after those three that came to meet him. They are practitioners of black magic and witchcraft. They are ruining many lives."

Sophia spoke with some determination, "Then I'm sure I can help you. I want him to go to prison for a long, long time. Meanwhile, listen to this recording.

"Those three have been hired by Santino to increase his power in the underworld. Rather to make him the supreme leader of his world. He will not only reward them with money, but also coerce people to help them in their mission."

"And these unholy conjurers will use their Satanism to work things in his favor. Santino is just as dangerous as they are," I surmised.

She agreed with a knowing smile and turned on her recording.

Sophia: *Hello Darling! Can I help?*
Santino: *Just sit with me. You help by being next to me.*
(Patronizing laughter…)
This is my beautiful wife, Sophia.
Oscar: *Hello ma'am.*
Santino: *Please continue.*
Oscar: *As I was saying, your Caporegime, Louis Bruno met me a few days ago and asked if I will be able to help you grow in your business using my special talents.*
Santino: *And…?*
Oscar: *Most definitely! My sorcery has powerful, lasting effects.*
Santino: *How much do you want for your services?*
Oscar: *There is one big ceremonial procedure that I will have to perform, for which I expect US$ 500,000. But it would also require continual*

reinforcing methods for at least one year, till you steel up your position. For that, a suitable monthly remuneration I leave for your consideration.
Santino*: I will consider your proposal and finalize the details in a couple of days.*
Oscar*: Also, sir, we would need some of your soldiers with people skills to intimidate folk for our mission.*
Santino*: And what is your mission?*
Oscar*: (laughs lightly) These are my associates Selene and Sybil. Like you, we too intend to gain ultimate power, but in various realms. (Pauses) Don't worry, our worlds do not overlap.*
Santino*: I find your initial price unreasonable.*
Selene*: No, sir, not at all! That first ceremony will eliminate your rivals. It is, in fact, underpriced because we need your help with our plans as well.*
Santino*: Hmm…Okay, I see your point of view. And I'll let you know soon.*
Oscar*: I look forward to working with you, sir. Ma'am, it was good to meet you.*
Santino*: I think we will have a fruitful partnership. Happy to see all of you. Sophia darling, can you please see them to the car? I'm going for a swim.*
Sophia*: Sure! I'll come to the pool in half an hour. Ladies…sir…please come, I'll call the driver.*

"Will this help?" Sophia asked.

"I think it's enough to alert the law enforcers to keep an eye on his activities. If possible, keep sending us anything you find that can incriminate him. For now, just forward this audio file to my phone please. I'll make sure the FBI gets this." I was excited that we managed to find something to get started.

"I have to go now," she said. "How are all of you going to find your way out? In fact, how did you even get in? So many of you… Are you part of some theatre group; some of you are in costumes?" She darted a look at the Toon boys and Aunty Tee.

Aunty Tee laughed. "You can say that; it's all a big drama. Don't worry about us getting in and out. You can join your husband, or he'll get suspicious. We'll be gone before you know it."

Chapter 58
Alerting the FBI

In a flash, we were back at Mike's place and ready to do a celebratory dance. Getting evidence against Oscar was the tough part. We were contemplating how to get the wheels in motion with the law, when Mike walked in.

"Mike!" I almost shouted. "What a pleasant surprise!"

"I thought I'd pass by and see how you guys are doing," he said.

I introduced him to everyone and asked him to join us for dinner. His awestruck expressions on meeting the Toon boys and Aunty Tee were hilarious. I told him about our day's win – gaining the damning clues that Oscar was involved in nefarious activities.

"Sid, I know the Director of the Criminal Investigation Division in the FBI. If you forward that conversation to me, I can give it to him to check it out. He may also want to meet you personally to know more." As usual, Mike came to the rescue. His support was unwavering.

"Yeah, sure!" I forwarded the audio file and felt assured that the wheels were definitely going to be set into motion. We relaxed and enjoyed the rest of the evening. I could see that Mike was having a good time.

Before leaving, he turned to Aunty Tee. "Your majesty! I would really like to travel dimensions with all of you someday. Sid has made me envious of his adventures."

"Of course, Mike!" Aunty Tee welcomed him. "Once we have this situation under control, it would be a pleasure to have you as a guest in the Magus Forest."

"…And in the Toon World," added Jim extending his hand for a shake.

Mike bid an excited 'Good Night' and left.

The next morning, we started discussing what would be the best strategy to weaken Daemon in the Toon World. I asked the boys if there were laws or rules against cults there.

They said it was pretty much like here. They would need to prove that criminal activities were practiced in the cult home. The authorities would then swoop down on them and incarcerate them.

"They were ready to kill me in a sacrificial ceremony!" I blurted.

"We know that, but the law does not. We can't prove anything now. Perhaps we should've approached them at that point of time," Steve stated, in a matter-of-fact manner. "Now it's our word against theirs."

"Yeah, you're right," I agreed. "But they kidnapped us. Surely, they've done that to others as well. We need to weed out those who've been forced into the cult, and they can give statements against Daemon."

The boys agreed, this may work. But we'd have to go back to the cult home and question the inmates. And that was no mean feat.

"They're in a different location now…more open…not hidden anymore behind a nondescript warehouse area," Roy informed. "Even if they were forced into it, they may be accepting of it now, or fearful of consequences if they deflect."

Aunty Tee, who was listening quietly till now, shared her thoughts. "We should go there when Selene goes. If she's there, I know she's going to do something big that can put them in trouble. We'll get proof enough to inform the authorities. Just like we did with Oscar here."

Everyone felt that was the best way to tackle the situation, and we decided we'd keep our eyes on Selene now.

The next two days we followed them around to various coven-steads. It was an eye opener how much of a network she had created with Oscar and Sybil. The Ely wiccan meeting was not the only source of increasing their manpower.

I also got a call from the FBI, confirming an appointment with them along with Mike. I told the others to continue their surveillance of the witches, while I was at the meeting. Mike picked me up and it was an intimidating interview at their headquarters.

At times, it felt like I was the suspect. The questions and cross-questions were probing and disconcerting. But Mike's presence gave me a lot of confidence. He had prepped me to not be nervous and just tell the plain truth.

I didn't involve the presence of the Toon boys or Queen Titania to avoid complications. They questioned the source of the proof. I told them it was the Don's wife.

They asked me how I know Sophia. I told them we were following the wiccans, who we suspected of killing my friend's mother. And we bumped into Sophia, while the wiccans met her husband. Only, I changed the location from their house to a café. It would be hard to explain how we got through so much security.

They questioned why his wife wanted to put him behind bars. I told them domestic violence was the reason.

They asked if she would testify against him. I assumed probably not before he has been arrested.

They also asked about the wiccans and if I have any proof of the murder I mentioned. I told them unfortunately, that happened many years ago. And we only recently overheard them admit to it, while we were following them. There was no proof.

They wondered how Mike was involved. And I said he was my boss who was just helping me reach the authorities. He had no knowledge of any of the people involved.

After the grilling interrogation, they seemed satisfied with my replies and agreed to look into it. They reminded me that they may call me again if necessary. I was relieved that it was working out and I did not find it as daunting as I did earlier.

I returned to give the good news to my friends. I also messaged Sophia to let her know the gist of the meeting. And corroborate that the location we met at was the café. She was happy that it was taken seriously. I cautioned her to remain normal, so that Santino does not suspect any treachery or breach of faith.

My group informed me they suspected that the big ritual Oscar intended to hold for Santino's benefit, was going to be held in three days. They had followed him to specialized vendors of witchcraft ingredients. The kind that is usually required when a there is a spellcasting ritual and raising of the 'cone of power'.

'Cone of power' refers to the method of raising energy to a peak above the circumference of the wiccans' circle and then releasing it upwards towards their goal.

I immediately informed the officers that I had just met, with these new details. They assured me they would act immediately.

Chapter 59
Back to the Toon World

We continued our vigilance, and a day later we followed them to another wiccan meeting. Selene left quickly though, and on her tail, we realized she was off to the Toon World to meet Daemon.

Here was our opportunity to debilitate Daemon's hold over his cult members. We would have to fragment them if we are unable to pin him down for the authorities to take over. We reached the Toon World.

Roy took us to the new location, and it was bewildering how much the cult had grown. It was like a small town on its own. It was a gated community and the entrance to the community had a life size cut out of Daemon in his trademark black robes. As usual, Roy got us in, and we stayed shielded by a wall of greenery.

A couple of thousand devotees of Daemon went about their everyday chores. I noticed they all wore a uniform black bandana. No more of the black robes as we had seen earlier. Their attire was regular and casual, with the black bandana creating their identity as disciples of Daemon. The bandana had 'Apollyon Abode' printed on it in white.

There was no way we could mingle with the crowd here as disciples. Only the Toon boys would be able to blend in. The rest of us would stand out like a sore thumb. We'd have to stay hidden where we were, until we were required.

The commune was dotted with small, prefabricated homes, almost like trailers. In the center, of the land was a large structure, which I assumed was used for the daily congregation of the disciples and their group activities. Next to it was a larger home, most likely for Daemon.

The boys walked into the crowd and found their way into a small home that was open and empty. They emerged wearing the bandanas and walked towards the larger building. After completing their recce of the area, they returned to give us the information.

The central structure was a huge hall, as we had rightly guessed, for the activities and gatherings. The big home was indeed for Daemon. Selene and Daemon were in a meeting inside.

Steve had realized it wasn't safe for us to be standing around the way we were. He found a spot to draw up a little trailer home for us to hide. It was close to the central building but hidden in shadows. Roy zapped us into it and told us to keep it locked.

Soon a series of short sirens blasted from loudspeakers. We could see from the windows that it had a strange impact on the disciples. They dropped whatever they were doing and zoned out, walking like zombies towards the central hall.

They were being hypnotized!

I looked at Aunty Tee to share my thoughts and saw that the Toon boys seemed affected as well. The rest of us felt normal. Maybe the sound waves were customized to affect the Toon people.

They were about to walk out of the trailer, when Aunty Tee waved her staff around them. An electrical impulse emanated from it and surrounded the boys. They broke out of their reverie.

"What happened?" asked Jim, looking lost.

"You almost walked out like zombies, like the rest of them," I told him.

"So that's how the community has grown," remarked Narissa. "Selene has been hypnotizing them. That way, they get the people to do whatever they want without any dissent."

"We need to break this hypnotic spell," said Aunty Tee. "I managed to get these boys back, but I can't handle this large crowd with my staff alone. What do we do?"

Amanda and Jacob had been silent spectators all this while as they took in the environment in wonderment. Amanda finally spoke up, "We saw that your staff can break the hypnosis. Now we need to figure out a way to amplify it enough to interfere with that hypnotic siren."

Jacob added, "The amplification will block the siren from reaching the people and break the thread drawing them in. If we amplify it a bit more, it may erase previous effects too."

"In any case, if it doesn't erase the effects of the past reverberations, I may know something that could work. Don't forget I've been learning from them." Amanda smiled. "But we still need to amplify it."

The sirens stopped as all the community members reached the hall. I decided to send Roy to check up on their activities there.

"Roy, you go ahead and attend that assembly. Aunty Tee, will he get affected now?" She shook her head in the negative. I sent Roy off to keep an eye. "Tell us whatever happens. We'll try to figure out this thing here."

"We will need plasma to magnify that electron wave you emitted Aunty Tee. We can create the plasma from normal air, though helium would be more effective. But we'll need a large amount of energy for that." Jim apparently was good at Physics too, apart from his communication. I was impressed.

"What do we need to do?" I asked.

"Steve, can you draw a transparent box with a suction pump? Like a vacuum cleaner." He looked at the rest of us and explained, "We have to use pressure to fill it up with air like a gas cylinder. Then we run electricity through it to ionize it. It would be similar to a storm cloud."

Steve created the box attached with an electric wire and Jim filled it with air. "Now we connect this to an electric socket." He plugged it in, and we waited for some time. "Aunty Tee, can you direct the electron wave from your staff towards this box?"

Aunty Tee waved her staff and we saw a lightning type of effect in the room. We were taken aback and excited. It worked but wasn't strong enough to block the hypnotic sirens. More power was required.

Narissa brought a glass of water and asked Steve to use the suction and put it into the box. "The moisture will help heighten the effect, like the storm cloud you mentioned. Plus, I can create more power in that water now."

I understood now how this was going to work. Narissa's power over water would definitely outshine the electricity from a socket. We placed the box on the windowsill. Narissa concentrated her powers and got the water moving in circular motion.

Gradually, the speed of the water increased to such a level, it was like a cyclone in a box. Aunty Tee directed her staff once again toward the box. The electron wave passed through the box and burst out of the window like a gigantic lightning bolt.

Roy, who was present in the hall, returned to tell us what happened. "That huge flash of lightning, was that you?" Our broad grins confirmed our success to him.

"Wow, that thing really worked! As soon as that happened, the people looked around like they were woken up from a stupor. Some of them looked angry and wanted to leave. Daemon threatened them to stop. They did not leave out of fear, but there was a mini pandemonium and protest was growing in a section of the community."

Oh my gosh! The hypnosis had worn off!

Chapter 60
End of the Cult

"I know what I have to do!" Roy exclaimed and disappeared.

We were left wondering where he went. Jim went back to the hall to search for him but returned, saying there was no sign of him there. He did, however, tell us that the protest was gaining traction.

About twenty minutes later, we saw the authorities raid the commune and head directly towards the congregation room. In the midst of the commotion, we saw Roy running towards our hiding spot.

"Where were you?" Everyone pounced on him simultaneously as he walked into the little house.

"I went to call the police," he panted. "I was rushing because I didn't want to lose time, just in case Selene managed to control the situation. It was the best time to weed out those who are here against their will."

"Ha-ha! You're a hero, Roy." Jacob was amused and impressed. "Now Daemon and Selene will get arrested too. That's the end of their clique."

We told the Toon boys to go and check out the goings on from a distance, and not get involved with the ruckus. The rest of us finally saw from our window, a handcuffed Daemon Dickens being hauled away along with a few more members. One of them was that burly guy...

What was his name? ...

"Walter!" Narissa exclaimed, as though reading my mind. She was pointing out to him. "That's the guy who locked us up the first time, on Daemon's command."

Right behind was Selene...also in handcuffs! We stared at each other in disbelief.

Aunty Tee noted, "So it all ends so easily? I'm finding this hard to believe. Selene in custody?"

As if on cue, the moment they reached an area with less crowd, Selene did a little turn around and vanished. The air had magically opened up a bright hole and sucked her in.

Okay, this is more believable.

As expected, she had jumped the realm. The boys came back to tell us that Daemon and the main administrative members had been arrested. Selene, as we all saw, had been apprehended too. But she managed to escape. Some of the dissenters were questioned and required to be witnesses.

"Our work here is done. Let's go back now," I said.

Aunty Tee waved her staff, and we were back, but near Oscar's home. "Wait for me…" she said and disappeared.

She reappeared a few minutes later. "Selene is back too, and Oscar has pried her cuffs open. But it is to our credit that her Toon World strength has been neutralized. She's really upset about it. It's a major setback in her quest for absolute power."

Back home, we all had a peaceful night's rest. Our little success was like a calming and soothing balm. But there was more work to be done. And we felt energized the next morning.

Before we started our day's surveillance, I felt it would be nice for everyone to contact their families. The emotional strength would also help in our mission.

Amanda and Jacob had left their kids at Nora and Paul's place. Narissa joined the conversation with them. Their parents were happy that the sisters were getting along and enjoying a holiday together. Well, at least that's what they thought!

The Toon boys did a short and quick tour of Toon World to catch up with their families with the help of Aunty Tee. And Aunty Tee herself, tried to catch up with her royal duties. She had already delegated the necessary work and was trying to update herself on the news. She also informed Archon about our success and how much we missed him.

As for me, I spoke to my parents, and I was relieved that they were much happier than I'd seen them in a long time. Dad's physical therapy was showing good results.

The morning was a family affair. And by afternoon, everyone was all set to tackle the villains. We set off on their tail as usual and found out that the big ritual was to be conducted on Santino's private grounds.

We had overheard their strategy, that they were going to use the ritual not only for Santino's benefit, but also to push their own agenda. And this little detail was not conveyed to the Don, because gaining their own supremacy meant dominating the underworld as well.

So, Santino was actually being set up for a backstabbing ceremony. True he would rise above his rivals. But he would not be the ultimate power in his business. He would be subservient to the Evil Trident.

The 'Trident' was their symbolic reference. Oscar, Selene, and Sybil…the three prongs of a unified power over three universes. They would become like the ultimate weapon…only this weapon was laced with poison.

There was a communication tower close to the property, and the triple jeopardy intended to magnify their controlling powers through the tower. They wanted to harness the extensive reach of the communication tower for their own gain. It apparently wasn't linked to Santino's ritual. But they didn't tell him that.

Selene had also not disclosed to Oscar that she had lost out on two of the universes – the enchanted Magus Forest and the Toon World. She explained her cuffs as a minor hiccup with the law. Perhaps she didn't want to risk losing his confidence and the opportunity to take over at least one world.

Unbeknownst to them, it was our mission to break this 'Trident' never to be used again. If the FBI foiled this ceremony, they would be quashed for good. We had to make sure that the ritual was impeded until the FBI arrived.

The following day was going to be the 'Grand Finale' of the whole show. We had to be prepared mentally and physically. I forwarded the location to the officials and was happy to note that they were already in the know.

I checked with Sophia, who informed me that two officers had contacted her and prepared her for the 'big day'. She was going to be given security as well.

We were all set from our side. We only had to wait for the action to roll out…

Chapter 61
The Final Countdown

The sun rose bright and warm on the day of the ritual. As far as I was concerned, it was a positive sign and I felt upbeat about handling the day with a fair amount of ease. We had managed very well so far. It wouldn't be too tough to just create obstacles in their ceremonial procedures until the FBI swooped down on them.

I pepped up our team and we were off to Santino's home. Energy seemed to be running high there as well. Santino was on tenterhooks and had his men running around with insane instructions. Sophia was not involved in any of the preparations.

I guess, in this case, his disdain for her abilities worked in her favor. In any case, she had been advised by the authorities against getting involved. She must have kept herself busy at home preparing for 'other' eventualities.

Oscar wore a very intense and formidable expression. Selene was by his side preparing the area for the procedure, while Sybil executed Selene's bidding. The demarcated area to hold the proceedings was close to the servants' quarters.

There was a large set up for a bonfire within a circle. Inside the circle were drawn small pentagrams at five points, forming the five points of a large pentagram. Crystals were placed in the center of each small pentagram.

A large Citrine was placed in the center of the small pentagram forming the top point or apex of the large star. This was for personal power.

The two points forming the base of the star had a Garnet and a Carnelian. These were for inner strength, energy, and confidence.

The crystals placed on the points forming the two arms of the star were the tiger's eye stone, which is called stone of courage, and the Leopard skin Jasper, which serves as a catalyst for personal growth.

"These crystals have been chosen and placed to enhance inner strength, vitality and confidence, and with the help of courage and stability, to attain maximum power," Amanda explained to us all about the crystals and their placement.

Herbs, oils, pen, and paper were placed on a little table next to several photographs of random men. We learnt later that these men were Santino's rivals in business. Oscar did a spiritual cleansing of Santino, and then Selene and Sybil. Selene did Oscar's spiritual cleansing too.

By the time they had completed all the necessary procedures to start, it was almost sundown and the perfect time to get the spellcasting into motion. I also noticed Oscar had his magic staff and his grimoire with him. Sybil held her small grimoire as well.

All the while, we had been hiding in a little quarter next to the designated spot. As usual, we kept an eye on the events from the windows. The quarter was the dwelling of the personal maid for Sophia. She locked us in, to avoid anyone entering while we were there.

She had been instructed, beforehand, and promised a suitable reward for her cooperation. She also had her own vested interest. Her son had been drawn into this world of crime against her will. She was willing to do anything to get him out of it.

Oscar motioned to Santino to come and sit with them. I began to get worried, because there was no sign of the FBI. I whispered to Amanda, "Do something to stall them, please."

She nodded and opened the window just enough for her to poke her head out a little. Luckily, they were all focused on the rites and didn't notice. She concentrated hard and looked up at the sky. She started to mouth a spell to invoke rain. Narissa joined her.

Soon it started to drizzle, and we could hear Oscar curse the weather. We quickly shut the window and hid. The drizzle turned to light rainfall. It was impossible to light the bonfire now. Satisfied, we waited, hoping the law would come charging in soon.

By the time the rains stopped, the skies became dark, and there was still no sign of the officers. I tried calling but no one answered.

Oscar had managed to light the bonfire and they started their black magic ritual. He anointed Santino with some oil and herb mix and started reciting his spell from his grimoire. We couldn't figure out what else to do at that point.

He threw into the bonfire, a handful of the ingredients on the table. The flames rose high and almost licked the high branches of a nearby tree. While continuing his incantation, he instructed Santino to write the names of his adversaries.

He mentioned one of those names – Vito Morelli – and threw a picture of the man into the burning pyre. Within moments of doing so, Santino got a call. He listened for precisely a minute and broke into a broad smile. "Vito has met with an accident. He's dead!"

We were taken aback with the kind of power this ritual had, even though we knew what to expect.

Black magic is so frightening!

They continued the process until just two more pictures remained. Santino's phone continued to inform him of the deadly or incapacitating fate of each man, after his name and photo were turned to ashes in the flames.

Just then we heard cars screech to a halt outside and some commotion at the entrance. An FBI task force of five to six men barged in and headed towards the bonfire. Santino's men tried to stop them in vain. They dragged Santino out of the ritual and arrested him and a couple of his main men.

Then they radio-ed the local police to come with back up. The ritual had halted with Santino's arrest. We heaved a sigh of relief that it was all over. The police too would be here any moment and arrest Oscar.

With our attention towards the lawmen, we didn't notice that the triple menace waited for an opportune moment, as the officers led Santino and his men into their waiting cars. They had restarted their ritual to complete their own objective.

Oh no! How do we put a stop to this?

We were left praying that the police arrive in good time and obviate the impending disaster.

Chapter 62
How to Save the World?

Oscar and Sybil both chanted the incantation for personal power, while Selene supported with her now-weak powers. We could tell that she was out of sorts without her own grimoire.

Her contribution here was her power as an individual…the powers she was born with, which was enough energy to strengthen the circle. Her hold as a witch had diminished with the loss of her grimoire. Like a predator without claws. I was so glad I had the foresight to take it away from her back then.

Maybe we should have incapacitated Oscar and Sybil too by taking their grimoires.

My rueful thoughts heightened as I saw Oscar lift his staff and create a fortifying blaze of current, emitted from the crystal on his staff. It connected all the crystals around the fire with a circular band of light. As we watched, it rose slowly but surely upwards forming a cone. Once the cone was complete it became a strong beam that rose towards the communication tower.

I darted a bewildered look at Narissa and saw an equally wide-eyed girl, worry write large on her face. Aunty Tee was pacing the room frantically. Everyone was thinking hard how to destroy the rising beam.

"Shall we make it rain again?" Jacob suggested.

"We can try, but I doubt it will stop the flow of that current." Narissa joined hands with Amanda and again made the skies flow. This time the downpour was heavier.

The raindrops falling to the ground touched the rising beam and created little nerves of current that spread randomly in the air, like lightning. Narissa took a chance and directed the raindrops like a high-pressure streaming jet towards the beam.

A large part of the current began to deviate and turn back towards the bonfire. Soon the electrical shock hit the circle of light around the fire and threw the trio almost a meter away.

They looked hurt and shaken, but the strength of the current wasn't fatal. And it didn't stop the beam from rising towards the tower either. Against the night sky, the huge flash of light gleamed liked a menacing weapon.

Steve immediately asked them to stop the rains. "It may turn fatal once the ionic intensity increases. And there's no telling which direction it will take and who will get hurt."

Narissa and Amanda made sure, the skies dried up. The three sorcerers were now in no position to do more harm, but they had already unleashed the demon.

If the current reached the tower, the effect of their black magic would spread far and wide. Their evil would become too powerful to control. And we had to find a way to terminate that streaming catastrophe.

Aunty Tee, without a word to any of us, zapped out of the quarters near the bonfire, and picked up Oscar's staff and the grimoires that had dropped when they were thrown off.

Selene saw her and screeched loudly, "Noooo…!!!"

Aunty Tee threw the staff and grimoires into the fire. There was a dramatic blast in the fire. A shrill scream filled the night air as we saw Sybil disintegrate into little fragments, that dissolved into the atmosphere like smoke. The stream of current that was progressing towards the tower also broke and ended. As though a light had been switched off.

Police sirens added to the sounds of the night. Several policemen filled the grounds and sealed the property. They were arresting all the armed men and questioning the servants.

Aunty Tee zoomed back into the room and all of us zapped back to our home, once we saw Oscar being arrested. There was no sign of Selene at all.

We were too exhausted from the drama of the entire day. Everyone was too tired and solemn to even rejoice the triumph. The FBI officers called me to inform me that their operation was successful, and everyone had been arrested.

They had no idea that we had been there the whole time. I enquired about Sophia, and they informed that she had been placed under a witness protection program. She would be given a new identity and was free to live a new life.

We were satisfied with the way things had ended. No one was surprised that Selene had disappeared yet again. At least now, we were sure that we had quashed all her strength and her lofty ambitions to rule the universe.

With half the night over, all of us just crashed into our beds within minutes. No one was up until noon the next day. Some weariness was still hanging over. But it was still a bright and beautiful day. Our chatter was light-hearted and free of worry.

I called Mike to share the good news and invited him to join us, so we could play out the denouement of this whole drama to him. He was intrigued to say the least. Our victorious celebration was a little sedate, but fun, nevertheless.

Amanda and Jacob started to arrange for their return to Ely. Aunty Tee wished them to delay one more day as there was something she wanted to do with the gang. She asked Mike to hang around for a day as well. To please her, he made the necessary arrangements.

When we started pounding her to tell us what was on her mind, she picked up her staff and waved it around. Within moments, we found ourselves in the enchanted forest, in Fairyland, in her castle. Amanda, Jacob, and Mike were thrilled to see the wonder before them. The rest of us felt a rush of pure joy.

She asked her attendants to call for Archon and also prepare a lavish feast for her guests. Archon was so happy to hear that we have come, he didn't lose a minute to be at the castle as soon as he could.

As soon as Archon arrived, we scampered towards him for a group hug. He was just as receptive and his green eyes glowed with love, as his wings enclosed us in an embrace. His physicality intimidated the new guests, but seeing our love and comfort around him, they felt more secure.

"Archon why don't all of you spend some time around the forest," said Aunty Tee. "Give the new guests a tour and then return to the castle for a grand meal."

"With pleasure." He smiled as he looked at them.

Making the introductions, we flew around on Archon's back, met some of our old friends and ended the day with a sumptuous royal dinner.

As Aunty Tee got ready to take us back to our homes, I knelt down in front of Narissa. "Narissa, will you marry me?"

The unexpected proposal was met with shouts of glee and support from everyone.

Her eyes shone as they misted over, and she accepted. "YES!!!"